I0764750

OTHER BOOKS by KASSANDRA LAMB

The Kate Huntington Mysteries
Psychotherapist Kate Huntington helps others cope with trauma, but she has led a charmed life...until a killer rips it apart. (10 novels)

The Kate on Vacation Mysteries
Even on vacation, Kate Huntington can't stay out of trouble. (4 novellas)

The Marcia Banks and Buddy Cozy Mysteries
Marcia Banks trains service dogs for veterans, and solves crimes on the side, with the help of her Black Lab, Buddy. (12 novels/novellas–1 more to come)

The C.o.P. on the Scene Mysteries
Eight days into her new job as Chief of Police in a small Florida city, Judith Anderson finds herself one step behind a serial killer. (spinoff from the Kate Huntington series; 2 novels–more to come)

Romantic Suspense
written under the pen name of Jessica Dale

LETHAL ASSUMPTIONS

A C.o.P. on the Scene Mystery

Kassandra Lamb

a misterio press publication

Published by *misterio press LLC*

Cover art by Melinda VanLone, Book Cover Corner

Photo credits: background © Alex Grichenko | Dreamstime.com; woman on shield © Photoeuphoria | Dreamstime.com (permission to use through Dreamstime.com)

Happy families are all alike;
every unhappy family is unhappy in its own way.

~ Leo Tolstoy in *Anna Karenina*

CHAPTER ONE

Eight days on the new job, and here I was, at my first homicide scene.

I stared down at the young woman who had once been attractive, before someone had gone at her with the proverbial blunt instrument.

It was the middle of the night, of course. And it was raining. Spritzing really, drizzle with some umph behind it.

Swiping moisture from my face, I noted the position of her hands. Resting on her thighs, on top of a short tan skirt that was *not* shoved up. But there was blood on it. Odds were fifty/fifty whether she'd been sexually assaulted. "Any sign of a weapon?"

"No, ma'am," the uniform beside me said, shaking his head forlornly. Or maybe the shadows cast by a nearby lamp pole just made him look forlorn.

The uniform's name badge read *Collins.* The stripes on his sleeve put a sergeant in front of that name. Mid-thirties, medium height, thin, dark hair. I knew the name but not the face, until now. He'd been on vacation for the last week.

Helluva welcome back.

"What've we got?" I directed this to Lieutenant Nathan Jacobs, my second in command. He oversaw the other detectives, but the department was so small, he was also in the major crimes rotation. And he'd apparently caught this miserable case.

"No purse, no ID." Jacobs ran a hand over his blond buzz cut. "Could be a working girl. Blunt force trauma, but also ligature marks on the neck, so COD's a toss-up. The ME is on the way."

I'd tensed at *marks on the neck*. Hiding my reaction behind a neutral mask, I stared at him.

"No witnesses." He paused. "Yet. Uniforms will start canvassing shortly."

Yeah, good luck with that at two in the morning.

Said uniforms were currently walking a grid, scanning for evidence on the damp ground of the park, shining lights up into the palm trees. Between the rain and the humidity—outrageous even at night, and in *October*—the officers were a bit wilted.

Except for Jacobs. Fortyish, slender, and slightly below average height—he only had a couple of inches on my five-seven—he looked like he'd stepped out of a men's fashion magazine. Tailored pinstriped suit, crisp white dress shirt. He shot his cuffs, and gold cuff links glinted, catching the weak light.

I scanned the crime scene again—a small park that had seen friendlier days. Not much I could do to be useful, without getting in the way. "Keep me posted."

I turned away, then intentionally glanced back over my shoulder. "And don't be jumping to conclusions, gentlemen. For all we know she was a UNF sorority sister out with friends for a night on the town."

Both Jacobs and the sergeant bowed their heads. You would've thought I'd said the victim was a nun.

I chuckled internally.

As the new Chief of Police of Starling, Florida, population roughly eleven thousand souls, it wasn't absolutely necessary for me to go to crime scenes. But I'd told the dispatchers that I wanted to be called for all major crimes.

I needed to get a feel for the types of crimes my department encountered. While Starling is a small city—or medium-sized town, depending on your perspective—it's only a few miles from

Jacksonville, which has all the big-city problems as my hometown of Baltimore.

Plus, one of the many reasons I'd taken this job was to get back into the field some. I'd considered it providence when I'd seen the recruitment ad for a new police chief of a town big enough to match my salary but small enough to allow me to be more hands-on.

Of course, that salary in Baltimore County had been for a homicide lieutenant, while here it was for the police chief. But the cost of living was lower, so it was still a step up.

I contemplated my feelings about providence—fate, or whatever—as I drove through Starling's minuscule red-light district.

Do I still believe in some sense of order and direction in the universe? I suppose I do.

The image of that young woman's battered face flared across my mind.

One thing for sure, I didn't want to think that I was in this battle against evil alone.

Mid-morning, Jacobs knocked on my half open door.

I was working on my third cup of coffee. I hadn't slept well, during the short period of time I'd been able to return to my bed.

"Might have something," the lieutenant said.

I motioned for him to come in.

He closed the door. "I ran the crime past JSO. They've got three possible matches."

Ah, thus the closed door. He didn't want his detectives hearing him admit that my new policy was working. I'd informed them that I expected to develop a far better working relationship with the Jacksonville Sheriff's Office than my predecessor had.

The JSO was an odd set-up for a big-city police department. I assumed the name was a compromise when the city consolidated with Duval County years ago and their law enforcement agencies were blended. The head honcho was called the sheriff, but the rank and file were police officers, not deputies. Their cars said *Sheriff* on the sides and *Police* on the back end. It was confusing as hell to newcomers to the area like me.

"One case was about two years ago," Jacobs was saying, "and another two months later. SA and homicide, beaten and garroted. And the third one five weeks after that, but just SA. The girl survived."

I winced inside at the "just SA." There is no such thing, in my book, as *just* sexual assault—it's a crime equally heinous as murder. But now was not the time to lecture the man.

"So, we know our victim was sexually assaulted?"

"Oh, uh, yes. I checked with the Jax ME's office. Full autopsy's tomorrow, first thing."

I stifled a sigh. Downside of a small city, no ME of our own.

"You tell them it might be related to some of JSO's open cases?"

"Yeah. That's why they moved it up from Wednesday."

Say what? That would've been over forty-eight hours after she was found, way longer than normal. I swore under my breath.

Jacobs grinned. "Welcome to Starling, the stepchild of Jacksonville."

I frowned at him.

His face smoothed into a neutral expression. "Anyway, I was gonna go talk to the gal who got away. She lives in Starling now."

"I'll go with." I pushed up out of my desk chair, grabbing the jacket of my black pantsuit off its back.

"Wha'?"

"I said, I'll go with you." There was a terse edge to my voice. I decided that was okay.

I resisted shaking my head as I turned toward the door. It might take awhile for this crew to get used to the idea that I wasn't a retired-in-place burnout like their old boss.

Darla Monkton was a month out of rehab, living with her sister. "Temporarily," she was quick to point out.

Her sister, Arliss, rolled her eyes from behind her, and left the room.

Darla was too thin, her face gaunt. Her collar-length dark hair was tipped with blonde. The file—which I'd quickly reviewed during the ten-minute drive—had said she was a blonde at the time of the assault.

I'd introduced myself only as Judith Anderson, no title, letting her assume I was just a detective. Knowing the police chief was taking a personal interest in the case might reassure her, or it might freak her out.

"Ms. Monkton," Jacobs began, "we're sorry to stir up bad memories, but we need to ask you about the assault you reported on April fourth of last year."

Darla's body was rigid as she settled into an armchair, across from where Jacobs and I sat on her sister's overstuffed green sofa.

I leaned forward. "We have a fresh case," I said in a gentle voice, "and we think there may be a connection."

She didn't relax completely, but kind of unstiffened, in response to my implied message that we believed her. "What do you need to know?"

"What," Jacobs said, "were you do–"

I shot him a cease-and-desist look. We knew what she'd been doing, working the streets to support her drug habit. No need to humiliate her with a reminder. "Your report said the assailant came up behind you. Can you tell us what happened from there?"

"He grabbed my hair, and shoved me down face first on the sidewalk." A shudder rippled through her body. "He told me if I screamed, he'd kill me. He showed me the tip of a knife. Then he punched the side of my face a couple of times...and did me right there."

She closed her eyes. "I was half prayin' someone would come along, and half prayin' they wouldn't. I didn't want no one seein' me like that."

Jacobs shifted slightly. "Even–"

"Then what happened, Ms. Monkton?" I quickly said.

She turned toward me, poking a skinny shoulder out as if to exclude Jacobs from our conversation. "It was pretty dark. Not many streetlights in that part of town. All I could see was the lower part of his face. His features were all weird, kinda twisted."

She shuddered again. "I realized later that he was wearing a woman's stocking over his face."

That was new. I hid my reaction behind a neutral expression.

She stared my way without really seeing me. "He pulled off the thing on his head and tried to strangle me with it." Her voice was now rote. "I fought him, and then this car came down the street. The headlights hit us, and the car stopped. A man yelled, 'Hey, what're you doin'?' And the guy ran off."

"The report said you couldn't make out his features and that he tried to strangle you," I said. "No mention of a woman's stocking."

Darla shrugged. "Honest, I don't remember what I told the cops that night. I was pretty rattled."

"Of course you were." I paused. "So, the headlights hit you—did you get a good look at his face then?"

The report had said she hadn't, but...

"The lights did shine on him for a second, but I was so relieved that help had arrived. It's all kind of a blur."

I ran through the usual questions, probing for more details about his appearance, what was he wearing, did he speak again, etc. Jacobs had gotten the hint and didn't say much.

"What was his voice like?" I asked.

"Kinda low and gravelly." She glanced toward the kitchen, separated from the living room by a breakfast bar.

I followed her line of vision to a wall clock. Ten to twelve.

"Um, I've got a meeting in ten minutes," she said. "Can we finish this later?"

Jacobs opened his mouth.

"Sure," I said, standing up. "Can we drop you there?"

She shook her head. "It's only a few blocks."

"Then I'll walk with you, if that's okay?"

Jacobs pushed up off the sofa. I gave him a quelling look.

"I'll wait in the car," he said.

Good boy, I thought.

Out on the sidewalk, I walked alongside Darla Monkton, a little reluctant to push her for answers.

"Congratulations on getting yourself to these meetings, on staying clean and sober." They were basic twelve-step, rah-rah words, but somehow I felt like a phony. I knew damned well she was struggling, every minute of every day.

I knew the signs—the shaking hands, the darting eyes, the defeated expression.

She shrugged. "I was doin' okay for a while. Getting out of Jacksonville helped. But I had a slip a couple of months ago. Somehow it's harder this time."

"Don't let this bastard win," I said.

She gave me a half smile. "If only he were the main thing driving me down the wrong path."

I resisted the urge to ask what that meant. I wasn't her therapist nor her sponsor.

"Do you remember anything more about the perp's appearance? Anything that might indicate race perhaps?"

She shook her head. "Could've been Hispanic, or light-skinned Black. He wasn't real dark-skinned, but the stocking, it was kinda dark-colored."

"So he could have been Caucasian?"

She nodded.

Doesn't narrow things down much.

"How about his hands?"

"He wore gloves."

Which I already knew from the file. I was fishing, stirring her memories to see what might surface. Even though I hated doing so. What if she relapsed, because of us?

The old, familiar guilt tightened my chest. I shoved it aside, took a deep breath. *Only the addict is responsible for his or her choices.* The mantra a counselor taught me decades ago, the one my stepmother'd made me go to, after...

"Wait." Darla suddenly stopped walking, turned to face me. We were in front of a church.

"His wrist." Her voice was excited. "I saw it as he was starting to pull off the stocking. He was rolling me over onto my back with one hand and taking it off with the other. I saw a little bit of his wrist. It was white."

Awesome. Out loud, I said, "That's really helpful. Thanks."

"Ya know," Darla said, "it's weird how things work out. It was the worst thing that ever happened to me, but it literally scared me straight. I wasn't able to work the streets anymore, so no money for drugs..." She trailed off, turned, and headed for a door on the side of the church. A hand-made sign, taped to the inside of the door's window, read *NA Meeting Here.*

The preliminary autopsy report on our victim arrived mid-afternoon Tuesday. It contained a couple of surprises. The cause of death was asphyxiation, due to strangulation.

But that wasn't the surprise—the blunt force trauma to her head had been administered *postmortem*.

And she had been sexually assaulted with an object, most likely with a rounded end. Perhaps a soda or beer bottle, the ME had speculated.

Hmm, did the perp have a limp wee-wee, and he took his rage out on her corpse *after* he strangled her? Maybe.

The *postmortem* abuse could mean the crime was personal and not random. Did somebody hate our girl? Yet the object wasn't inserted all that forcefully—it hadn't done much damage.

No finger marks on the neck. The ligature used to strangle her was something cloth, like a scarf, the ME said. That fit with Darla Monkton's description of the rapist trying to wrap the stocking from his head around her neck.

I dropped the autopsy report on my desk and rubbed my eyes, pretending that they were only tired. After all, I hadn't slept well last night, again.

Damn! I'd wanted hands-on, but not to the point of the nightmares returning.

I shook my head to clear it.

A knock on my office door. "Come."

Jacobs stuck his head in first. "Chief, you're psychic." His tone was downright gleeful. "She *was* a sorority girl at North Florida."

CHAPTER TWO

I gestured for Jacobs to come in. “Close the door.”

He did so and sat in the chair in front of my desk. “I had a couple of uniforms canvas the sororities on UNF’s campus. One of them talked to a girl named…” he consulted his phone, “…Natalie Bancock. She said her roommate has disappeared.”

I gave him a well-practiced neutral stare, not about to let on that my comment at the crime scene had been a wild-ass guess, a glib remark to keep him on his toes.

My stare didn’t seem to affect him. Not surprising. He’d been a cop for fifteen years.

“Have you interviewed her?” I asked

“Not yet. About to now.”

I put my palms on my desk to push myself to a stand.

“Lemme guess,” he chuckled, “you’re coming with.”

Once in his car, a white SUV, I said, “You went to the autopsy?”

A beat of silence, Jacobs gazing out the windshield. Then he glanced my way, a neutral expression on his face. “Of course.”

“Anything you noticed that wasn’t in the ME’s report?”

Another brief pause. “Nope.”

“Her clothes. Did you bring them back to our guys or send them to the state lab?”

He looked my way again. “The latter. That okay with you?”

Damn! I needed to stop acting like a homicide unit chief. I couldn't micro-manage this guy. He hadn't shown any blatant signs of resenting a female boss, but all cops were at least a little macho, even the female ones.

I swallowed a snort. *Pot...kettle...black.*

Out loud, I said, "Sure, that's fine. I hear they're good."

He nodded, his eyes on the road.

I might not have gotten much in the way of an orientation from my predecessor, but I had done my homework. The state equivalent of the FBI was the Florida Department of Law Enforcement. They had several offices, scattered around the state. And they had state-of-the-art labs, including the one located in Jacksonville.

We were silent for several miles of thick green flora lining country roads, palmettos and palm trees interspersed with weeds and tall sparse pines. Then suburbs, and eventually city streets that could be in any American metropolis.

At the outskirts of the University of North Florida's campus, Jacobs glanced over. "You know what the uniforms have started calling you?"

"What?"

"C-O-P 10-97."

"What does that mean?" Did Starling still use ten codes?

"It's an old Jacksonville code for 'on the scene.' The first officer who spots you discreetly says it into his radio, letting everyone know that the Chief of Police is on the scene."

I hadn't noticed, but I'd only been to a few scenes so far.

I gave a small shrug, trying for nonchalance, but the mantle of top cop did not sit all that comfortably on my shoulders yet. "Can't blame them for wanting a heads-up."

Was I hampering my people's ability to do their jobs? Anxiety from the boss looking over your shoulder wasn't conducive to top performance.

Unless you're a goof-off.

I reined in a sigh. I wasn't going to change my strategy just yet.

Jacobs turned onto a side street. "Welcome to Sorority Row."

The older brick buildings we were passing sure looked like dormitories to me. I shot him a con-fused look.

"I was being facetious. UNF doesn't have houses for their Greek chapters. The one Natalie and her roommate are in is the poor folks' sorority, as the mean girls call it."

"How do you know so much about UNF's sororities?"

"My niece is in one of them, and she's a talker." He rolled his eyes. "Every family gathering, we hear all the latest sorority news."

He pulled into the parking lot of one of the nondescript buildings.

In a small sitting area off the main entranceway, two girls slouched on either end of a dingy maroon sofa. One was reading, a textbook by its size. The other was fiddling with her phone.

"Ladies," Jacobs said, "could you direct us to Natalie Bancock's room?"

The one with the textbook raised her eyes and waved a hand toward the back of the building. "Down the hall, second door on the right."

The first door was open, the room tiny, with bunk beds and not much space for anything else.

The second door was closed. Jacobs knocked.

"Come in."

These girls had opted not to bunk their beds. There was barely enough room to walk between them. A young woman of about twenty—Natalie, I presumed—was propped up against the wall at the far end of one bed, a book in her lap.

Jacobs introduced himself, then said, "And this is–"

"Judith Anderson." I took a step forward, offering my hand. No point in alarming her with the fact that the chief of police of a neighboring city had taken an interest in her roommate's disappearance.

Natalie leaned forward and shook my hand. It was a firm grasp, which surprised me a little. College-aged kids often were hesitant about shaking hands. They weren't quite used to the adult ritual.

"You told one of our officers that you're worried about your roommate," I said.

She gestured toward the other bed, which was unmade and quite rumpled. Hers was made up with a plain navy comforter. "Have a seat."

I sat gingerly. Jacobs opted to stand at the end of the bed.

Natalie shifted around to put her feet on the floor. "Pearl left here late Sunday afternoon, and I haven't seen or heard from her since."

Jacobs consulted his phone. "Pearl Altman, twenty-three, a junior."

Natalie nodded. "We're both juniors, but she's older. She worked for a few years after high school, before her parents talked her into trying college. Turns out she loves it."

She gave a slight shake of her head. "She's missed her classes for the last two days, which is totally not like her. And I keep texting and calling but get nothing back."

"Calls go to voicemail right away or it rings first?" Jacobs's voice was a bit brusque.

But Natalie didn't seem to be the fragile type. "Right away, which says to me that her phone is off. That's also not like her."

Jacobs had been taking notes on his pad. Now he was scrolling on his phone, looking for something. I suspected what it was.

"Natalie, do you have a photo of your roommate?" I quickly asked.

"Sure." She leaned behind her and grabbed up her own phone, tapped the screen a few times and turned it toward us.

It was a selfie of Natalie and another girl, one who looked a lot more cheerful and alive than the one in the autopsy report.

But it was the same girl.

In the photo, they stood in front of a light gray rancher, a middle-aged woman on the lawn in the background.

"Last Thanksgiving. I spent it with Pearl and her family."

"Do you have her parents' contact information?" I asked gently.

"Sure." Then her face fell. "You know where she is, don't you? She's been hurt."

I glanced at Jacobs. He was stone-faced. Keeping my own expression neutral, I said, "It's an ongoing investigation. We–"

"She's dead, isn't she?"

Neither of us said anything.

Her eyes grew shiny but she didn't break down. She swallowed hard. "I've had a bad feeling since yesterday. Well, since Sunday, but especially since yesterday."

"Did you call her folks?" Jacobs asked, following my lead with his own gentle tone. Or maybe he would've gone there on his own.

Natalie shook her head. "I was going to until that officer came around, asking if any of the female students were missing. I didn't want to worry her folks until I talked to you."

Tears pooled in her eyes. One broke loose. "This is going to kill them, especially Mrs. A. Pearl's their only child." She took a deep breath. "I should call her."

"No," I said quickly. "We'll contact them. Just give us the info."

She found the number on her phone and read it off for Jacobs, gave him the address as well.

"Tell us more about Pearl," I said. "Who are her friends?"

"She doesn't have many. I'm probably her only close friend. She's kinda shy. But she and I have been like sisters since we were paired up as roommates last year." She choked on a suppressed sob, swiped at her eyes with her fingers.

"Boyfriend?" Jacobs asked. "Friends with benefits?"

Natalie shook her head again.

"How was she Sunday?" I asked, "Before she left. Did she tell you where she was going?"

"No, but she had a manila envelope with her. She'd been carrying it around with her for days." Natalie stopped, grabbed a tissue from a box on a tiny table between the two beds. She blew her nose.

"She wouldn't tell me what was in it. She'd gotten kinda secretive lately. Which hurt a little, that she suddenly wouldn't talk to me. We shared everything." Her eyes pooled with tears again.

We asked more questions. Did Pearl drink, use drugs? Had she had any arguments with anyone lately? We got negative answers to all of them.

Jacobs looked around the tiny room. One side, Pearl's, was cluttered. Natalie's side was immaculate. "I don't see a computer. Did Pearl have a laptop or tablet?"

"Yes." Natalie squared her shoulders and stood up.

I had to stand as well and walk to the end of the bed, to let her out. "They don't even have enough room in here for desks?" I commented.

"I guess they wanted to get as many rooms in as they could." She started to move toward a built-in unit by the door—two rows of white drawers, under a chest-high ledge, a mirror on the wall over it.

I stepped into her path. "We'll get it."

"The left side is hers," she said, although that was obvious. The left end of the ledge was covered with makeup, hair ties and other detritus. While Natalie's end was bare and spotless.

"Her tablet should be in the top drawer."

Jacobs donned latex gloves and carefully opened the drawer. He took a couple of photos of the inside of it.

I stepped over and looked in. The tablet had a ratty pink cover. Beneath it was a jumble of clothing. "Do you mind if we take a look through her things?" I asked.

Natalie shook her head. "That's her closet." She pointed to the first of two narrow white doors at the end of the dresser unit.

I donned gloves as well, and Jacobs and I searched the drawers and the closet. More jumbled clothing, and a backpack with spiral-bound notebooks and four textbooks in it. I ruffled through them. Nothing tucked inside. The notebooks had only class notes in them, best I could tell.

"How do you want to handle this, Chief?" Jacobs said in a low voice.

I thought for a few seconds. "We contact the campus police. Ask them to put an officer on the room until we can get parental permission to take the tablet and such, or a search warrant. And I want our crime scene team to go through her things."

I turned to Natalie. "Can you find another place to hang out for tonight?"

She nodded.

"And don't say anything to anyone about Pearl yet," Jacobs said. "Give us a chance to talk to her parents first."

She nodded again, and almost lost it. Her face crumpled for a second and a half-sob escaped. Then she visibly pulled herself together.

She gathered a few things and we all exited the room.

Jacobs held out a hand for the key. He gave her his card, along with the spiel about calling him if she remembered anything else, no matter how seemingly irrelevant.

"We'll try not to inconvenience you too long," I said. "You'll get a call when we're done."

She nodded one more time and mutely turned away.

Outside, we both paused on the sidewalk and took deep breaths. "So, are you *going with* for the death notification?" Jacobs asked.

"No, thank you."

"Oh, I see. You only want to be part of the fun stuff."

I raised my eyebrows at him. "That..." I tilted my head toward the dormitory building, "was not what I'd call fun."

His face sobered. "No, it wasn't. And I guess rank does have its privilege."

"Exactly. There are two things I hope I never have to do again."

"What's that?"

"Drive in the snow and notify a parent that their child is dead."

Jacobs shot me a small grin, then his face settled back into a somber expression.

Back in his car, we both made phone calls, mine was to the UNF campus police.

"The family's in Clover County," Jacobs said, "so I sent Cruthers to notify them. That way I can take you home. Then I'll come back here with the crime scene team later tonight."

"Okay." I resisted the urge to point out that he too was delegating the notification.

He glanced at his watch. "It's rush hour, though. If we leave now, we'll only sit in traffic. What do you say to a bite to eat first?"

I opened my mouth to say no, but my stomach rumbled a loud yes. I'd never gotten around to eating lunch.

The end of his mouth turned up in a half smirk. "My treat."

I waved a dismissive hand. "No way."

"Consider it a welcome-to-Florida meal. And I know just the place, not far from here. You like Japanese food?"

I opted to give in for now. "Sure." We could argue over the check later. Now that I'd thought about food, I was ravenous.

Perhaps it was my imagination, but I could've sworn Jacobs was flirting with me over dinner. When the check came, I laid my hand on it before he could pounce. "I have an expense account. You don't."

He shrugged, didn't argue.

As we entered the outskirts of Starling, he offered to take me home.

"Then how would I get to work in the morning?"

"I could give you a ride?"

"Thanks for the offer. Just drop me at my car."

There was that half smirk again, or was it meant to be a smile. "Sure, Chief."

He stopped near my car in the municipal parking lot.

"We have a tech person, right?" I asked. Damn the previous chief for his totally inadequate orientation, which had lasted roughly two hours and consisted mostly of him bragging about all the bad guys he'd caught in his day.

"Sure do," Jacobs said. "I'll get him to go over the tablet tomorrow."

"Sounds good. See you in the morning."

At home, I stripped and headed for the shower. I imagined the hot water—beating against my skin—washing away the depravity of human nature I'd encountered that day. Some nights, it worked.

Tonight, it didn't.

I gazed into the steamed-up bathroom mirror, my face a softened mirage.

Why shouldn't Jacobs be attracted to me?

Slowly, the glass cleared. A pale face, surrounded by dark hair in a short bob, stared back. A too-thin, sharply defined face.

You have such lovely cheekbones, Judith... My mother's vague voice in my head. *If only you weren't so thin.*

I clenched my teeth and used the sleeve of my ratty white terrycloth robe to wipe away the remnants of steam—and the image of those cheek-bones—from the mirror.

In the living room, the stacks of moving boxes I'd yet to unpack bore witness to my lack of domesticity.

Maybe I should get a cat.

Where had *that* thought come from? I shook my head and headed for the kitchen.

I poured a glass of wine and returned to the only piece of furniture in my living room—a black leather sofa that was starting to crack on the arms.

Nonetheless, I'd moved its shabby chic self with me from Maryland. It was big and comfy.

I picked up the remote from one of the cushions, pointed it toward my TV perched on a box across the room, and found the sitcom I'd been binge-watching lately.

I was nodding off by the second episode. I went to bed early and, thankfully, slept dreamlessly.

Ringing woke me. I groped on my bedside table for my phone, held it to my ear. "Yeah?"

"Chief, we've got another homicide." The dispatcher's voice was neutral, a finely honed skill.

I shook my head to clear it of sleep. "Hold on."

Sitting up, I swung my legs off the bed and grabbed the pad I kept on the table. My alarm clock informed me it was three in the morning.

"Where?"

The dispatcher gave me the address. I didn't recognize it, but I didn't yet recognize many streets in this city. My GPS would figure it out.

I thanked her, disconnected, then threw on clothes. My phone went into a back pocket, my keys in a front one.

I grabbed up the thin wallet my cousin had sent me last Christmas.

A faint smile hovered on my lips. Paulie knew me well. I hated purses. Although I often carried a briefcase with my laptop in it.

Random childhood memories of playing with my cousin—the closest thing to a sibling I had—kept me company as I rode the elevator to the ground floor of my building.

In my car, I programmed my GPS and headed for the crime scene, in yet another small park.

The face of the uniform handling the crime scene log was neutral as he recorded my presence, but I spotted another officer muttering into his radio.

I could guess what he was saying. *C-O-P 10-97.*

I grimaced and marched toward the pair of uniforms standing near a dark bundle of clothes.

Of course I knew it would materialize into a corpse as I got closer, but when I looked down into the face... I swallowed a gasp.

"Detective's on the way," a uniform said.

"Who?" I managed to get out.

"Bradley."

I took a deep breath. "Call Lieutenant Jacobs."

Silence. I looked up.

The uniforms were as different as night and day. One tall, thin and young, the other short, stocky, and middle aged.

"Related to one of his cases," I said.

The older one nodded.

Why had they hesitated? Was it that unusual for Jacobs to be called out to a homicide, even if it wasn't his case?

I shook my head, turned again to the body.

And clamped down hard on my emotions as I stared into the battered but familiar face of the only victim who'd escaped Jacksonville's serial rapist/killer...until tonight.

CHAPTER THREE

Detective Bradley showed up a few minutes later. He gazed silently down at the corpse.

I didn't really know him. And suddenly it struck me—how was I supposed to run a department of thirty-some officers, detectives, and civilian personnel when I didn't know a thing about any of them?

"You called in Jacobs?" Bradley said, his tone bland.

"Related to one of his cases."

He nodded, still staring at the young woman.

He gestured toward the battered face. "Those happened awhile before death."

I looked more closely. There was considerable swelling around the cuts.

Bradley gestured toward the young woman's hands, resting in a semi-remorseful pose on her jeans-clad thighs. "That like the other case?"

"Yes. We're holding that back from the press, though."

He pointed to one of her wrists. "She's been tied up."

I leaned closer. Yup, red marks on her wrists. That *wasn't* like Pearl.

I tilted my head in the direction of a small crowd gathering in the parking lot on the other side of the park. "See if anybody saw or heard anything useful."

Bradley headed that way.

So far, the civilians were staying behind the crime scene tape that was guarded by a single uniformed officer. But as Bradley approached, a woman ducked under the tape to intercept him. Even from a distance, I could tell she was better dressed than the other looky-loos.

Reporter. And a pushy one at that.

Confirmation came in the form of a man with a video camera on his shoulder, trailing behind her.

Bradley herded them back beyond the tape.

The apartment building's hallway smelled musty. A bare window at the end framed a predawn square of charcoal gray.

Jacobs rang the sister's doorbell.

I swallowed hard. *Damn!* I'd hoped to never go through this again, and not just for the obvious reasons.

He rapped knuckles against the door.

I jerked.

Two burly county cops on the porch, the afternoon sun beating down. "Is your mother home?" Me, a scrawny teenager, staring at them, my throat so tight I couldn't talk.

I shook my head slightly, brutally shoving the memory away.

Jacobs's back was rigid. Had he picked up that I'd had a brief flashback? More likely, he was bracing himself for the task at hand.

The sound of a deadbolt being turned. I arranged my face into a sympathetic expression.

The door swung slowly open and the dead woman's sister stood in front of us, in a fuchsia robe that clashed with her carrot-colored hair.

There was no blanching as realization dawned. Arliss Monkton's face was already ghost-white. No wide-eyed look of shock.

Only a down-turned mouth and resignation in her gray-blue eyes.

"You found her?" Her voice was barely above a whisper.

"May we come in, ma'am?" Jacobs asked.

She peered past his shoulder at me. "The bastard got her, didn't he?"

A lump had formed in my throat. "Ma'am, I'm afraid your sister is dead."

She turned and walked away, leaving it to us to follow or not. I gently closed the door behind me.

She sat in the only armchair. No alternative but the couch. I perched on one end, carefully allowing space between myself and Jacobs.

He sat down, unbuttoned his suit jacket, and leaned forward. "Ms. Monkton, when's the last time you saw your sister?"

"A few minutes before eight. She said she needed a meeting. There's one at the church a few blocks from here that meets at eight."

The same church Darla and I had walked to two days ago.

"And she never came home?" Jacobs said.

Arliss shook her head. "I went to bed early, with a migraine, but I couldn't get to sleep. Even after the medicine kicked in and the headache eased some. I was worried about her, out alone at night, after that girl..."

She turned her gaze toward me, her eyes wide. "But it's only three blocks and they're well lit, and there's a convenience store across the street," her pitch rose, "with cars and people coming and going." She choked a little on the last few words.

She bit her lower lip. "I wanted to drive her, but she wouldn't let me. Told me not to fuss, to go to bed and take care of myself."

"What time does the meeting let out?" Jacobs asked.

"They're usually an hour. I finally got up around ten-thirty and checked her room. I hadn't heard her come in, but I was hoping maybe I'd drifted off and she had come home..." She trailed off again, looked away.

"She had a phone with her?" I said gently.

She nodded. "I called and called. It went straight to voicemail. She must've turned it off during the meeting."

I glanced at Jacobs.

He shook his head slightly. No phone at the scene.

"Could we see her room, please?" I asked.

She stood, pulled her robe tight around her, and trudged toward a hallway.

Darla's room had obviously been a study originally, lined with bookcases on two walls and a small computer desk in a corner. No computer.

A sofa bed, open, took up a third wall. The bed was unmade, sheets twisted.

Arliss stood in the doorway, her hands clenched in front of her.

Jacobs and I did a quick search. Nothing useful. We'd have a crime scene tech go over the room again, but I doubted they'd find anything.

"What was your sister wearing this evening?" I asked.

The woman's brow furrowed. "Jeans and a tee shirt, light blue." Her voice was impatient.

The corpse in my mind's eye wore the same clothes. My throat tightened again.

"I assume she has a sponsor in NA," I said. "Do you have their contact information?"

Her face contorted into an odd expression, half confusion, half anger. "Look, I get that you cops ask the same questions again and again, but really, I gave y'all this info earlier. Why aren't you out there catching the bastard that did this?" She spat out the last few words.

"What do you mean *earlier*?" I said.

"When I reported her missing."

I'd called a meeting for this afternoon. Jan Richards, the senior dispatcher was just coming off night shift. She'd grumbled that she needed some sleep since she was on again from three to eleven.

To at least pretend that I gave a crap, I slid the meeting to three. Things would go more smoothly if she wasn't in a sour mood.

The phone calls setting up the meeting had taken over an hour, which did not improve my own mood. I needed to hire a secretary, although I had no idea how I would pay her, or him.

Or maybe... A small seed was germinating in my brain.

I shoved those administrative thoughts aside and perused the crime scene photos I'd arranged on my desk. Computerized files are all well and good, but sometimes you need to print things out and look at them side by side.

Five sets of photos—the first two almost identical. Known prostitutes. Both blondes, skimpily clad, faces battered, ligature marks on the necks, sprawled on the pavement of two different alleys in Jacksonville. All showed signs of sexual assault—by a human, not an object. Traces of lubricant and the lack of semen indicated the rapist wore a condom. ME reports said the women had died where they were found.

Then there was Darla Monkton's SA, that hadn't ended in murder, the first time. Photos had been taken of her injuries at the hospital. She'd declined to do a rape kit but had reported she thought the guy wore a condom. The attack had occurred at the edge of a small park, around midnight.

Victim number four, corpse number three, Pearl Altman, was different in several ways. The blows to her face were post-mortem and she was assaulted with an object. *And* she was a brunette. Her skirt was on the short side, but otherwise her attire was fairly demure. Plus her body had been neatly arranged, with her hands on her thighs.

The main similarity, they were all garroted with something smooth, like a woman's stocking, rather than strangled by hands.

The ME wasn't sure if Pearl was killed where she was found, but time of death was six to eight p.m. I doubted she'd been lying out in the open for that long, without someone noticing her earlier.

Next, Darla again, with similarities to all of them. Neatly arranged, hands on thighs, like Pearl, but the blows to her head had happened before death, like the others. The preliminary report said she was assaulted by a human—if you could call the bastard that—but again, no semen. No word yet if she'd been killed where she was found—autopsy was later today—but dead or alive, she was most likely transported to that park. It was two miles from the church. And there were signs of restraint on her wrists and ankles.

New developments—she'd been kidnapped, held somewhere for a while, then taken to the park, either before or after she was killed.

A tap on my office door. I glanced up. The occupants of several desks in the bullpen—detectives and a couple of uniforms—stopped what they were doing to stare.

I need some blinds. The fish-bowl effect of this office was already getting old.

"Come," I called out, none too friendly.

The door cracked open and Detective Bradley stuck his head through the opening. "Good morning."

I grunted but waved him inside. He closed the door behind him.

"Take a look at these, Bradley."

He sidled up beside me and looked down. He was several inches taller than me—at least six foot.

After a moment, I tapped the last two photos. "What do you see?"

"A copycat, with some semblance of a conscience. The poses are almost, but not quite, remorseful."

"Yeah." I paused. "Her facial wounds," I touched Pearl's photo, "were *postmortem* and she was penetrated by an object." I pointed to the photo of Darla's corpse. "Last night's victim was beaten and sexually assaulted before death, like the first two women."

"A copycat who's escalating *really* fast?" He shrugged. His well-tailored navy jacket shifted effortlessly back into place on his broad shoulders.

He obviously spent a larger percentage of his salary on clothes than did his fellow detectives. With the possible exception of Nate Jacobs.

His eyes were blue, matched by his pale blue dress shirt. Light brown hair, medium length, recently trimmed. His skin was fair, no doubt an avid user of sunscreen.

Sharp as a tack this morning, aren't you, Anderson? I sneered at myself internally.

I shook my head slightly. I needed to do something to improve my mood or I'd be taking somebody's head off by lunchtime.

"You got anything pressing on your plate right now?" I asked Bradley.

"Nope."

"Good, you can help Jacobs with this case." I grabbed my black pantsuit jacket from the back of my desk chair. "I want to visit the scene where she was most likely taken."

My door opened—I hadn't heard a knock.

Jacobs leaned in. "Did someone say my name?"

"Yes. Bradley's gonna help you out."

Jacobs's upper lip curled slightly, then his expression quickly shifted to neutral. "The more the merrier. One car or two?"

Bradley was now stone-faced. These two did *not* like each other.

"Three cars," I said. "We all might need to scatter to different places to follow leads."

The three of us walked slowly down the sidewalk, traveling the same three blocks as Darla had last night, between her apartment and the Methodist church where the NA meeting was held.

I noted the contrasts in our footwear. We all wore black, but otherwise... Bradley wore heavy Oxfords, with velcro straps—rather out of sync with the rest of his sartorial splendor but quite appropriate for fieldwork. Jacobs wore expensive-looking black wingtips. And in between were my well-worn, low-heeled pumps—*not* particularly appropriate for fieldwork. I made a mental note to start carrying some sturdier shoes in my car.

Jacobs had already tracked down and talked to the young woman's sponsor. Darla had never made it to the meeting last night.

I picked up a cigarette butt with a pair of tweezers. Jacobs held open a small evidence bag. I dropped it in. We'd found four more by the time we reached the church, and three outside the side door.

Smoking is the lesser of evils for addicts trying to clean up their act.

"Bradley," I said, "see if you can find the pastor. Find out if he knew Darla."

I gestured for Jacobs to follow me.

We crossed the street and walked down the other sidewalk, stopping in front of the convenience store Arliss had mentioned. The sign read *Pronto's*.

Was that somebody's name? If not, why the apostrophe s? I suppressed my inner grammar nazi and looked around.

The store had a tiny parking lot that might hold eight cars on a good day. At the moment, four were lined up near the doors. We headed that way.

"You talk to the clerk?" I asked.

"Yes and no. The guy on this morning was not the one who was here last night. He said the owner usually closes, then comes back mid-morning the next day to do the bank deposit."

"It's not open twenty-four/seven?"

"Nope. It's independent, not part of a chain. Open every day, but closes at eleven p.m."

I nodded. "Any surveillance cameras?"

"Not outside, sadly. Clerk said they kept getting vandalized, so the owner took them down. The inside ones didn't show much of the outside, only the fronts of the cars lined up."

We entered the store. The air conditioning was a welcome relief. It was October, for crying out loud. When *did* it cool down around here?

The young man behind the counter was slightly taller than average and lean, an athlete's body. He sported a surfer's tan and blond streaks in his light brown hair.

Jacobs walked over and spoke to him. The kid shook his head. No, the owner hadn't come in yet.

Jacobs poured us each a cup of coffee. We sipped caffeine for a few minutes, as a parade of customers came and went.

I was about to suggest Jacobs call the owner, when a medium-height, slightly stocky man entered the store. He wore a short-sleeved white polo shirt and dark slacks. Unnaturally black hair was thinning on top.

He went behind the counter, and we started toward him.

His gaze shifted our way and he leaned down slightly, feeling around for something under the counter.

Jacobs's hand moved under his suit jacket. Mine went to my gun in its waistband holster at the small of my back.

The clerk quickly whispered in the guy's ear.

The owner relaxed some and turned toward us. "How can I help you, Detectives?"

I let out a pent-up breath.

"Detective Jacobs." He held up his badge. "This is Chief Anderson."

The man's head bobbed up and down, a smile plastered on his face, but his eyes were wary. "Frank Tremont. Happy to meet you." He didn't extend a hand to shake.

"Do you know this young woman?" Jacobs held up a photo of Darla Monkton we'd gotten from her sister.

"Well, yes and no. Don't know her name but she lives around here. Comes in every few days, usually to buy smokes."

"Did she come in last night?" Jacobs asked.

"No, but I saw her, across the street, walking toward the church."

"What time was that?" I asked.

"I didn't look at the clock, but it was likely around eight. That's when the NA meeting starts over there."

"So you knew she went to that meeting?" I asked.

"Oh, uh, yeah. I'd seen her goin' in there before."

"Did you see where she went last night?" Jacobs asked.

The guy shook his head, dislodging his comb-over some. "A customer came up to the counter, and when I looked out again, she was gone."

As if on cue, a big guy in jeans, tee shirt and a hard hat plopped several wrapped sandwiches and two sodas on the counter.

The owner turned toward him.

I glared at the clerk, who was looking a little pale under his tan. He took the hint and stepped in front of his boss to help the customer.

The owner turned back toward us, the overhead florescent lights glinting off beads of sweat on his forehead.

Interesting. I was actually a bit chilly now, in the aggressively air-conditioned store, and I was wearing a long-sleeved jacket over my shirt.

"Think for a minute," I said. "Did you see anything else around the time you noticed the young woman?"

He closed his eyes for a few seconds. Then they popped open. "There was a car. It stopped near her."

"Can you describe it?" Jacobs said.

"A dark sedan. Too far away to see a plate and the driver was just a silhouette. But... she leaned over some, like he'd rolled his passenger window down and she was talking to him."

"Did anyone get in or out of the car?" I asked.

"Not that I saw, but it was about then when the customer came over."

Jacobs extracted a card from his jacket's breast pocket. "Give us a call if you think of anything else."

I nodded at the surfer-boy clerk as we left. He gave me a shy smile, but his eyes looked worried.

Out on the sidewalk, I turned to Jacobs. "I want an extra uniform patrolling this block tonight."

He smirked. "You wanna know why the owner's so squirrely."

"Yes, and also to see if some john's trolling around here for pickups at night."

"Could be. This is one of the areas on the cusp. Safe enough during the day, but not the best place to be at night."

"Which is probably why the owner does his bank run during the day."

Jacobs nodded.

"And get a hold of that sponsor again. See if you can get any names of the people at that meeting. Maybe one of them got a better look at that car, and/or saw if the victim got into it."

He frowned. "I doubt I can get names, because of the anonymous thing."

"Ask the sponsor if she can call the others and see if they'll agree to talk to us. You know how to play it—help us find the bastard who killed their friend."

CHAPTER FOUR

Back at the precinct...uh, the station—Starling only had one police station, on the third floor of the municipal building—I stared again at the crime scene photos.

A soft knock on my office door.

"Come."

Bradley opened the door, then closed it behind him. He cleared his throat. "Are you sure you want me working this case with Lieutenant Jacobs?"

I waved him to a chrome and black leather visitor's chair. "I take it you two don't get along."

"That's putting it mildly."

I debated asking what was behind their animosity, suspected I wouldn't get a straight answer.

"Yes, I want you on this case. I may even set up a task force and ask the Jacksonville detectives who worked the earlier cases to join us."

"Jacobs doesn't like people messing with his cases."

Well, maybe it's time he learned to play nicely with others.

I leaned back in my desk chair and changed the subject. "Who do we have in our rookie pool right now?"

Bradley tilted his head to one side. "Three officers, two male, one female." He rattled off their names and I jotted them down.

"May I ask why?"

I waved a hand in the air, not quite ready to share my half-baked idea. "You find the pastor?"

"Yup. He recognized the victim's photo, said she'd come to church on Sundays a few times, but she always ducked out the back door as soon as the service was over."

"So he never talked to her."

"Correct, but his impression was that she was a lost soul, trying to find her way back to God."

I snorted softly. "Hardly a leap to figure that out."

He smiled. It made his boyish face look even younger.

I'd pegged him as mid-thirties, but he could be younger than that. If he'd made detective in record time, that could explain Jacobs's rancor. The lieutenant didn't seem the type to like "pretty-boy hotshots," as my former partner, Dolph Randolph used to call them.

Dolph never resented my rapid ascent in BCPD, though. Indeed, as my mentor, he took partial credit for it. Credit well deserved.

A wave of longing washed over me. I froze for a second. Was I homesick?

Shaking off the feeling, I said, "Anything else from the good vicar?"

"Not on our victim, but he had contact info for the person who runs the NA meeting. I think he's called the secretary of the meeting."

"Excellent. Track him down."

"I thought Jacobs was talking to the sponsor again."

"He is but it doesn't hurt to attack the problem from two angles."

His expression was skeptical.

My stomach tightened. Was I buying trouble here, maybe alienating my second in command?

Probably, but I didn't rescind the order. Women were dying. These guys would just have to suck it up and work together.

"Have you looked over the case files?" I asked.

Bradley nodded.

"Any insights into where to go next?"

"The envelope the roommate said Pearl was carrying. I'd love to know what was in it."

I stood, grabbed my suit jacket. "Let's go talk to the roommate again." She might be motivated to remember more, to impress tall and handsome Bradley.

That reminded me... I texted Jacobs as we walked to the parking lot. *Anything on Pearl's tablet yet?*

Not yet. I'll check when I get back.

I also hadn't asked him how the parent notification went. Had Cruthers found out anything useful from them?

And why did I have to ask about these things?

Maybe because he isn't used to a police chief who wants a blow-by-blow. I mentally cut Jacobs some slack.

Cruthers get anything from the parents? I texted.

Only permission to take any of her things we wanted.

"One car or two?" Bradley asked.

"One. It's a longish drive."

"Could you drive so I can call the NA group's secretary?"

"Good idea." I led the way to my car.

Bradley made his call and apparently got voicemail. He left a message.

"Mind if I move this seat back?" he said.

"Go ahead."

He did so and stretched out his long legs, although there still wasn't quite enough leg room for him in my compact. He gave me a small smile. "I guess I don't know you well enough to make jokes about clown cars, huh?"

"No, you don't."

But I found myself smiling back.

I contemplated the car issue. It was very unusual for a department to *not* assign PD-owned vehicles to their detectives and high-ranking members, such as the police chief. I'd asked about it at my interview, and had gotten some mumbo-jumbo about cost savings from the mayor.

"So, why were you asking about the rookies?" Bradley interrupted my reverie.

I answered his question with one of my own. "Did Chief Black have a secretary or aide?"

"More or less. We used to have a clerk who handled the phones, kept things organized in the office. She retired when he did."

Then what happened to that line item in the budget?

"Do you know anything about the rookies? Do any of them have clerical backgrounds?"

Bradley was silent. I glanced his way. His expression was neutral.

He cleared his throat. "The female one does."

"Do you know her?"

He nodded.

"Do you think she'd be interested in being my temporary assistant?"

"I don't know."

There was something about his tone. "What's your best guess?"

"I think she'd resent being asked."

"Because she'd assume I was asking because she's the only female."

He nodded again.

"How long has she been on the job?"

"Eight months."

"Would you be willing to talk to her, feel her out? If I call her in, she may assume she's obligated to say yes, even if she hates the idea."

A beat of silence. "I guess."

I glanced his way again. Still the neutral expression, staring straight ahead.

"Tell her there will be tedious stuff, like phone calls, but she'll learn more about the department in a few months than would normally take years."

He turned toward me and raised one eyebrow. "Years? We're not that big of a department."

"Okay, a few months versus a lot of months."

"I'll ask her," Bradley said.

It was an unorthodox approach, to say the least, but with the staffing and budget constraints I had, I needed to get creative.

"How do you know her, by the way? Just from the department?"

"No, I knew her before she went to the academy."

I looked his way, my eyebrows in the air now.

His face softened. "She's my kid sister."

We found Natalie in the dorm's dining hall, at a large table with a scarred and sticky top. But the end where she sat was clean. Books and notebooks were spread out in front of her.

"Sorry to interrupt your studying." I introduced Bradley.

Natalie gestured toward two chairs on the side of the table. We sat.

"We've been wondering about the envelope Pearl had," I said, "when she left here Sunday. Any guesses as to what might've been in it?"

"Yeah. I think I've put a couple things together. Pearl told me once that she was adopted. This semester, we're both taking this biology class, ya know, and one of the first units was on genetics. Like, that's when she got kinda secretive."

Bradley leaned forward. "You think she was searching for her biological parents?"

Natalie nodded. "One time, when I got the mail for both of us, there was a letter from one of those ancestry companies. You know, the ones that test your DNA."

She stopped, took a deep breath. "She acted like it was junk mail, threw it in the trash. But when I went to empty the can later, the envelope wasn't in there."

"Do you remember the name of the company?" Bradley asked.

She shook her head. "It wasn't one of the real popular ones though, that you see advertised on TV." She rushed on. "I'm sorry I didn't think of this sooner. None of those things really registered as related, until she..."

"Of course they wouldn't," I said. "Did you call Detective Jacobs?"

"No." Her cheeks pinked. "I, um, was going to, after I finished studying for my test tomorrow."

I nodded, thinking that Jacobs maybe needed to work on his interview skills, at least when it came to young women. His somewhat brusque approach didn't work well with them.

I gave her my own card this time. "If you think of anything else, do let us know right away."

"Um, are y'all finished with our room? I told Pearl's mom I'd pack up her stuff, what your crime scene guys didn't take, that is."

"Let me double check that for you."

Out on the sidewalk in front of the dorm, Bradley asked, "You want me to track down the DNA company?"

"Yes, please."

We walked in companionable silence to my car. My stomach rumbled, complaining that I'd never had breakfast.

Bradley grinned.

"Let's catch a bite before we go back." I glanced at my watch. One-ten. "But maybe we'll get out of the city first."

CHAPTER FIVE

We grabbed a booth in a restaurant off of Route 301 that served breakfast all day. The waitress tried to hand us menus.

Bradley shook his head. "Coffee, black. A stack of pancakes and turkey sausage."

"Coffee," I said, "also black. Scrambled eggs and bacon, from pigs, not turkeys."

"Oink, oink," he said softly, as the waitress turned away.

The snicker that snuck out belied the stern look I was giving him.

"I'm paying, by the way." I shouldn't have to say it, since the senior officer always pays—we make more money. But after the scene with Jacobs last night, I wanted to nip in the bud any notion that I should be treated differently because I'm female.

Bradley lifted that one eyebrow. "Sure, boss."

I hadn't had time yet to get through all the personnel files, but I had skimmed those of the sergeants and the detectives. Bradley's file indicated he had passed the sergeant's exam shortly before Chief Black announced his retirement.

But Black had not promoted him. Was that an oversight—he hadn't gotten around to it before he retired? Or was it intentional? There hadn't been any complaints or reprimands in Bradley's file.

So, now I had two potential openings to get to know this guy better. Wimpy turkey sausage or kid sister. The latter should produce more useful info.

"How do you feel about your sister becoming a cop?" I asked.

He grimaced. "Mixed emotions. Proud she got through the training. Empathy for her reasons for wanting to be a cop. Scared to death she's gonna get hurt. Even more scared that our parents will blame me if she does."

"Are they likely to do that?" An only child, with a family that was Dysfunctional with a capital D, I was curious about how "normal" families worked.

"Probably not, but I'll blame me." His gaze rose. "Ah, saved by the coffee."

We were silent while the waitress poured. "Your food'll be right out."

I liked the southern drawl but missed the "hon" that would've been tacked on the end back in Maryland.

Okay, time to find out more about how the department worked. "Pretend you're a training officer and I'm a new recruit, fresh out of the academy... Where do our recruits go to the academy, anyway?"

"In Jacksonville."

I rolled my eyes. "Of course."

His mouth quirked up on one end. "No, it's not JSO's academy. The Northeast Florida Criminal Justice Center is *in* Jacksonville, but they're affiliated with a college, not the city. They train for most of the smaller departments in the area."

"How long's their program?"

"Six months."

My mouth fell open, just as the waitress delivered my eggs and bacon.

She smiled—seeming to think my reaction was to the gigantic pile of food on my plate—then she deposited a plate with a stack of hot cakes a half foot high in front of Bradley. "Enjoy." She bustled away.

"Six months! Baltimore County's academy was over two years."

He nodded. "I was with Tampa PD for several years before coming here. Theirs was twenty-six months. But I've heard of other departments where it's six months to a year."

My stomach growled, objecting to my ignoring the food in front of me. I ate some eggs. "Back to my scenario. Pretend I'm a new recruit and tell me about the department. How does it run?"

The old chief had been so sketchy about details, I suspected he hoped I'd fall on my face. I had no intention of doing so.

Bradley was looking confused. "As in, you know nothing?"

I nodded, scooping more food into my mouth. The eggs were delicious, the bacon under done. *Should've asked for extra crispy.*

"Um, we've got fifteen full-time officers and three sergeants. Each shift consists of five officers and a watch commander. An officer's assigned to each quadrant of the city, and one is at large, ready to assist where needed. Six of our officers have had SWAT training."

I already knew most of that, but I didn't interrupt.

"Four part-timers work a few shifts a week, on the full-timers' days off and they cover the evidence room." He paused to take a bite of pancakes.

"A trained officer is willing to work only a few shifts a week?"

Bradley gave me a small smile. "Welcome to the land of retirees. They're all drawing pensions from departments up north." He ate a chunk of sausage, before continuing, "There are four detectives, including Jacobs. Then the civilians—our two-man crime scene team, the tech geek, and the public information officer...she's part-time. The dispatchers technically work directly for the city, but the police chief has traditionally supervised them."

Damn! The dispatchers! I jerked my arm around to look at my watch. Two-fifteen.

"Eat up. Speaking of dispatchers, I have a meeting with them and the watch commanders at three."

He arched an eyebrow but said nothing as he demolished the rest of his pile of pancakes.

We were back in my car in fifteen minutes.

"So," I asked, "what brought you up here from Tampa?"

"My partner got a great job offer in Jacksonville, but I didn't particularly want to work for JSO."

Partner?

"Why not?" I asked.

Bradley gave a small shrug. "Higher crime rate, pays not that much better, *much* bigger bureaucracy."

"What's your partner do?"

"He's an accountant for a good-sized company."

Ah, "he." Bradley was gay. "He got a name?"

Silence. I glanced over.

One side of his mouth was quirked up in a half smile. "Would you believe Bradley."

We both chuckled.

"Brad Montgomery. We're talking about getting married, but he's insisting I take *his* last name." He chuckled again. It had the feel of a long-standing joke between them.

"How long have you been together?" I asked as we entered the outskirts of Starling.

"Eight years."

"And you haven't gotten married?" I blurted out, then wished I'd kept a better rein on my mouth. We were getting a little too far into personal territory. But this guy was easy to be with.

I caught another shrug out of the corner of my eye. "It's complicated," he said.

"You don't want to be that blatant at the department."

"I don't hide anything, but... Let's just say, Florida is not always the most tolerant state in the union."

I wondered if his sexual orientation was part of the animosity between him and Jacobs. And/or part of the reason Black hadn't promoted him.

"How about the other detectives? What's the scoop with their families?" It would be helpful to know who might be dealing with problem teenagers or having marital problems.

"Cruthers is married, two teenage kids."

I was trying to figure out how to probe for more info, when he added, "Seems to be a happy marriage. The kids have never been in trouble."

I almost chuckled, but caught myself. He knew why I was asking. And the fact that he knew that was a sign he might be good leader material.

"Patterson's divorced," he said.

"Kids?"

"One daughter. I think she's sixteen or seventeen."

"Any issues that you know of regarding her?"

"She seems like a good kid. But he and the ex get into it sometimes over the custodial set-up."

I nodded.

Bradley fell silent.

"What about Jacobs?"

I caught a grimace out of the corner of my eye. "He *was* married. His wife committed suicide two and a half years ago."

I stiffened, then covered with an empathetic wince. "That's rough."

"Yeah. No kids. He didn't say much about it, but I got the impression that was the reason. She had some kind of biological-clock crisis when she hit thirty-five and still no kids, threw her into a tail-spin."

I nodded and quickly changed the subject.

The meeting was in the dispatch center, since one of the dispatchers had to monitor incoming calls.

The head dispatcher, Jan Richards, was sitting at one of the terminals when I walked in. Her eyes darted back and forth between several computer screens.

I cleared my throat and gave her a hard look when she glanced my way.

She took the hint. "Jenny, take over." She changed places with the youngest of the dispatchers, who had to be at least ten months pregnant. Jenny had to sit semi-sideways at the terminal.

I looked at the group, gathered around a small conference table—male sergeants on the right, female dispatchers on the left. The public information officer had taken it upon herself to attend. She sat at the far end.

Standing at the head, I discreetly pulled in a deep breath. "I called you all together because I need your help. We need to develop a better system of communication."

"How so?" said Sergeant Lewis, third down on the right.

"We had a missing person report last night, on Darla Monkton. I would like to know what happened to it?" I tried hard to keep my tone neutral but I was doing a slow burn inside. If a BOLO had gone out on Darla, maybe she wouldn't be dead today.

The sergeant two down from me, Collins, said, "I caught that one, toward the end of my shift. I didn't send the BOLO out right away because she was only an hour and a half overdue. She could've gone for coffee with her sponsor or something."

"You know Darla?" I intentionally used present tense. Apparently, he hadn't received his change-of-shift briefing yet.

Johnson, the day-shift sergeant, right in front of me, closed his eyes. He knew what was coming.

"Yes," Collins said. "I used to be with JSO. I picked her up a few times in Jacksonville for soliciting." There was compassion in his voice.

Which made me feel a little guilty about what I was going to spring on him. But only a little.

I looked past him to Lewis. "And the report was passed on to you."

"Yes."

"What did you do with it?"

"Nothing." He was stone-faced, with a hint of disdain in his tone. The words, *She was an addict and a prostitute, whaddaya want?* hung unsaid in the air.

I moved my gaze back to Collins. "I hate to have to tell you this, Sergeant, but your missing person *was* a key witness in a homicide case." I paused, glared at Lewis. "And she was found early this morning, sexually assaulted and strangled."

Collins's face blanched. Lewis lowered his gaze. The hand he had on the table curled into a fist. Was he angry at me or the killer? Or himself?

I ground my teeth, wishing I knew these people better. I let my own anger off its leash. "Damn it, we're not that big of a department! We need to communicate better. If there had been proper follow-up on this case, that young woman might be alive today."

I turned to Jan Richards. "For the time being, I want to hear about all missing person reports."

"When they come in?" she asked.

"Definitely."

She nodded.

I turned my gaze back to the sergeants. "And there will be no ignoring MP reports or delaying responding to them, regardless of the individual involved. Am I clear?"

Nods along that side of the table, Lewis's a bit stiff.

"Dismissed." I beckoned to the public information officer and left the room.

She caught up outside the door and walked with me back toward my office.

"I need you to put together a press release right away. Something that doesn't scare the bejeesus out of the public. But I want them to know they should report any missing persons as soon as they become concerned. Maybe make it sound like we're clarifying that the forty-eight-hour thing is a myth. That we don't wait to start investigating an MP case and they shouldn't wait to report it. It needs to be worded strongly enough to get people's attention but, like I said, not cause panic."

We entered my office. "Try to get it on the six o'clock news."

The PIO closed the door behind her. "What's this all about?"

I peered into her eyes, wishing I could remember her blinkin' name!

To her credit, the attractive thirty-something didn't squirm under my gaze. Instead she stuck out her hand. "I'm Phyllis Gladstone, by the way. We haven't had a chance to meet formally."

I shook the hand. "Pleased to meet you, Ms. Gladstone."

She smiled. "My friends call me Phyl."

I stared at her again.

This time she did squirm a little. "I mean, you can call me that, if you want. In private at least." The briefest of pauses. "Florida isn't a very formal state."

I suspected the last part was a veiled message about the image I was projecting to my people.

"Okay, Phyl. You can call me *Chief* in private."

She chuckled. "Got it, Chief." Her eyes sparkled.

I found myself smiling at her.

Then my mood sobered. "Be prepared to work extra hours for the next week or more."

"Why? What's going on?"

I took a deep breath. "We have a serial killer on our hands."

CHAPTER SIX

A soft knock on my door. "Come in."

Sergeant Collins stepped hesitantly into my office. He held two pieces of paper in his hand.

I'd anticipated this, but I wasn't going to let the man's guilt deprive my department of an experienced officer.

"If one of those is what I think it is," I said in a firm voice, "you can tear it up right now."

He looked startled, as I'd suspected he would. "Ma'am?"

He stepped to my desk and handed me one of the papers—a printed-out copy of the report on the missing person case. It said basically what I already knew.

I glanced up. Collins was clutching the other paper in his hand, his eyes shiny. "I would also like to tender my resignation, Chief."

I dropped the report on my desk, sat back in my chair and sighed loudly.

"Sit down, Sergeant."

He gingerly perched on the edge of a visitor's chair.

I let the silence spin out, to see what he would say.

He looked down at his hands, clutching the paper in his lap. "I meant to call Arliss back..."

Arliss. He knew the sister too.

"Things got hairy at the end of my shift. A couple of drunk and disorderlies came in, from one of the bars downtown. When the officers and I had finally wrestled them into the holding cell, Sergeant Lewis was standin' by the desk."

"What did you tell Lewis in the change-of-shift briefing?"

"That I'd meant to call the reporting party back. I assumed he would, and then put out a BOLO if her sister wasn't home yet."

I leaned forward. "When you come on duty, are you briefed in detail about the major cases the detectives are working on?"

"Not in detail, just their status, and any personnel or resources the detectives are requesting."

I tapped an index finger against my lips. "I'm thinking you should read the lead detectives' most recent reports on all active major cases at the beginning of each shift."

How many could there be, under normal circumstances.

"Maybe keep a list of names of all witnesses, victims, and persons of interest. Do you see any downside to that becoming part of the procedure?"

He jerked his head off to the side, looked at me out of the corner of his eye. "Some detectives might not like having info about their cases bandied about."

"I'm not talking about making them public knowledge," I said, a little impatient. "Only the watch commanders would see the reports."

Collins's face was pointed in my general direction again, but he wasn't making eye contact.

What was he not saying? Did he think the sergeants would resent the additional work? Or was one of them a blabber-mouth—might not keep things confidential?

"Okay, I'll have to give the issue some more thought," I said. "And I officially refuse to accept your resignation. Your decision to hold off on the BOLO was not out of line, since you didn't know that she was a witness in another case."

Lewis's lack of follow-up, however...

Collins finally made eye contact. "Yes, ma'am." His tone was half relieved, half forlorn.

"Not much luck with the genetics company yet," Bradley reported, lounging in one of my visitors' chairs. "I finally waded through the menus and got a live person, who transferred me to a supervisor, who admitted this was all above his pay-grade. I'm waiting for the CEO of the company to call me back."

"How'd you figure out which company?"

"Got lucky there. The student worker who puts the mail in the slots at the mail center has almost a photographic memory. He saw the envelope to Pearl Altman—said it's not every day that someone gets DNA results so it stood out in his memory."

I nodded, fighting to concentrate. It had been a long day.

"We also tracked down some of the folks from the NA meeting–"

"We who? You and Jacobs?"

"No, me and a uniform. I got phone numbers and first names from the group's secretary. Three people remembered seeing Darla near a dark sedan. None thought to look at the license plate. Two of them said they couldn't see the driver, only shadows inside the car. One woman said she thought it was a man, but he was silhouetted against the convenience store's outside lights behind him. She said she wondered if Darla was up to her old tricks, literally, as in prostituting to get money for drugs."

My door opened. Jacobs stuck his head in. "Did I just hear my name?" he said cheerfully.

I swallowed a sigh. I needed to speak to him about knocking first. And his name hadn't *just* been mentioned. Had he been eavesdropping at the door?

He came in and plopped down in my other visitor's chair.

"Turn up anything interesting?" I kept my voice carefully neutral.

"About the same as Bradley here," he said in a sarcastic tone, "who seems to have been duplicating my efforts." He turned to Bradley. "I thought I told you I would deal with the NA folks."

Bradley visibly sucked in a deep breath. "Sarge assigned a uniform to help–"

I held up a hand. "My fault. I told Bradley to talk to the NA group's secretary."

Bradley gave a slight nod. "The uniform and I worked the phones. Found some–"

"Well, I talked to people in person—better to see their facial expressions, you know."

"The NA secretary only had first names and phone numbers," Bradley said, "not addresses."

Jacobs smirked.

Why did I feel like a mother with squabbling siblings whenever these two were in the same room?

"Anyhow," Jacobs said, "one of the gals I talked to wondered if Darla was using again, and the guy was either a john or her dealer."

"Did she get a good look at him?" I said.

He shook his head. "Too dark. But I say, trust these gals' instincts. They were probably on the streets themselves at some point, to feed their habits. They know the body language."

Bradley bristled. I suspected I knew why. It was a bit of a leap to assume all female addicts were whores.

"I say we roust Darla's old pimp," Jacobs continued, "and her dealer. Bradley, you take the pimp."

Bradley pursed his lips and turned to me. "You were going to form a task force with JSO?"

Jacobs scowled at him.

"That's my plan." Then I got what Bradley was trying to convey. The pimp and the dealer would be in Jacksonville. Not our jurisdiction.

"I've got a call in to their Chief of Investigations," I said.

Bradley and Jacobs exchanged a look, suddenly co-conspirators of some kind. Neither said anything for a full beat.

"What?" I demanded.

"Uh," Bradley said, "he didn't exactly get along with your predecessor."

A second exchanged glance.

Jacobs cleared his throat. "How about I touch base with the detectives over there who worked the first cases?"

I nodded, even though I was confused as hell by his sudden alliance with Bradley.

He stood. "Later." And he was out the door, closing it behind him.

"What is going on?" I demanded of Bradley.

He slowly shook his head. "Chief Black, despite his last name, didn't play well with certain people."

Ah, the man was a bigot as well as a sexist. Why am I not surprised?

It looked like I had a lot of fences to mend with my neighbors.

The rookie, hat tucked under her arm, stood stiffly at attention in front of my desk—slightly shorter than average but sturdily built, dark hair in a tight bun low on her neck. She saluted. "Officer Barnes, reporting as ordered."

"*Requested*," I said, leaning my chair back to look up at her more comfortably. "At ease, Officer."

She relaxed slightly.

"I assume Detective Bradley explained what I have in mind."

"Yes, ma'am."

"There will be no hard feelings, no repercussions, if you don't want the assignment. Understood?"

"Yes, ma'am." Her voice still sounded like a raw recruit answering a drill sergeant.

"I'm thinking six months." I was considering having a rookie rotate into the position periodically. It would be a good way to assess their potential, as well as solve my lack-of-an-assistant problem. Again, unorthodox, but you do what you gotta do.

"There'll be some tedious stuff involved. Answering phones, opening my snail mail and such, but I want you with me whenever I'm out in the field. You'll learn the department along with me."

No response.

"When we're at a crime scene or discussing a case with another officer, I want you paying close attention. I'll want your take on things afterwards. Any questions?"

"No, ma'am."

Was that a glint of anger in her brown eyes?

"Are you thinking that I'm asking you because you are the only female rookie?"

A slight hesitation. "No, ma'am."

"Okay, *that* is not allowed."

She blinked. "What, ma'am?"

"Lying to me. I always want to hear what you truly think, even if I won't like it."

She blinked again. "Yes, ma'am."

"I asked Detective Bradley if any of the rookies had admin experience. You were the only one who did."

"With all due respect, ma'am, that is *because* I'm female. Men don't usually take clerical jobs, except maybe in a mail room."

"So why did *you* take a clerical job?"

"To pay the bills while I got my training. If you're female, warm and breathing, you can usually get a file clerk or receptionist gig, without any experience."

I nodded. Not much had changed in that respect since I was a young woman.

She cleared her throat. "I've handled the phones, typed correspondence, filed, set up meetings, fetched coffee." Her lip curled slightly.

I gestured toward my personal coffee maker at the end of the credenza behind my desk. "I keep my own stash of coffee, and you're welcome to share it."

"Yes, ma'am."

I blew out air. "You're giving me a crick in my neck, Officer. Please, sit down."

She hesitated again, stared at the visitor's chair like she thought it might bite.

"Sit."

She sat, perched on the edge, wiggling some and rearranging the accouterments on her duty belt that had caught on the metal arms of the chair. She placed her hat on her knees, looking no more comfortable than she had when standing.

"So?" I said.

Two blinks this time. "Ma'am?"

"Do you want the assignment?"

She opened her mouth.

My phone rang. I held up an index finger. "Hold that thought." I grabbed up the receiver. "Anderson."

"Chief, this is Jenny. Jan said you wanted to know about any missing-person calls."

I visualized pregnant Jenny, sitting sideways in front of the dispatch terminal. "Yes."

"We got one, just now. I passed it on to the sarge."

"Name?"

Movement in my peripheral vision. Barnes had taken out her notepad and pencil.

Jenny said the name and my heart stuttered in my chest.

I repeated it out loud for Barnes's benefit, but I didn't need it written down to remember it.

Francis Tremont—the owner of the convenience store.

CHAPTER SEVEN

I looked at Officer Barnes, pointed my chin at the pad in her hand. "I take it that means *yes*."

She nodded.

"Jenny," I said into the phone, "text the address to Officer Barnes's cell phone."

"Yes, ma'am." Jenny disconnected.

I shoved myself to a stand and headed for the door, hiding a smile when Barnes was right on my heels.

We exited the front doors of the building. The outside air hit me in the face like a hot, wet blanket. Early October and almost seven p.m., and still the temperature hovered around eighty-five.

Once in my car, the AC blasting, I said, "Radio Sergeant Collins that I've reassigned you. We'll deal with the paperwork, and a desk and such for you, tomorrow."

Barnes did as instructed.

"Out of curiosity, what's with the different last names?" I asked. "Bradley said you were his sister. Are you married?"

She shook her head. "We're half-sibs. Same mother, different fathers. But we were raised together." Her tone was still a bit clipped.

Which was fine. I didn't need to get too cozy with her.

Ten minutes later, we pulled up behind a cruiser, in front of a cement-block rancher in a middle-class neighborhood.

An officer I didn't recognize stood on the front porch, talking to a petite, dark-haired woman in the doorway. She wore khaki capris and a light green tee shirt.

When we were about ten feet away, her worried brown eyes in a pale face turned toward us. The officer whirled around. "Chief, wha…" He trailed off.

"At ease, Officer." Slightly uncomfortable that he recognized me when I didn't know him from Adam, I pointed toward the half-open door. "Shall we take this inside?"

"Where are my manners?" the woman said in a Southern accent. She opened the door wider.

I glanced at the officer's name tag as I walked past him. *T. Armstrong*. Under his name was *serving since 2006*. A fifteen-year veteran. His rugged face pegged him as at least forty.

He and Barnes exchanged a nod of recognition.

As he entered, he removed his hat, revealing a completely bald head, which, ironically, made him look somewhat younger.

Barnes and I settled on a sofa covered in tropical flora, Armstrong on a matching loveseat. We all declined Mrs. Tremont's offer of tea or coffee, and she sank onto the edge of a stuffed armchair, bright red like the hibiscus in the other pieces' upholstery.

I nodded to Armstrong.

He led the woman through her story. Her husband hadn't shown up for his daughter's soccer match after school, and then hadn't come home for dinner.

"I saw on the six o'clock news that y'all had just changed the rules, that we shouldn't wait to report a missing person, so I thought I should…" her soft voice trailed off.

Armstrong reassured her that she had done the right thing.

Actually, we hadn't *just* changed the rules. The forty-eight-hour waiting period had been abolished nationwide decades ago, after a young woman was kidnapped and killed while the local cops refused to take the parents' report. In Baltimore County, I'd worked a case where the father in a similar scenario had sought twisted revenge for his daughter's death by becoming a serial killer himself, kidnapping people and then killing them exactly forty-eight hours later.

I tuned back in as Armstrong cleared his throat. "I know this is awkward, but is there anyone else Mr. Tremont–"

He stopped abruptly when I shook my head slightly. No need to get into the possible girlfriend on the side.

"Mrs. Tremont," I said, cutting to the chase, "your husband owns a convenience store, correct?"

Armstrong's eyebrows went up to where his hairline would be, if he had one.

"Yes. This is his night off, though," Mrs. Tremont said. "He always takes Sundays and a weeknight, whenever the girls have something happening." She shook her head. "I called the store. Ronnie said he hadn't been in, not since he came for the bank deposit this morning."

"And I assume you've been calling him?" I asked.

"Again and again. It rings several times and goes to voicemail."

"Could we have his cell phone number, please?" I reached for the pad in my pocket, then noted Barnes's pencil hovering over hers.

I suppressed a smile.

Mrs. Tremont rattled off the number.

I looked at Armstrong and raised my own eyebrows, silently asking if he had more questions.

He shook his head slightly.

We all stood, Mrs. Tremont a beat behind us.

"Try not to worry, ma'am," Armstrong said. "We'll be in touch." He gave her his card. "Call if you hear from him or think of anything else that might be helpful."

Out on the sidewalk beside our cars, I filled Armstrong in on the serial killer case, and how Tremont was a potential witness in Darla Monkton's murder.

"Shit, that don't bode well for Mr. Tremont." He quickly added, "Sorry, Chief."

"Armstrong, I've been a cop for twenty-five years. My ears are not the least bit sensitive."

I paused, glanced at Barnes, who was chewing on her lower lip.

"And you're right," I added. "This doesn't bode well for Tremont."

At the convenience store, the three of us hovered off to the side, trying to look casual, while waiting for a lull in customers.

I considered getting a cup of joe, but it was getting late. I was hoping to be able to go home soon.

Who am I kidding? I grabbed the nearest pot and poured black caffeine into a thick cardboard cup. I held the pot up toward the others. They both nodded, Barnes half a beat behind Armstrong.

I poured two more cups.

Barnes doctored hers with cream and half a packet of sugar. She carefully bent over the top of the packet and put it back in the square container on the counter. *Really?* Did she think someone would use that half a teaspoon that a stranger had opened?

Barnes caught me watching and her cheeks reddened. "Sorry. My mom taught me to be frugal." She pulled the half packet out and threw it in the nearby trash can.

When the line of customers was down to two people, I stepped forward. "Ronnie, isn't it?"

The kid behind the cash register glanced my way. "Yeah."

"What time did Mr. Tremont come in today?"

"'Bout eleven, as usual." He gave his customer some change and picked up one of the next person's items.

I was trying to be discreet, but time was ticking and the sun had already set. The sky was now the dull gray of dusk, and getting darker by the second. "And what time did he leave for the bank?"

Ronnie shrugged. "A few minutes later. I didn't notice the exact time." He said goodbye to the customer, apparently a regular—he gave us a curious look.

Ronnie turned toward us. "Mrs. T's been calling, but I haven't seen him since then." His tone had shifted from matter-of-fact to worried, now that the customers were gone.

"Which bank does he use?" Armstrong asked, his pad and pencil out, as was Barnes's.

"Belmont Bank. It's independent. He likes to support locally-owned businesses."

I nodded as the other two scribbled. Armstrong gave Barnes a sideways glance.

Ronnie pulled out a zippered navy-blue canvas bag from under the counter. "He had the deposit in one of these."

The bank's address was printed in small letters on a lower corner of the bag. The officers wrote on their pads.

I thanked the young man and headed for the door.

"Ma'am, ya gonna find him?"

I turned back. Ronnie's eyes were now shiny.

"You like him," I said.

He nodded. "He's a good boss."

"We're going to do our damnedest to find him."

Once outside, the door fully closed behind us, Armstrong said, "whether or not he'll still be alive is another matter. Uh, Chief, do I need to take notes, or just let the rookie do it?"

The chuckle in his voice saved him from a reprimand for being flip. "You take your own notes, Officer," I said in a stern voice. "It's your case. The rookie's my new assistant."

Armstrong's eyebrows shot up, but he didn't say anything.

We drove in tandem to the bank. It was now closed, but a white sedan sat in the parking lot.

I got out of my car and stretched, hoping for a second wind. The coffee had helped, but only a little.

Barnes climbed out of my passenger seat, pad in one hand, phone in the other.

Armstrong trotted up. "Ran the plates." He gestured toward the sedan. "It's Tremont's."

"Shit," I said.

He gave me a lopsided grin.

Barnes held her phone out in front of her and started walking toward the side of the small brick bank building.

"Get a search warrant to process the car," I said to Armstrong.

"Wife would probably give permission."

"Probably. Get the warrant. Just in case the wife turns out to be involved." Although I doubted that would be the case, in this instance.

"Chief," Barnes called from behind the building.

We jogged around the corner to join her in a smaller back parking lot, well lit by two streetlights.

She punched a button on her phone, and a faint ringing came from the direction of a dumpster in the near corner of the fast-food joint's lot next door.

"Time for your first dumpster dive, kid," Armstrong was saying as I walked toward the sound. I almost stepped on the phone, in a clump of weeds.

"Either of you got gloves?" I called out. Mine were in a pocket of my jacket, which was slung across the backseat of my car. It was too fricking hot to drive in it.

I took several pictures of the phone, from different angles.

Armstrong appeared beside me, with a pair of blue latex gloves and an evidence envelope in his hands.

Barnes went on past us toward the dumpster. "Shit!"

I jerked my head in her direction. She'd clamped a hand over her mouth.

"Back up, Rookie, before you contaminate a scene," Armstrong said.

She shook her head, one hand still over her mouth, pointed with the other.

A man's dark brown sandal stuck out from behind the back of the dumpster.

It was strapped around a foot.

CHAPTER EIGHT

After Jacobs and the ME arrived, I figured it was time to get out of the way and let my people do their jobs. So I went home.

But I left Barnes there to keep track of what was going on, since she was still on shift anyway.

She had *not* contaminated the scene. Indeed, she'd handled herself better than I had when I'd seen my first corpse, years ago.

Inside my apartment door, I kicked off my shoes and wished again that I had a cat.

Where did that thought keep coming from? I hadn't had a pet in my twenty-eight years of adulthood...although we'd had cats, and a dog for a few years, when I was a kid.

I'd never felt lonely living alone before either, but now I guessed that's what I was feeling.

Maybe it was because I wasn't comfortable with my coworkers yet, as I had been in Maryland.

Up there, after a long day of interacting with others, I'd been ready for the peace and quiet of my own space. But down here, there wasn't a sense of connection yet with my fellow cops.

I shook my head. There might never be. I was the big boss now. I needed to maintain a certain distance, keep a wall up.

I snorted. *Or should I say, a* thicker *wall.* I'd never been good at letting people in.

I shed clothing, took a hot shower, and curled up on the couch in my robe, a glass of wine in hand.

I'd stick to one glass, in case I had to go out again later. I found a Netflix show that looked interesting and leaned back with a sigh.

The woman on the floor got up, as she sometimes did. "Are you hungry? I'll fix you a snack." She walked toward the fridge, and I sat at the tiny kitchen table.

My long legs barely fit under it. She called it our postage-stamp table.

A buzzing sound. Was it the microwave?

Another buzz.

I opened one eye. My cell phone was vibrating across the cardboard box I used as a coffee table. I jolted upright.

Since I recognized none of the people on the TV, I assumed the show I'd been watching had ended and something else was now on.

I picked up the phone and checked it. A text message from an unknown number.

Chief, you awake?

I glanced at the time on the phone. Who the hell was texting me at eleven-twenty?

Yes, I texted back, while thinking, *I am now.*

No response. The phone rang and I jumped, almost dropping it in my lap.

The same unknown number.

"Anderson," I barked into the phone.

"Barnes here, Chief. Um, the ME says Tremont was probably strangled first, until he passed out, then knifed. He's been dead for a few hours. That's all he'd say for now."

"Any sign of Tremont's bank deposit bag?"

"Not around him, or in his car. Officer Armstrong thinks it might be in the dumpster... You want me to search for it in there?"

"No," I said emphatically. "You are my assistant. Let Armstrong get someone else to go dumpster diving."

"Phew. Thank you, ma'am."

I suppressed a chuckle. "What about the video from the bank's surveillance cameras?"

I very much wanted to know how Tremont ended up in the back of the bank when his car was parked out front.

"That's really weird, ma'am. Jacobs got the bank manager out here, and he checked for the footage. There was none for the entire day. Apparently, the back cameras were tampered with last night."

Hmm... interesting coincidence.

"Aren't you off shift now?" I asked.

"Yes, technically."

"Then go home, because as of tomorrow, you're on day shift. Oh, who's doing the notification?"

"Jacobs was going to, and Officer Armstrong said he should go too, since the missus already knows him."

"Good. See you in the morning."

"Yes, ma'am."

I arrived early, but Barnes was already there, ensconced at the metal desk nearest my door.

"Good morning, Chief." Her expression was neutral. "I got your coffee maker going, and I've ordered a new phone for this desk, that will have your extension on it as well as mine."

"Get me a new phone too, with two lines. I want the new one to be totally private, with a different number from the department's, if that's doable."

She nodded briskly.

"Once that's set in motion, come into my office."

Another brisk nod was interrupted by a loud voice, "Hey, Rookie, that's my desk!"

"Sorry, Detective Cruthers." Barnes smiled sweetly past my shoulder. "I'm the Chief's new assistant so I have to be nearby. I moved your things to an empty desk over there." She pointed across the bullpen.

I turned slightly. Cruthers was middle-aged, tall and husky, with shaggy brown hair. He growled like the bear he resembled, then made eye contact with me.

"Sorry, Detective," I added my apology, but straight-faced. Sweet smiles are not my thing.

"Harumph." Still scowling, he stomped off to his new desk.

I'd poured myself a cup of coffee and had barely sat down, when Barnes was in my office. I gestured toward the door, as I took my first sip.

Bleck! I stared down into my cup. Pale brown water.

Barnes had closed the door and was now standing in front of my desk, looking nervous for the first time since I'd met her yesterday. "I, um, I'm not much of a coffee drinker myself, ma'am. I wasn't sure how much to use."

I flicked my hand to indicate it wasn't a big deal, even though it was. I didn't run well in the mornings without my caffeine lubricant. "Sit," I said, pointing to a visitor's chair.

Barnes sat. But first, she removed her baton—which had gotten stuck sideways in the chair's arm yesterday—from her duty belt.

"What's your take on the Tremont case?"

"No sign of the bank bag," she said, "so it *looks* like a robbery gone bad."

I noted the emphasis on *looks* and suppressed a smile. This gal was bright and observant. "What do you think?"

"The ME commented last night that he was garroted from behind. There was a smooth red mark on his throat." Barnes ran a finger straight across her own neck. "He wasn't willing to speculate about what the garrote was made of yet. *But* it's quite a coincidence that a witness in another case involving garroting happens to be robbed just now—and is also garroted."

I sat back in my chair and let a small grin escape, briefly. "I had an excellent training officer when I was a rookie, and a great mentor as a novice detective. The latter, my partner in homicide for ten years, used to say that he's allergic to coincidences."

She gave me a half smile.

"What are your thoughts about the garroting?"

She frowned. "If I were a crook, and I had a knife, why would I waste time strangling the guy and then stab him? I'd poke him some with the knife, so he'd cooperate, grab the bag and run."

I nodded. Those were my thoughts exactly.

"And," Barnes continued, "how did Tremont get from his car out front to the dumpster in the back? The assailant wouldn't have dragged him there in broad daylight."

"Highly unlikely, so he was lured back there somehow. Any other thoughts?"

"I called Officer Armstrong this morning."

Bet he loved that! It was now barely seven-thirty, so that call happened quite early, after Armstrong had been up half the night. But I didn't say anything.

"He said the notification went as well as could be expected. Jacobs..."

Was that a slight curling of the lips I detected?

"Officer Armstrong said Jacobs questioned Mrs. Tremont about her whereabouts yesterday. She doesn't have a very solid alibi. She was out running errands until her daughter's game at three."

I sat back. "What's bothering you, Barnes?"

She shook her head, but then blurted out, "Officer Armstrong said that Jacobs really pushed her hard." Her voice was disapproving. "But the woman seemed legitimately devastated."

"Did he say anything else about the alibi?"

"She had a couple of receipts, but there was a big time gap in between the times on them. Jacobs was going to check them out today, Officer Armstrong said."

"He was quite chatty, wasn't he?"

Her cheeks pinked slightly. "He was my training officer, for my first six months."

"Ahh." I paused, wondering if I should ask the next question. What the hell... "So tell me, why do you refer to just about every cop in the department by their title and last name, but with Lieutenant Jacobs, you only use his last name?"

"Not to his face," Barnes said quickly.

"I'm not chastising you. I only want to know why you don't like him."

She started to shake her head. "I–"

I held up a finger. "What is my number-one rule?"

"To always tell you the truth." She let out a low sigh. "Yesterday was the first time I really interacted with him."

A beat of silence.

"But?" I said.

"But my brother doesn't like him. He told me to stay clear of him as much as I could, that Jacobs was a suck-up big time with the old chief, while..." She trailed off.

Hmm, I would've said big bro, Bradley was more of a suck-up than Jacobs. Well, maybe that wasn't fair. Bradley's friendliness seemed like his genuine personality. Jacobs—I wasn't sure what his true personality was yet. He was more guarded.

Was he a suck-up? I'd felt he was flirting with me the other evening. Was that sucking up?

"While what?" I said.

Her cheeks were pink again. "Um, I'd rather not repeat what Detective Bradley told me in confidence."

I considered pushing her, but decided that wasn't fair. I nodded and picked up my pen. "That's all for now."

Barnes stood and headed for the door.

"Oh, and from now on," I said, my tone casual, "I'll make the coffee."

Her cheeks pinked yet again, but there was relief in her eyes.

"You're welcome to help yourself whenever you like," I added.

Her eyes darted around some. She gave me a wan smile and hustled out the door.

I swallowed a chuckle.

An hour later, a knock on my ajar door. Bradley stuck his head in. "Chief, Detectives Foster and Edwards are here from the JSO for the first meeting of the task force." His face was blank, but there was a tightness around his eyes.

Was he mad about something?

I pressed my lips together to keep a sigh from escaping. When would I know my people well enough that I could stop being so hypervigilant with them?

My chest felt heavy. I realized with a start that I was homesick for the Baltimore County PD—where I knew the personalities and quirks of every member of my precinct, and quite a few of the other BCPD cops as well. But the department was not the same as it had once been.

I shook my head slightly to disperse those thoughts. Not the time to be rehashing my recent grievances, even though it would help ward off the homesickness.

"I'll be right there."

Bradley's head disappeared, and I closed the report I'd been reviewing on my computer.

Barnes was gone from her desk. Slightly annoyed, I found my way to the smaller of our two conference rooms.

And she was already there.

I couldn't completely suppress my smile. She was passing out steaming cups, with the logo of a nearby coffee shop on them. From the aroma alone, I felt more energized.

Good girl! If it's not in your skill set, hire someone who can do it well.

There was also a board already set up, with crime scene photos from each case tacked on one side, and a white-board area next to it for notes. A box of thumb tacks and three markers of different colors were on the conference table near the board.

I was about to give Jacobs mental credit for the display when I noticed he was *taking down* the photos from the Tremont scene.

I cleared my throat.

Jacobs froze, the last of the photos, of the dumpster, in his hand. He carefully placed it on the table, face down. "That's getting a little ahead of things," he said, as if to himself.

But I knew it was aimed at me.

After greeting the Jacksonville detectives, I moved to where Barnes was now leaning her butt against the wall, her own cup in one hand and a legal pad in the other.

A steaming cup also sat on the table at one of the two empty seats in front of her. I gave a slight shake of my head, looked meaningfully at the other empty chair, and sat down.

She took the hint and sat beside me.

Jacobs frowned at her.

"Lieutenant," I said, "bring us up to speed. Gentlemen, feel free to add anything as he goes along."

Still standing, Jacobs ran through the details of the earlier cases in Jacksonville. Foster and Edwards remained silent, until he mentioned the woman's nylon that the perp had tried to strangle Darla Monkton with.

"We didn't have a type of murder weapon before," Foster said, his tone neutral. "Some kind of cloth was all the ME had said."

He was the older but the less fastidious of the two, his dark suit rumpled when it wasn't even lunchtime yet. And his medium brown hair, liberally sprinkled with gray, stuck up in a few places, probably due to his tendency to finger-comb it out of his face.

Another shot of homesickness. He reminded me some of my former partner.

Dolph isn't even in Maryland anymore, I told myself.

Jacobs had moved on to Darla's murder.

"Do you think y'all going to interview Ms. Monkton again triggered the perp to get rid of her?" Edwards asked, in a Southern accent that pegged him more as a Georgia man originally, rather than a Floridian. He was mid-thirties and nattily dressed in a light grey suit, his blond hair cut short.

I opened my mouth to say yes, but Jacobs was shaking his head.

"We don't know," he said. "Could've been that. Or he could've been watching for an opportunity to get to her, to complete unfinished business."

The Jacksonville detectives gave slight nods. His explanation was also plausible.

Bradley was silent, his face blank. Barnes was keeping her head down, scribbling away on her pad.

When Jacobs had run down, I said to Bradley, "Where are we on the ancestry angle with Pearl Altman?"

He leaned forward and explained how the roommate had remembered Pearl's search for her biological parents, wondering if that was somehow connected to her death.

"Unlikely," Jacobs interrupted him, "since the MO was so similar to these others."

Bradley glanced his way.

"But not exactly the same," I said.

Bradley's gaze flicked toward me, annoyance in his eyes. I suspected it was about Jacobs, not me.

His tone was smooth, however, as he continued, "No luck getting a subpoena for the ancestry company's records. Judge said we don't have sufficient probable cause. I'm gonna talk to the company's CEO again today." The end of his mouth quirked up in a half smile. "See if begging works, though I doubt it will."

I nodded, then turned to the Jacksonville detectives. "You gentlemen have anything to add?"

"Nothing that isn't already in the case files we sent over," Foster said. "But we'll go back a few more years. Now that we have the woman's stocking piece of the MO, might be other cases that could be the same perp. He most likely didn't start out killing his victims, so maybe some older SA cases will pop and produce more witnesses."

I nodded again. "Thank you."

Foster smiled, but his eyes remained grim. "No problem. We've got a couple of dogs in this race too."

"Also," I said, "in case Darla Monkton had fallen off the wagon, can you check out her old pimp and her drug dealer? See if she had any recent contact. Maybe she got crosswise with one of them."

Foster nodded.

I turned back to Jacobs. "Tremont?"

"I'm not sure he's relevant," Jacobs said.

I raised my eyebrows. "We look at all angles." My tone was deceptively mild. My subordinates in BCPD would've known what that meant.

His face slightly flushed, he picked up one of the crime scene photos and tacked it to the bottom of the cork side of the board. It was the one showing Tremont lying on his back behind the dumpster, a knife wound in his side. "Francis Tremont, convenience store owner. Robbed and knifed yesterday as he was about to make a bank deposit."

Foster frowned. "What's the connection?"

"Ligature marks on his neck," Jacobs said, his tone slightly impatient. "He was partially strangled to incapacitate him, then knifed."

"Garroted from behind," I added, "as the women likely were, according to the ME."

Chest tight with annoyance, I waited for Jacobs to continue, but the silence spun out.

Edwards shifted in his chair. "I don't get it. How's this guy related to the other homicides?"

Jacobs opened his mouth but I spoke first. "Officer Barnes, how are the cases connected?"

She jerked her head up, eyes wide, mouth hanging open. But she recovered quickly, straightening in her seat. "Tremont was a witness in the Darla Monkton case. He saw her talking to someone in a dark sedan outside the church where her NA meeting was about to start. She and the car were too far away for him to give us details, but she never showed up at the meeting. Three people headed for the meeting also saw the car but couldn't tell us any more than Tremont did."

Foster was nodding slowly now.

"Anything from the interviews of the bank personnel?" I asked Jacobs. "Or from the canvassing of neighboring businesses?"

"Haven't had time to read the uniforms' reports yet," he said. "I was prepping for this meeting."

My teeth clenched behind closed lips. Now he was really pissing me off.

"Besides," Jacobs added, his tone casual, "I'm pretty sure it's a coincidence that he happened to get robbed right now."

"Barnes," I barked, "how do I feel about coincidences?"

The corners of her mouth twitched. "You're allergic to them, Chief," she said in a mild voice.

To Jacobs, I said, "Assign another detective to the Tremont case. Tell him to loop us all in on his reports." I swung an index finger in a circle to indicate everyone in the room.

"I can't have all my men tied up on this," Jacobs shot back.

I narrowed my eyes at him, furious that he was arguing personnel issues in front of the Jacksonville cops, even though I'd started it.

In the low, firm voice my detectives at BCPD had learned to fear, I said, "You got something more important than a serial killer for them to work on?"

He blew out air. "No. I'll put Cruthers on it."

"Good." I stood up. To Foster and Edwards, I said, "Thanks for coming over to our house, gentlemen." They rose and I shook their hands.

Edwards gave me a slight nod as he shuffled past. Foster stopped and leaned in close. "You go see Darla," he said in a low voice, "and she dies. Then your best witness to what might've happened to her dies. You might have a leak, Chief."

"I know," I whispered back, even though I hadn't totally admitted it to myself until today.

"And your lieutenant..." He rolled his eyes.

Foster was somewhat out of line, but I liked him, so I let it pass.

Barnes followed the detectives out the door. I was headed out after her when Jacobs cleared his throat.

I turned back.

"Sorry for being testy, Chief. I'm a bit sleep-deprived." He gave me an ingratiating smile.

I could certainly relate to that. "Yet another good reason to bring more hands on deck."

"Uh, are we approved for overtime on this?"

I sighed. "Of course."

The mayor and city council would probably forgive me for blowing my budget right out of the gate, *if* we actually caught this killer.

"Can we handle this, Nate?" I used his first name intentionally, to show no hard feelings since he'd apologized. "Or should I be calling in the FBI?"

He gave an exaggerated shudder. "Not yet. Hopefully not ever. I think we can handle it."

"Good, because I don't really want to have to run to the feds with my panties in a wad over my first major case as chief."

He grinned, and I left the room, figuring the fences were mended.

But something was still bothering me.

I walked back toward my office, down the long hallway that stretched across the front of the third floor of the municipal building. Someday, if I succeeded here as chief, I hoped to have our own building, but for now 3MB was our home.

Floor-to-ceiling windows along one side of the hallway made it an oven. The glass was tinted, but predated modern glass products designed to filter out most of the sun's heat. Maybe we could get an additional tinted coating on the inside of the glass?

As so often happens, when I stopped thinking about a question, the answer popped into my head. I knew what was bothering me. If Jacobs didn't believe the Tremont case was related to the others, why hadn't he already assigned it to another detective, instead of keeping it himself?

Was he a control freak?

That would explain some of Bradley's dislike of him.

"Chief?" A familiar voice broke into my reverie.

I turned my head but kept walking, anxious to get to the cooler climes of the detectives' bullpen ahead.

Bradley trotted up to me, fell into step. "If the ancestry company's CEO doesn't cooperate, I'd like to go talk to the roommate again. Cruthers interviewed the adoptive parents?"

"Yeah. They had no idea who might have wanted to harm Pearl."

"Do you think they knew their daughter was looking for her biological parents?"

"I doubt it," I said. "Pearl didn't even tell her roommate, slash, best friend."

"If the roommate hasn't thought of anything else, I'll swing by and talk to the parents again."

I nodded, sighing internally. Such was police work sometimes. Talk to witnesses, explore leads, talk to the same witnesses again. Rinse, repeat.

We entered the bullpen.

Barnes sat at her desk by my door, savagely ripping open envelopes with a letter opener. Her expression was beyond stormy.

"What's up, Sis?" Bradley said as we approached.

"Don't call me that here," she hissed, without making eye contact.

Then she carefully put down the opener and pulled a newspaper out from under the pile of envelopes.

She flipped it to the below-the-fold side and slid it toward us.

A brick of dread formed in my stomach as I read the bold headline over a two-column story.

Shit! The mayor and city council would *not* forgive this.

And I definitely had a leak in the department.

CHAPTER NINE

"Damn that woman!" Bradley said, pointing to the byline under the obnoxious headline.

Is Our New Police Chief Sexist? by Marly Davis

The phone rang on the desk.

I held up my hand. "Don't answer that, Barnes."

I marched into my office, tossing the door shut behind me. It slammed, shaking the glass wall.

Keeping my back to the glass—I really needed to get some kind of shades up in here—I picked up my ringing desk phone.

As I'd suspected, it was the mayor, asking what the hell was I doing pulling the only female from the rookie pool to be my admin. "Don't you know anything about optics?" he blustered.

"Apparently not, Mr. Mayor," I replied, as blandly as possible. "I'm a cop, not a politician, and a damned good cop at that. Which is why you all hired me."

"What's with the *you all*?" he said. "You makin' fun of Southern accents now too?"

"No, sir. I'm from Maryland, and we say *you all* up there, two words. I guess it's because we're on the cusp between the North and the South." I was tempted to add a *hon* to the end of the sentence, also a Marylandism, but I clamped my teeth together to resist the temptation.

My guess was Mr. Mayor would not be amused.

A pause. "Well, you need to address this, in a press conference. Today! And say something to soothe the public's concerns about these killings."

I groaned internally. I hated press conferences, but I'd known they would be part of the job.

"I will hold a press conference, sir, but I'm not sure calming the public is the best approach. People, especially women, need to be on guard."

"Then you need to tell them you've got leads, that you're close to making an arrest. You know how bad this makes me and the council look? Here we hire this hot-shot Northern detective and next thing we know, we got a killer on the loose." His voice had gone screechy.

I pulled the receiver slightly away from my ear. "But sir, we're *not* close to making an arrest. Yes, we do have leads, but–"

"Then I suggest you find somebody to arrest pretty damn soon." He hung up.

My door latch clicked behind me. I whirled around.

Barnes stuck her head in. "Press conference?" she said in a low voice.

Either she reads minds—which I wouldn't put past her—or she'd heard my end of the conversation through the glass.

"Yes, set one up for three. And find out if there is such a thing as soundproof window shades."

"It's the door that's the problem. It's wood veneer, hollow inside."

"Fine, then order regular shades and a different door that's soundproof."

She nodded. "Can I write up some comments for the press?"

I opened my mouth to say no, closed it again. *Sheez Louise.* I now looked like a fish, in my fishbowl of an office.

"Sure. Why not."

Barnes pulled her head back. The latch clicked shut.

I wanted to rant, maybe throw a couple of objects to vent my fury. But I was the boss and my office was made of blinkin' glass... So I sank into my desk chair, woke up my computer and pretended to be reading reports.

At one-thirty, Barnes brought me her notes and stood in front of my desk.

I read the first few lines, then looked up, eyebrows in the air. These weren't notes for what I should say. They were her words, a statement about the job she had willingly agreed to take on, for the sake of the department and because it was an excellent way to get to know its workings more quickly, from the inside out.

I got a lump in my throat. "You want to say this at the press conference?"

She shook her head rather vehemently, her cheeks turning bright red. "Can you read it for me? I, um..." she stammered. "I'm not the best public speaker."

I considered pushing her to speak for herself, but her discomfort seemed close to phobia level. "Only if you're there to vouch for these being your words."

Her face paled, but she said, "Should I go home and get my dress blues?"

I glanced down at my own somewhat rumpled white blouse. At least I hadn't dribbled any coffee or lunch on it today. "No, we don't want folks to think we're all worried about appearances. Leave that to the mayor. We want to look like we're focused on doing our jobs, which we are."

She nodded, one firm up and down of her head.

The beginning of the press conference went better than I'd expected. I'd managed to avoid saying *serial killer*, but I'd conveyed the need for caution and vigilance.

The ten members of the press, seated in the larger of our conference rooms—seven men and three women—were mostly polite. Bradley and Barnes stood on either side of me, behind a podium.

For some reason, PD press conferences always called for a show of several officers working the case. Which meant those officers *weren't* actually working the case while cooling their heels during the press conference.

I had no idea where Jacobs was at the moment, but I was glad he wasn't here. The reporters would've tried to get more info out of him, as they had with me in Baltimore County, when the police chief wouldn't tell them *everything* about a homicide case.

As it turned out, the PIO, "call me Phyl" Glad-stone, had crafted my remarks. I'd forgotten she existed. Having a public information officer who puts words in my mouth would take some getting used to. But they were good words.

Only one reporter—Marly Davis, of course—raised her hand while I read said remarks. She was fiftyish, carefully put together and well preserved, with a dark bob. Not a hair out of place.

I ignored her as I concluded, "If members of the public see anyone or anything that doesn't look right, please trust your instincts and report it."

More hands went up, but I raised my own in a stop gesture. "I also have a statement to read, on behalf of my new assistant, Officer Gloria Barnes." I read her statement to them.

Some scribbled notes; others held up small recorders or cell phones.

I'd barely finished, when Marly Davis called out, "Are those really her words?"

I turned partway toward Barnes.

Face flushed, she took a step forward. "Y-yes, those are my words. I'm, um, honored to serve as Chief Anderson's assistant. She's an excellent police officer and I know I'll learn a lot from her."

Several reporters nodded.

Marly scowled. "What about the coffee?"

Damn, how the hell did she know about the coffee?

Barnes opened her mouth, but I cut her off. "What coffee?" I asked with exaggerated innocence.

"The coffee she *fetched* for the men this morning."

"I did that on my own," Barnes blurted out. "Out of my own pocket."

"She brought one for me too, and one for herself," I said, letting a little snark creep into my voice, "so not just for the men. And she sat in on the meeting as a contributing member."

"Well, isn't she the good little helpmate," Marly mumbled, none too quietly.

Something snapped inside. I scrunched my forehead up in mock confusion. "So, let me get this straight. If a woman *chooses* to use her skills to help others do their jobs, knowing that will help *her* learn how to be a better police officer more quickly, then she's to be denigrated?"

"How's she going to learn anything fetching coffee and answering phones?" Marly shot back.

"Because she also goes with me when I visit crime scenes and sits in on the briefings I receive." My voice was angry. I was good with that.

"This is a six-month assignment," I continued, somewhat more calmly. "Then she will be rotated out of it and spend some time on the streets. After which, my guess is she'll quickly advance to detective."

I turned to Barnes, expecting her to be smiling.

She looked crestfallen. "Do I have to rotate out?" she whispered.

I gave a small shake of my head—now was not the time for that discussion—and turned back to the podium. "I suspect when other rookies see how this program works, they'll be fighting for the opportunity to be my assistant." I hadn't really thought of it as a "program" before, but the word sounded good to my ears.

And apparently to several of the reporters who were now nodding more vigorously. One raised his hand. "Getting back to the case–"

"Please do," I said.

A low titter rippled through the room.

"How close are you to apprehending this serial killer?" he said.

Damnation! I'd intentionally avoided mentioning the cases in Jacksonville. We'd been able to keep that connection under wraps so far. I'd presented the murders of Pearl, Darla, and Tremont as cases we thought might be related to each other, but we didn't yet know by what.

"Well, if these crimes were indeed committed by the same person, they would technically fit the definition of serial killings. But as I said, we don't know the perpetrator's motives yet. We are pursuing several avenues and leads and will bring this person or persons to justice as soon as possible."

Several reporters called out questions at once. I waved a hand and headed for the door. "That's all for today, folks. This case is ongoing and I can't divulge specifics at this time. We'll keep you posted as best we can."

I swept down the hallway, Bradley and Barnes on either side. The latter had hesitated at the door, perhaps thinking she'd clean up. But Phyl Gladstone had firmly shooed her out of the room.

A good thing. No doubt the reporters would've tried to grill her if she'd stayed, not to mention that her looking like a maid was not the "optic" we wanted right now—or ever.

"You made an enemy of Marly Davis," Bradley said, his tone sympathetic.

"Oh, I think we were already enemies. I just engaged in the battle."

Barnes let out a low snort.

I'd asked Barnes to print out some reports for me. She came into my office and handed me the stack of papers. "New door and shades are in the works," she reported. "Phone company's coming tomorrow, and Detective Foster from Jacksonville is on my line."

"Thank you, thank you, and transfer him over. You can call it a day, Barnes."

She scrunched up her face. The meaning of the expression escaped me, but she left my office before I could ask what was going on.

My desk phone rang and I picked it up. "Detective Foster, how're things going?"

"Pretty good. We've got three SA cases from 2019 that may be our boy's earlier escapades. Two teenagers—one in May, the next in July—grabbed from behind by their hair, threatened with a knife they didn't see, dragged into alleys. Couldn't give much of a description because the guy had a woman's stocking over his face, distorting his features. The next, a month later, Shelly Trent, seventeen, also dragged into an alley. She got a quick glimpse of his face, said it was all distorted. The detective who caught the case speculated it might be a Halloween mask. When she felt something smooth sliding around her neck from behind, she fought him and got away."

"Good work."

"Thanks. We've got a five-month gap between Shelly and the first murder, so we might find other cases in there. I was calling to see if you wanted to send someone along when we talk to Shelly."

"Definitely. What about the other two girls?"

"They've both moved away, one to south Florida. I've got a call in to the Miami PD to go talk to her again. The other gal we've lost track of."

"Okay, when did you want to interview the Trent girl?"

"This evening."

"Let me call Lieutenant Jacobs." Tagging along with my own detectives was one thing. Undermining Jacobs' position as task force leader—any more than our tit-for-tat this morning already had—was another.

"I just did. Went to voicemail. We *want* to go tonight." He came down hard on the *want*, the implication being they would go without us.

"Okay. He must be in the middle of something." Excitement bubbled in my chest. That meant I was free to go with.

Bradley's head appeared around my doorframe. I held up a finger in a *wait* signal.

He pulled out his pad and started scribbling.

"I'll send someone or come myself," I said into the phone.

Bradley slipped a note in front of me.

No luck with the CEO. Off to talk to roomie.

I shook my head, held up my finger a second time.

"One of my guys is coming to Jacksonville," I said into the phone, "to talk to Pearl Altman's roommate again. Would you or Edwards like to go with him, and I'll go with the other to see Shelly?"

"Sounds like a plan," Foster said. "She lives with her aunt on your side of town. Meet us there."

He gave me the address and I jotted it on the bottom of Bradley's note. "See ya there."

I disconnected, stood and grabbed my jacket off the back of my chair.

"Who's Shelly?" Bradley asked.

"I'll explain in the car. You're driving."

I hastily stuffed the pages Barnes had brought me into my briefcase, alongside my laptop. As I breezed past her desk, I said, "Go home!"

She got up and followed us out of the building, but in the parking lot, she headed for her brother's burgundy sedan.

"It's okay, Barnes. You can go home."

She turned, her face screwed up again. "Do I have to?"

Startled, I said, "Well, no. Not if you don't want to."

The Trents' house had a Victorian flavor to it, with gingerbread trim and a wide porch. It reminded me of Kate Huntington's house back in Maryland.

A tugging sensation in my chest. Good heavens, was I missing *Kate Huntington*? I mean, yes, I'd been thinking about her because of this damn serial killer case, but we weren't exactly friends.

She'd just consulted on a few of my cases...and stuck her nose in a few others without my permission. And I certainly wasn't missing her pain-in-the-butt P.I. husband.

Although I owed him one, after he'd helped my former training officer out of a jam. And caught the asshole who'd almost killed Dolph.

Foster and Edwards piled out of their unmarked sedan as we pulled up. Barnes and I got out of Bradley's car, and Edwards took my place in the passenger seat.

I stared a bit longingly at the unmarked, something Starling could not afford, I'd been told. We paid our detectives mileage instead, to use their own cars. I wasn't convinced it was less expensive.

"Be back as soon as we can," Bradley called out of his open window.

Foster, Barnes and I approached the house's covered porch.

"Did you call ahead?" I asked Foster.

"No." He ran his hand through his already disheveled hair. "Didn't want to give her the chance to say she didn't want to talk to us."

"What if she says it to our faces?"

He gave me a smile and rang the doorbell. “I can be quite charming when I want to be.”

A dog yapped inside.

After a moment, the door opened partway and a thin, middle-aged woman stood in the opening. “Can I help you?”

The dog, an off-white mop, tried to slip past her feet, still yapping.

“Shut up, Princess.” She nudged the dog away with one foot.

Foster introduced himself and showed the woman his badge, along with a friendly smile. “We’d like to speak to your niece, please.”

“So would I.” Her tone was crisp. “Haven’t seen her in days.”

CHAPTER TEN

"Can we come in, ma'am?" I asked.

The woman looked me up and down, her brown eyes hard. I pegged her for five to ten years older than me. There was a lot of gray in her dark hair.

Finally, she said, "Y'all vaccinated?"

Three nods.

Since Covid, that had become a common question before people would let law enforcement officers in the door.

"Lemme deal with the dog." The door closed almost all the way, then opened again a minute later.

No sign of the dog as we entered, but her yapping echoed from elsewhere in the house.

The living room was neat, the furniture aging but well cared for. A colorful quilt covered a long sofa. The woman flipped it off and tossed it in a corner. "That's to keep the dog hairs off the couch." She gestured toward said couch and a matching armchair.

Barnes and I took the couch, Foster the overstuffed chair.

Mrs. Trent perched on the front edge of a recliner across from us.

"I'm Judith Anderson, Starling's Chief of Police, and this is my assistant, Officer Barnes. We're working with the JSO on a case that might be related to your niece's assault."

The woman leaned forward and offered a hand. "Julianne Trent."

I shook the hand. "How long has Shelly lived with you?" I knew the answer—Foster had sent the case file to my phone—but it was a good place to start, to get her talking.

She sighed. "My husband's sister was a single mom. She died when Shelly was nine. Cancer. The girl's been with us ever since. We never had kids of our own."

"And she's about nineteen now?" Foster said.

The woman nodded. "As of last month. She was already a handful, before the *assault.*" She didn't make finger quotes but they were there in her tone. "But the last couple of years..." She trailed off, shaking her head.

"So, a lot of arguments..." I trailed off myself, on purpose.

"Don't know why I bother. It's always the same routine. I ask her an innocent question like where she's off to. She yells that she's an adult now and stop bossin' her around. I yell back that she's still under my roof, yada, yada."

"Has Shelly ever talked to you," I asked, "or your husband, about the attack?"

"Not to me, but maybe to Nick. They were thick as thieves."

Hmm, past tense. What did that mean?

"When's the last time you saw Shelly?" Foster asked.

"Tuesday morning. She said she was goin' to lunch with a friend."

"Has she ever taken off like this before?" I said.

"Yeah, but usually only for a day. She comes in, says she stinks and needs a shower, then she changes clothes and takes off again."

"Does she work?" I asked.

"Part-time, waitress at a diner not far from here. Gives her spendin' money."

"Do you know what friend she was having lunch with Tuesday?" Foster asked.

She shook her head, but said, "Might've been Lori. They've been besties ever since Shelly came to us."

"Do you think your husband might have any ideas about where she's gone?" I asked.

She shook her head again, her face sagging. "He passed two years ago. Heart attack. A couple a months after Shelly's..."

My throat ached. This woman had seen more than her share of loss. And if the bad feeling in my gut was right, she was about to see more.

Foster asked her for Lori's phone number and that of the diner. The woman went off to get them.

We sat quietly, not making eye contact. I suspected Foster's gut was in agreement with mine.

Mrs. Trent finally came back, a yellow sticky note on her finger. Her eyes were red-rimmed and puffy.

She handed me the note, which I passed on to Barnes. She stuck it in her notepad.

"You think that sonuvabitch finally made good on his threat?" Mrs. Trent said, venom in her voice.

Foster looked startled, then his expression quickly shifted to neutral. "What threat?"

"He called here, 'bout five months after it happened. Said he was watchin' her and he'd come back for her someday."

"Was the call reported?"

"No. Shelly laughed it off, said one of her friends was playin' a trick on her. It was after that, though, when she got really out of control."

We sat in Foster's car, waiting for the others to come back. We'd talked to friend Lori and to Shelly's boss. They'd confirmed what we'd already suspected. Shelly had never shown up for lunch on Tuesday nor for her shift the next morning at the diner.

Lori had told us that Shelly wasn't bothering to get a full-time job or go to college because she figured she was going to die young.

I'd managed to maintain an outward calm, but that had hit me in the gut.

"You've definitely got a leak," Foster said now, from the driver's seat.

I shook my head. "Maybe, but this info didn't come from the leak. We hadn't even *thought* about previous SAs in Jacksonville until our meeting this morning. Shelly disappeared two days ago."

"True. Maybe this guy knows we're hot on his trail, and he's cleaning up loose ends."

"Maybe. She disappeared the same day Darla Monkton was killed."

"So why haven't we found her body yet?"

"Maybe he hid her," I said. "Didn't want it to be obvious he was cleaning up."

Foster nodded, as Bradley's sedan turned onto the side street.

I grabbed the bag with the burger from the diner for Bradley—Barnes and I had already eaten ours. She and I climbed out of Foster's unmarked. Sticking my head back inside, I said, "We'll be in touch."

But my detective was exiting his car, along with Edwards. He had a paper evidence envelope in his hand.

He held it up. "Pearl's roommate had found some papers, right before we got there," he said, excitement in his voice. "She'd been cleaning the room for a new roommate, and apparently neatnik Natalie believed that should include taking the curtains down and washing them. The papers were rolled up in one end of the expandable curtain rod. It's part of the ancestry company's report."

Bradley gave us that half smile of his. "Pearl had found her mother, deceased, and her maternal grandmother, still living."

"There are pages missin'," Edwards said, in his heavy Southern drawl. "But there's a reference to someone who currently lives in Lawtey, who might be a cousin on her father's side. No name on that page, though, and the next page is one of the ones that's missin'."

"So," I said, "those missing pages may be what she had in the envelope she took with her Sunday. Where's Lawtey?"

"Small town on 301," Foster answered. "Between here and Starke."

"Bet she called him first," Edwards said, "to make sure he was home."

"You dumped her phone records?" Foster asked me.

"Jacobs would've," I said. "He didn't mention anything popping in them, though. But now, we know what to look for."

Bradley turned his nose up at the barely warm burger. Barnes, sitting in the backseat, demurred when I offered her half. I shrugged and ate the whole thing, while Bradley drove us back to Starling.

"Not to be obnoxious, but how do you stay so thin?" he asked.

"That *is* a little obnoxious," I said. "But I'll answer you anyway. One part good genes, one part I rarely get to eat three meals in the same day. I never got around to eating lunch today."

I left out that I did thirty sit-ups followed by twenty push-ups most mornings. And since I'd turned forty, I'd added a two-mile run several times a week, as weather and my schedule allowed.

I wiped my mouth with a napkin, then pulled out my phone. I called Jacobs, and got voicemail.

"Nate, a new lead in the Pearl Altman case, from the genealogy angle. Check her phone records for any calls to or from the area around Lawtey. She might have been chasing down a cousin of her biological father."

I disconnected.

"Nate?" Bradley said, one eyebrow in the air.

"I'm trying to cultivate my warm fuzzy side."

He threw back his head and laughed. A strangled snicker came from the backseat.

I'd meant it as a joke, but hadn't thought it was that funny. "And what exactly do you find so amusing about my warm fuzzy side?"

Bradley didn't answer. His mouth twitched.

"Or is the fact that I think I *have* a warm fuzzy side the amusing part?"

He shot me a grin by way of an affirmative answer.

Speaking of warm fuzzies... I contemplated the name issue.

I'd always called my detectives in my unit by their first names, since I'd been one of them for years, before being promoted to lieutenant. After that, they called me LT, and sometimes Judith in the privacy of my office.

I sure as hell didn't want my people down here calling me by my first name. At least not until my authority was well established, psychologically as well as on paper. Everyone seemed to have settled on calling me Chief, which worked fine.

But Phyl Gladstone had pointed out that things were more casual in Florida. Should I be using first names with the detectives?

I'd tried it out with Jacobs earlier, and it had seemed to help ease the tension after our confrontation.

I shook my head. My brain was too tired to sort it out tonight.

Once home, I tossed my briefcase on my sofa and made a call. It went to voicemail.

"Kate, hi, this is Judith Anderson. Um, hope you all are doing okay. I've got a big case. I'd, uh, like to run it by you, when you have a minute."

I disconnected, mentally kicking myself for the hesitant *ums* and *uhs*. I also made a mental note to somehow find some money in the budget for a consulting fee.

It was one thing to ask Kate to offer her professional opinion as a psychologist for free on cases that affected her. Quite another to call up from five states away and pick her brain.

Exhausted, I barely stayed upright long enough to shower. I flopped down on my sofa in my robe and clicked on the TV.

I jolted awake when my phone rang. My first thought was gratitude that I hadn't been dreaming.

Scrubbing a hand over my face, I sat up, muted the TV, and grabbed the phone off my makeshift coffee table.

I glanced at the screen before accepting the call. "Hey, Kate. Thanks for calling me back."

"No problem. Hope this isn't too late. I'm headed home from a night class."

I looked up at the driftwood clock Paulie had made for me years ago, the only thing I'd gotten around to hanging on the walls so far. Nine-thirty.

"No, this is fine. Um, how's the family?"

"Doing fine. Billy's in middle school now, which has me a little freaked out. And Edie's fifteen going on twenty-five."

"And Skip?" I asked, pretending to care.

"He's fine, and Rose and Mac are as feisty as ever."

Rose Hernandez, Skip Canfield's partner in their P.I. agency, and her husband, Mac Riley. I had a lot of respect for both of them. They were seasoned investigators. Rose had been with BCPD for a few years, before going private.

"So, what's the case?" Kate asked.

I took a deep breath. "Less than two weeks on the job and I've got a serial killer on my hands." I gave her all the history, as succinctly as possible.

"And today," I concluded, "our contact in Jacksonville found three old sexual assault cases there that may be related. The last one, the victim disappeared two days ago."

"Oh my," Kate said, distress in her voice.

My mind conjured up a mental image of her. Fair skinned, blue eyes, but dark curly hair, now streaked with grey, and her figure slightly fuller than it once was.

"She's a wild child," I added."She might have just taken off. But somehow I doubt it."

"Me too." Kate blew out air on the other end of the line. "Okay, the first sexual assault was how long ago?"

"Hang on a sec." I grabbed my briefcase and pulled out the copies of the files I'd had Barnes print out.

I gave her the timeline on the SAs in Jax, then said, "Shelly, the missing girl—he tried to strangle her, like the later dead girls, but she got away."

"And the first murder?" Kate asked.

"Five months later."

"He was escalating, but maybe got scared after the one he tried to kill got away."

"So he laid low for a while," I said. "We have another eighteen-month gap after Darla got away," I added *the first time* in my head, "before Pearl is killed."

My chest hurt. Other than the Forty-Eight-Hour Killer, as the press had dubbed him, I'd never worked a true serial killer case. Unless you counted the hit man who'd tried to take out Kate and her friends because they knew too much about a certain ambassador.

Contrary to popular belief, true serial killers are rare.

I took a deep breath. "How would you profile this perpetrator?"

"Statistically speaking," Kate said, "he's likely to be between the ages of twenty and thirty-five. Tell me again about the second one who got away."

I repeated my succinct description of the earlier SA and attempted murder of Darla, adding a few more details.

"Wait, she said he was flipping her over?"

"Yes."

"That was an escalation. The others he'd attacked from behind, kept them facing away from him. Now he's flipping her over. My guess is the attacks weren't satisfying his sick needs well enough anymore, so he wanted to watch her face as he strangled her."

I allowed myself a small shudder. "But why would he strangle Pearl first, then inflict damage to her face *postmortem*?"

"That doesn't make a lot of sense," Kate said. "Unless that's a copycat killing."

"We've considered that, but the detail about the woman's stocking wasn't common knowledge. Hell, we didn't even know about it until recently."

"Pearl was assaulted with an object, right? That's totally out of sync with the earlier MO. Either it's a male, who became impotent for some reason. In which case, how could he successfully assault the next victim a few days later? *Or* Pearl's killer is female, and/or a copycat."

I was a little stunned. I hadn't really considered a female, probably because we'd linked the case to the earlier SA/murder cases that we knew were committed by a male.

"It's even weirder," I said, "that Darla's homicide is a mix of the MOs. Body arranged like Pearl's but beaten and assaulted like the earlier cases."

"Viagra maybe?" Kate was still stuck on the impotence issue. "But young men don't usually go from virile to impotent in a year and a half. Unless he had some kind of medical issue."

I pondered that. Would identifying men with recent onset of erectile dysfunction help us? How would we even do that? We couldn't get subpoenas for medical records of every male between twenty and thirty-five in the city.

That brought up another question. *Aren't serial killers, by definition, crazy?*

"Would he have a history of mental instability?" I asked.

A slight pause. "Most likely not. While a few serial killers are paranoid schizophrenics, they wouldn't be as organized as this guy is. Most serial killers are not psychotic; they have antisocial personality disorder. Which is technically a mental disorder, but it won't score them any points in a court of law."

"They're psychopaths."

"Exactly."

"Aren't they typically loners?"

"That's a bit of a myth," Kate said. "They can be loners—living alone or with a parent, don't have friends, prefer to work alone, etcetera. *But* they can also be married, have families, seem perfectly normal to the outside world. Like the BTK Killer. They can be quite charming—the nice guy next door that no one would suspect was a stone-cold killer."

Kate sighed. "They're likely to be abusive with those families, though, who are usually too brainwashed or scared to report the abuse."

My stomach had tightened. "So they could be anybody." I blew out air. "Well, since there are way more seemingly nice married men out there, would it hurt for me to eliminate the loners first?"

A soft chuckle. "Might as well. But keep in mind, most loners are not psychopaths. There can be many reasons why someone prefers their own company."

Silence on the line. Then I got it. She was talking about *me*.

"I've been thinking about getting a cat," I blurted out.

She laughed, and after a beat, I snickered along with her.

"This has been really helpful, Kate. Can I call again if I have any follow-up questions? I *am* going to send you a small token of my appreciation."

Still with a chuckle in her voice, she said, "If it's anything like my previous compensations, it will be very small indeed."

"No, seriously, I have a budget now, and I..." My chest swelled with a warm feeling, even as my face heated. "Thank you for all the times you lent your expertise to my cases, but this time I can and will pay you."

"*Seriously*, that's not necessary. It's just good to hear your voice. Feel free to call me any time. Take care, Judith." She disconnected.

More warmth in my chest, offset by anxious butterflies in my stomach.

Talk about mixed emotions.

Maybe Kate was a friend after all.

A mental flash of a dark-haired woman, lying on a floor, seemingly asleep but not.

My chest constricted, the warmth gone. The anxiety prevailed. Letting people in was dangerous.

CHAPTER ELEVEN

Another glance at Paulie's clock. Almost ten. Did Starling have a local news channel?

I unmuted the TV and channel-surfed. I needed to know what the press had to say about my news conference.

Prime-time shows still on the Jacksonville stations. But I finally found what looked like a local station, just as the ten-o'clock news was announced.

No surprise that the serial killer was the lead story. The press had apparently made the connection with the Jax murder cases. They'd dubbed him the Midnight Killer.

Wait. I sat up straighter on my sofa. The news conference they were showing was *not* mine.

Great! The politicians are weighing in.

The City Council Chair, Mark Hayes was a prominent local lawyer. Why he wanted to dabble in politics was beyond me.

I studied him as he rambled on, admonishing the public not to panic, promising the killer would be caught soon, yada, yada.

He was tall and slender, mid-forties, with some salt sprinkled in his expensively coifed dark hair. His silver-gray business suit was custom tailored.

Beside him stood an attractive blonde woman. She wore a modest black dress with a discreet pearl choker, and looked like she went to the gym regularly. A dark-haired boy, mid-teens, next to her, and a blonde older girl on her other side. Another boy, older still, stood behind them, also blond and as tall as his father. His eyes were slightly glazed over, like he was stoned.

Okay, that's way too cynical. He's probably bored to tears.

I squinted at the TV. The wife seemed vaguely familiar.

No doubt, I'd met her at the reception held in my honor, when I'd first arrived in Starling.

I'd definitely met her husband. Councilman Hayes had sat in on my interview with the mayor in June. He'd struck me as a nice enough guy, but that could be his politician veneer.

He wound down with a promise that the city would provide the police with every resource possible to solve these crimes quickly.

Hmm, might be a good time to submit a supplemental budget request.

Like I have time to work on that right now.

My insides tightened, guilt and anxiety once again doing battle in my chest.

That's what I *should* be working on, instead of involving myself directly in the investigation.

But it was a serial killer! I could hardly step back now. Way too much was riding on this case, young women's lives and my career.

I sighed. I'd have to work even longer hours.

Finally, the larger of our conference rooms at 3MB appeared on the TV screen, with me at the podium. But the sound was muted while the male news anchor talked, implying that I'd said we weren't even close to catching the killer.

The shiny-toothed anchor stopped talking and the sound came up, as I was making my final statement. *Okay, good.*

Except they didn't stop there. They went back to the exchange with Marly Davis, starting with her, "What about the coffee?"

I groaned and flopped sideways on the sofa, burying my face in a leather cushion. I couldn't watch.

The female anchor's voice had me turning my head and opening one eye. "Officer Barnes indicated that she was pleased to be the admin of the new police chief and that she expected to learn a lot from the chief, whom she called an 'excellent police officer.'"

Bless you, Barnes.

A wave of...*something* washed over me. I couldn't pinpoint the feeling, but it made me squirm.

The news broadcast had moved on to other things. I clicked the TV off and went to the kitchen for a glass of wine. My mind was searching for something to analyze, something to distract myself from the news and that weird feeling.

I sat at the built-in breakfast bar with my wine.

The woman, the council chair's wife. Where had I seen her before? The sense of familiarity went beyond what one would experience after only a brief introduction.

I *knew* her from somewhere.

I woke up early and went for a run along the riverwalk. It was deserted. The sun was barely peeking over the horizon and the breeze coming off the Sofki River—a tributary of a tributary of the St. Johns River—was cool. Maybe autumn was finally coming to North Florida.

A couple of blue herons strutted among the tall grasses along the shoreline, ignoring the rhythmic slap of my sneakers on the boardwalk.

I focused on my breathing, trying to ignore thoughts of nightmares and serial killers.

Tired but exhilarated, I grabbed a quick shower, dressed, and still managed to beat Barnes to the office.

I was so early that a janitor was mopping the terrazzo floor of the bullpen, in front of the coffee station. He was tall, but thin—around thirty—with dark, longish hair pulled back into a ponytail.

How fortuitous. I approached, my hand extended. "Hi. I'm the new Chief of Police, Judith Anderson."

He stared at the hand, then wiped his own on his coveralls and shook mine. "Bill Walker." His grasp was about right, neither tentative nor bone-crushing.

"I'll bet you have quite a mess to clean up here most nights. My cops aren't all that neat when they fetch their coffee."

I hoped I didn't sound weird or condescending. All the glad-handing that came with the job was a bit out of my wheelhouse. It made my inner introvert shudder.

He flashed a quick smile—straight, white teeth.

Probably the offspring of a middle-class family who could afford orthodontics.

So why is he mopping floors for a living?

I shoved that question aside and asked, "Do you do the whole building?"

"No, ma'am. Just this floor."

Hmm...

"Well, you do a great job. It helps us do our jobs better to have a clean environment." *Okay, that sounded pompous as hell.*

But he flashed another small smile—so fast I couldn't tell if it was genuine or not.

"Thank you, Mr. Walker." I decided to stop now before I offended him, if I hadn't already.

With a nod I turned toward my office. I would be checking out Mr. Walker.

One lonely, bear-like detective sat at his desk across the bullpen. Shirt sleeves rolled up, cardboard coffee cups scattered across his desk, Cruthers leaned forward, squinting at his computer screen.

I walked toward him. "Must be fascinating reading if it kept you up all night."

He swiveled his shaggy head toward me. "Hi, Chief. Actually, it's a whole lot of boring repetition. The Tremont canvassing reports. Nobody saw nothin'. How could that be in broad daylight?"

I shook my head. I had no answer to that question.

Nor had I answered my own question about that weird feeling last night.

But during my run, I'd had a minor epiphany—maybe we didn't have an internal leak. Maybe what we had was a very observant, *local* perp.

I dragged a chair over and sat next to Cruther's desk, where I could see his monitor. "Can you pull up a map of Starling?"

"Sure." He clicked on a program icon and a map popped up.

"Where's the park where Pearl Altman was found?"

He hovered his cursor over a spot and clicked. A virtual red pushpin appeared above the words, Holly Park.

"And the church where Darla Monkton's NA meeting was? And the park where she was found?"

Two more pins appeared.

"And Tremont's store, home and bank?"

Three more pins.

"You're pretty familiar with that section of town?" He hadn't had to look up any of the addresses.

He gave me a tired smile. "I grew up two blocks from Holly Park. That area's called Starlingville. It was the original small town, established a hundred years ago. In the sixties, it incorporated, annexed a lot of the surrounding farmland and a couple other hamlets, and was renamed Starling."

I nodded. Good info to have.

Cruthers shook his head, his tired face sagging even more. "I hate what's happening to that park. I used to play there, even after dark. Now you can't walk through it in daylight by yourself, unless you're armed. The red-light district is just on the other side of it—where there was a factory, and then farmland beyond it, when I was a kid."

I studied the map. There was a faint dotted line around the area labeled Starlingville. The red pins were all within that line.

I debated, then said, "Don't share this with anybody else yet, but I think our perp lives in that area."

Cruthers grunted. "And that's how he's keeping up with our investigation."

"Maybe. I want you to do something, but only after you've caught a few hours of sleep. We're looking for men, between eighteen and forty," I expanded the age range some, just in case, "who live alone or with parents. Cross-reference the canvas reports for all three murders, Tremont's, Darla's and Pearl's. Anybody who was interviewed for two or more of them, start there. Check to see what jobs they have. Any of them who have loner-type jobs that take them out and about in the city—plumber, taxi driver—they go to the top of the list. Then check the rest of the guys that were interviewed during the canvassing for any of the murders, for the same parameters."

That would hopefully net our perp if he was the loner type. If he was a charming family man, I had no clue how we'd narrow that group down. Maybe start again with those who lived near one of the murder sites and/or had been hanging around them...

Cruthers was nodding. "The computer can do the cross-referencing for me, while I catch some sleep."

"Good. What's your take on Tremont's wife? Jacobs thought her alibi was shaky."

"I talked to her again. She's pretty broken up, and I drove to that supermarket that was her second stop that day. It's all the way across town. One of those ones that specializes in organic stuff. She said she was trying to make up for the junk Tremont ate at his store when he was working, so he'd live a long..." He trailed off, scrubbed a big hand over his stubbled face. "Anyway,

I don't see a hole in the time frame big enough for her to drive to the bank and lie in wait for hubs."

I rose, liking this guy because he still cared. Police work hadn't hardened him completely as it did some. "Send me a screenshot of that map, please."

"The program's on all our computers," he said. "I'll save it and you can access it."

"Okay." I hesitated. But Cruthers couldn't be the leak. He'd been added to the task force after the killer had somehow gotten wind of our movements. "Label it *Street Robberies 2019.*"

Dark, bristly eyebrows moved toward his hairline, but he nodded.

I turned away, then back again. "Hey, do you know if the cleaning people in the building work for the city, or are they from a service?"

"A service, I think. Don't know which one."

"Thanks."

Shouldn't be that hard for me to find out. I really didn't want someone, who worked for a cleaning service the city had hired, poking around 3MB.

Paranoid, much? I shook my head at myself as I headed for my office.

But I'd learned the hard way to maintain a healthy skepticism when it came to politicians and the big brass.

I snorted to myself. *I'm the big brass now.* So all I needed to worry about were the politicians.

At ten-thirty, I took a break from the budget request I'd been working on and did a search for janitorial services. There were two in Starling.

I called the first one from my cell phone and was immediately put on hold.

I felt a little guilty since my plan was to lure Walker away from the service and hire him directly. I wanted him loyal to the police department. But first, I wanted to make sure he was a good worker.

I'd decided a certain amount of subterfuge was called for. When someone in their HR department finally answered, I said, in a chipper voice, "Hi, my name is Judy Anderson. An employee of yours has applied to rent a room from us. I'm calling to check on his employment."

"What's the name?" the woman asked. She sounded bored. I hoped she'd stay that way and quickly forget this call after we hung up.

"William Walker."

He did indeed work for the service, had been with them for eighteen months and there were no complaints in his file.

"He said he brings home about four-fifty a week. Does that sound about right?"

"I can't discuss wages over the phone," her voice sounded wary now, and more alert.

"Oh, of course not. Thanks so much," I fake gushed and quickly disconnected.

I Googled *how much do janitors make in Florida*, added enough to make the amount enticing, and inserted that figure next to janitorial services in my budget.

My stomach rumbled, reminding me that breakfast had been skimpy and several hours ago. I'd slapped together a PBJ this morning and stuffed it in a paper bag, so I could work straight through lunch.

But first, I skimmed back through the budget request.

I'd done some research into the budgets from the past few years and had discovered another gift from my predecessor. Shortly before retirement, he'd submitted a budget far below the department's needs, and a good bit lower than previous years.

He'd not only eliminated the line item for the department's clerk, but also for the captain who had worked under him. Some additional research uncovered that said captain had resigned over two years ago, and Chief Black had never bothered to fill the position.

Of course, his ridiculously low budget had been eagerly accepted by the mayor and city council.

There had been two dissenting votes. One was Mark Hayes. He'd lobbied for a higher budget, matching or exceeding the year before.

I warmed a bit toward him. Now his specific comment about resources made more sense.

The old chief had also laid off two officers. My "emergency" request called for the reinstatement of all those eliminated positions, plus one new uniformed officer and another detective.

I figured I'd at least get back to the old personnel level.

I opened my desk drawer to retrieve the PBJ from my briefcase, hesitated, then pulled out my laptop as well. I needed a mental break.

I looked around. The chief's office had been carved out of one side of the bullpen, with three glass walls—except for one corner, partitioned off with actual wallboard to create a closet-sized private bathroom.

Another smaller cube of glass, on the opposite side of the bullpen, was for the second in command, Jacobs. It was empty at the moment, as were the other desks, except for Barnes outside my door. Everybody was either out in the field or out to lunch.

I leaned back in my desk chair and took a bite of the PBJ. As I chewed, I booted up my laptop, and on a whim, searched for local cat shelters.

I scrolled through cute pics and videos, munching on my sandwich. The tense muscles in my back relaxed some. I chuckled softly at one video. I felt like I was nine again, but in a good way.

It barely registered that Barnes had entered my office. She came around the corner of my desk, frowning, and glanced at my laptop screen.

I sat up abruptly, slammed the computer shut, ready to chastise her for taking liberties.

But she was scowling over my shoulder, through the plate glass behind me.

I whirled around. Two uniforms stood by the desk closest to my glass wall, big grins on their faces.

Heat crawled up my neck. I glared at them.

They ducked their heads and shuffled away.

"When are those blinds being installed?" I demanded.

"Friday," Barnes said.

"Tell the company there's a bonus if they get it done tomorrow." I'd pay it out of my own pocket.

"Um, the phone company's gonna be here shortly to install your private line."

Crap, I'd forgotten about that.

I quickly added another line item—phone upgrades—to my budget request, then sent it off to the mayor and Councilman Hayes, cc'ing the rest of the council.

The mayor would likely be pissed that I hadn't gone to him first, but there was no time for pussyfooting around.

I had a serial killer to catch!

CHAPTER TWELVE

I'd locked my desk, logged out of my desktop and was about to head to the conference room, where I could stare at the murder board and pray for fresh ideas, when Bradley showed up.

"Just got a call back from Pearl's grandmother, finally. I'm off to interview her. You wanna come?"

"Definitely." I gestured for Barnes to follow us.

She shook her head. "Phone company guys are here. They're on their way up."

As she spoke, two men in tool belts entered the bullpen, one middle-aged and bald, the other young, thin, and blond. The kid carried two cardboard boxes—our new phones. And he looked vaguely familiar.

Why were strangers suddenly looking familiar?

"Do you gentlemen need one of us to hang around?" I asked as they approached.

The older one said, "You got any special instructions?"

"The number of the new line, does it show up anywhere on the phone or on the other party's caller ID?"

"Not on your end, and it's set up right now to show up as *private* on caller ID. But you can change that if you want." He tapped one of the boxes in his assistant's hands. "It's all in the user's manual."

Which was probably written in geek-ese. I glanced at Barnes.

She nodded slightly, indicating she was on top of it.

"Okay then," I said. "Thanks, guys."

I waylaid Cruthers as he returned from his nap, asked him to keep an eye on the phone guys and make sure my office was locked after they were done.

"Sure thing, Chief."

Twenty minutes later, we pulled up in front of an older Cracker-style house in the Benson district on the eastern side of the city. It had been one of those small towns swallowed up when Starling incorporated.

I gave myself a mental pat on the back. I was starting to learn the lay of the land in my new city.

The older clapboard house sported a new-looking green metal roof, its line broken by two dormers. A small air-conditioner hung out of one of the windows.

The woman who answered the door was short and plump, with steel-gray hair and a wrinkled face. The embodiment of "sweet little old lady," until she opened her mouth.

"I didn't expect you to bring an entourage," she said to Bradley. But she held the screen open wide. "Well, come on in." Her tone was begrudging.

Bradley introduced us.

The woman, Charlotte Stiller, showed us to a small living room and excused herself.

Cabinet doors banged in a nearby kitchen. A couple of minutes later, she came back, carrying a tray with glasses and a pitcher of iced tea.

Barnes jumped up from her perch on the edge of an armchair. "Let me take that, ma'am."

The old woman gave her an approving nod and let her do just that. Barnes carefully put the tray down on a glass-topped, wooden coffee table.

Bradley had also stood. Mrs. Stiller impatiently waved him back down and settled herself into a rocker across from the sofa where Bradley and I sat.

"That girl, Pearl, I figured no good would come of her stirrin' up the past," Mrs. Stiller said.

Barnes had taken it upon herself to pour tea into the four glasses and pass them around.

Another approving nod from the stern-faced grandmother.

No sugar bowl on the tray. I braced myself for the tartness of unsweetened tea, and about gagged when I took a sip. It was sweet enough to make my teeth ache.

Barnes sat down in the overstuffed armchair, leaned back, and grimaced when the chair attempted to swallow her alive. She juggled her glass of tea, managed not to spill it.

Meanwhile, Bradley was patiently drawing Charlotte Stiller's story out of her.

It was a sad one, of a widowed mother who sent her child off to college, only to have her come home the next spring, pregnant and determined to marry the baby's father at the ripe old age of nineteen.

"Everything I'd dreamed of for her, everything she'd dreamed of for herself..." She made a swooping gesture with her hand. "All out the window. She's gonna get married and be a stay-at-home mom, raise her baby right, as if I didn't raise *her* right." Her voice dripped with bitterness.

"We had a terrible fight. I had visions of her living hand-to-mouth with some wet-behind-the-ears boy, working some menial job. She quickly and loudly reassured me that would not be the case. 'My *man* comes from a good family, old money,' she says. And she sashays upstairs to get herself ready to go meet this 'good family.'" She made air quotes, then sighed.

"Vivian came home that night, her face all blotchy and puffy. She refused to talk to me. I heard her pacin' around upstairs until the wee hours of the morning. The next day I found out what all that pacin' was about. She carried three boxes and two suitcases out to her car. Said she was gonna stay with my sister-in-law, her aunt—she'd already called her—until the baby was born...and she was giving it up for adoption.

"I tried to talk her out of it, convince her that she could stay with me, that I'd help raise the child. But she was adamant. She was going away and the baby, my grandchild, would be raised by strangers."

The woman's chin was tense, her lips a thin, angry line, but a tear had escaped one eye and trickled down her cheek. "I never saw my daughter in person again. Never even knew if the baby was a boy or a girl. Vivian got married three years later, up in Chicago. She'd started a business, a clothing boutique. It was a success. She had two kids, a boy and a girl. I get a Christmas card every year." She gestured toward the far wall.

I turned my head. Lined up along the top of a bookcase were photo cards showing a smiling family of four, the kids growing slowly from toddlers to preteens, the parents aging graciously.

"Sometimes we talked on the phone," she continued. "But she wouldn't come home to visit. One time I suggested I could come up there, to Chicago. She said that was a good idea, but not right then. They were real busy. Maybe later in the year. Neither of us ever brought the subject up again."

I had a funny feeling there was more to the story of why Vivian held her mother at arm's length.

The old woman had stopped talking.

"You told all this to Pearl?" Bradley said in a gentle voice.

She nodded.

After another beat of silence, I asked, "Vivian didn't want an abortion? Was that for religious reasons?"

Mrs. Stiller shook her head. "I would've been okay with an abortion. Not thrilled but okay, if it meant she went back to school and pursued her dreams. She'd been plannin' to go to medical school, become a doctor. But she wouldn't even consider it."

Hmm, taking time out to have a baby wouldn't have necessarily derailed that plan. Maybe becoming a doctor was more the mother's dream than the daughter's.

"What did Pearl Altman say to you?" Bradley asked.

She frowned. "I'm afraid I didn't give her a chance to say much. I told her what happened with her mother, and then I got mad that she'd gotten me all stirred up. I told her to go away, that it was too late. I felt bad later. I'd planned to call her."

And now it truly is too late.

"Did you give her contact information for her mom's family?" Bradley asked.

The old woman shook her head, fresh tears breaking loose from shiny, red-rimmed eyes. "There was no point. Her mother died last year in a car crash. I don't know if Vivian ever even told her husband about that first baby."

I'd known Pearl's mother was deceased, but still the grandmother's words gave me a jolt. I swallowed hard. The what-ifs in this situation were haunting...would no doubt, *be* haunting this woman for the rest of her life.

Bradley apologized for once again stirring up bad memories, and we said our goodbyes.

Watching Barnes struggle out of that chair provided some comic relief after the sad interview.

As we walked down the sidewalk to her brother's car, Barnes said, "The boutique. I'd love to know if it was started before or after Vivian's marriage."

"What are you thinking?" I asked.

She stopped and turned to me. "That the 'good family,'" she made air quotes, "paid Vivian off to go away and never come back."

Her brother and I exchanged a look, both of us nodding. "Distinct possibility," Bradley said.

Barnes shrugged. "Not that it helps us any."

"I'm not so sure about that," I said. "If someone wanted Pearl's existence covered up that badly, they might not take kindly to her poking around trying to find her parents."

Back in the car, Bradley pulled away from the curb. "If the pregnant daughter went off to Chicago," he said, "how did the baby end up back down here?"

"Should I call Mrs. Stiller and ask?" Barnes said from the backseat. "I have her number."

How did she get the old woman's number?

"Sure," I said out loud. "She seems to have a soft spot for you."

I glanced sideways at Bradley. He met my gaze, a twinkle in his eyes. "I didn't give her the number," he whispered. "We think she's part witch." He glanced over his shoulder at his sister, who didn't seem to hear him.

I turned slightly in the passenger seat, watching Barnes.

She already had her phone against her ear. "Ma'am, this is Officer Barnes. Sorry to disturb you again. We just have a few follow-up questions. Where did your sister-in-law live?"

A pause. "Uh, huh." A longer pause. "And the boutique, was that business started before or after Vivian married?"

A few moments of silence as Barnes listened. "Uh, huh. Yes, that's very helpful. Thank you, ma'am." Another pause. "Yes, ma'am. Again, we're very sorry for your losses."

She disconnected. "The aunt was in Jacksonville. *After* the baby was put up for adoption down here, then Vivian went to Chicago to go into business with a college friend. Neither had any money, according to Mrs. Stiller. She was surprised when the boutique was a big success right off the bat."

"It would be," Bradley said, "if she had a bundle of start-up cash, free and clear."

"Barnes, I gotta know," I said. "How'd you have her phone number?"

"There was a pile of bills, on the little table next to my chair. The phone bill was on top." She glared at the back of her brother's head. "And no, I'm not a witch."

I chuckled. "No, only observant. A good trait for a police officer to have."

Barnes's cheeks pinked.

"Did she have anything else to say?" I asked.

"No... Well, she told me never to have kids 'cause they'll break your heart."

My phone rang, saving me from having to respond. Caller ID said *Jacobs*.

I turned to face forward again. "Anderson."

"Hey, Chief. I did find a number in Lawtey that Pearl called a couple of times. I called it and got an old man. He remembered that she came to see him, but he couldn't help her. She thought he might be a cousin, but he didn't recognize any of the names she mentioned, people the DNA company had said might be related to her."

I sat up straighter. "Did he remember any of those names?"

"Unfortunately, no."

Damn. "How far is Lawtey from here?" I asked Bradley.

"About half an hour."

"You got an address for this guy?" I said into the phone.

Silence. Then faint road noise. "You there, Nate?"

"Yeah, hang on. I'm looking it up in my pad."

I dug out my own pad and a pen.

"His name's Benjamin Nelson." Jacobs gave me the man's address. He had to repeat it when a noisy truck went by on his end, drowning him out. He was apparently near a busy street.

"We're already out and about," I raised my voice a little to be heard, "so we'll swing by and talk to him in person. See if we can jog his memory."

"Out and about where?" he asked.

"The east side of town. We–"

More road noise on Jacobs's end drowned me out. I briefly wondered why he hadn't gone to see Nelson in person himself, since he was obviously out and about as well.

"Okay," he yelled over the rumbling. "See ya when you get back." He disconnected.

I hadn't told him about our visit with Pearl's grandmother, but that could wait. I plugged Benjamin Nelson's address into the GPS app on my phone.

CHAPTER THIRTEEN

Once out of Starling, the country roads were mostly deserted. We made good time.

Just before the Lawtey town limits, Bradley turned onto a sandy road, winding past weeds and palmettos and scraggly Southern pines.

We rounded a curve, and house trailers of various sizes and states of disrepair were scattered along each side of the road, on generous but mostly unkempt lots peppered with more scraggly pines and palmettos.

Bradley pulled up in front of a small trailer whose metal siding had once been blue. Now it was a sickly bluish-greenish gray. Except near the ground, where rust brown was the dominant color.

I swiveled my head, taking in our surroundings.

One pickup in a sandy driveway down the road apiece and a dark sedan two properties over, back near the curve. It was surprisingly clean, considering the moldy, decrepit state of the trailer it was parked next to. Those and the old compact in Nelson's driveway were the only vehicles.

We exited Bradley's car and approached the front of the trailer. It was eerily quiet, despite the trees and underbrush around the small community. No insect noises, chattering of birds, nor rustling of small animals. Of course, it was hotter than Hades so maybe all such critters were burrowed into various cool spots somewhere.

Still, the hair follicles on my neck prickled.

Bradley rapped on the trailer's door.

Silence.

He knocked again, then after a moment, tried the knob. It twisted in his hand.

He glanced my way. I nodded.

He cracked the door open and wrinkled his nose. He shot me another look, concern in his eyes. "Mr. Nelson," he called out as he drew his weapon. "Starling police, we have a few questions for you."

I caught a whiff of a putrid odor and shared his concern.

No response from inside the trailer.

Bradley eased the door open farther. "Mr. Nelson," he called out again, "we're coming in. We just want to make sure you're okay." He slipped inside.

Heart pounding, I pulled my weapon. Barnes had her gun in her hand. I nodded and we entered the trailer.

No humans in the cluttered living room. Not even Bradley.

Where'd the hell he go?

The kitchen was separated only by a breakfast bar. No Bradley in there either.

But the counters were covered with styrofoam food containers and pizza boxes, most of them not completely empty. The decaying food remnants explained at least some of the putrid smell that permeated the air.

There was a hallway off the living room and a closed door that was most likely a closet. Another closed door in the kitchen was probably a pantry, but it could be big enough to hide a person.

Bradley cleared these rooms that quickly? No way.

Barnes and I spread out to check the closed doors.

The sharp sounds of breaking glass, from the back of the trailer. "Stop! Police." Bradley's voice.

I swung around the corner from the kitchen. On high alert, we moved quickly down the hall to an open doorway. Another open door at the end provided a view of a disgusting toilet.

I poked my head around the first doorframe, hoping to find Bradley cuffing whoever he'd been yelling at.

No such luck.

A gaping hole where a window had been, wood splinters and glass shards on the sill. Bradley, standing next to a toppled wooden kitchen chair.

He stared across the room, at a king-sized bed, and the overweight old man, lying on it. Eyes closed, sweating profusely.

"Bathroom's clear," Barnes said from behind me.

"Go!" I said to Bradley. "We've got the old man."

He clambered through the window frame.

Barnes rattled off the address into her radio. "Ambulance and sheriff's department on the way." She glanced toward the window with anxious eyes. "Should I go too?"

A split-second debate. "Yes."

I prayed that she wasn't too green, that worry for her brother wouldn't cloud her judgment. But Bradley needed backup.

She vaulted over the windowsill and disappeared.

I ran to the old man on the bed, touched his neck to search for a pulse. His skin was slimy from sweat, even though the room was aggressively air conditioned. The putrid stench was less intense back here and competed with the odor of stale beer.

I found a pulse, weak, but it was there. And he was breathing.

On closer inspection, he wasn't as old as I'd thought. His broad, unshaven face was flaccid but not all that wrinkled, his whiskers and hair more pepper than salt. Most likely around fifty years old, but they had not been easy years.

I spotted an object on the floor beside the bed, crouched down without touching it.

Cylindrical, a syringe. Much cleaner than its surroundings.

I stood, leaned over to check the man's pulse again. My fingers against his neck felt nothing but sweaty skin. No pulse.

Damn! I knelt on the side of the grimy bare mattress—fortunately it was a firm one. No need to wrestle him to the floor and screw up the crime scene.

I started CPR.

Barnes and Bradley returned, Bradley puffing a little.

Barnes took over from me, counting her compressions under her breath.

"Nothing," Bradley said. "He got away clean."

"You're sure it was a man?" I asked.

"Pretty sure. I caught a glimpse of a pants leg and shoe, before he got all the way out the window." He sucked in air. "Both black. Probably dress slacks. The shoe was leather, with shoestrings."

"Tell me, from the beginning."

He took another deep breath. "I had stepped inside, was about to clear the front rooms, when I heard a moan from back here. Then a crash just as I got to the doorway. I came around it, gun out, but the guy was already most of the way out the window. The old man was convulsing so I was torn. Then you and Glori...Officer Barnes came in."

"I wondered how you could've disappeared from the front rooms so fast. We were only a couple of seconds behind you."

"I was in the hallway when I heard you coming in."

The paramedics arrived, forcing us to temporarily halt our discussion.

I sent Barnes with them when they took Mr. Nelson to the nearest hospital in Starke. Then I called that city's police chief to request a guard be put on Nelson's hospital room. The chief had seemed reluctant to do so, until I mentioned a serial killer was wreaking havoc a mere thirty miles away up 301, and this incident might very well be related.

We cleared out so the Bradford County Sheriff's Department could process the scene.

On the cement stoop, I stopped and took a deep breath. The heat actually felt good after the over-air-conditioned trailer.

Deputies were methodically checking each property, in case the perp was hiding on one of them. And the sandy road was now crowded with emergency vehicles.

Beyond them, two women with small children in tow, stood on the porch of the trailer across the street.

"Be right back." Bradley walked toward them.

I looked up and down the road. The pickup farther down was still there, but the dark sedan near the curve was gone.

Seriously? Someone had come out of their house, gotten in their car and driven away, not the least bit curious about the cause of the circus two properties down?

I flagged down the Bradford County detective who was the lead on the case, pointed out the trailer and told him about the car that had been there but was now gone. "I didn't see the plate, unfortunately."

He nodded. "I'll run the address through the DMV, see what vehicles are registered to the residents."

We exchanged cards as Bradley came back, shaking his head. "They didn't see anyone over here until we arrived."

"Our Lieutenant Jacobs had talked to Nelson by phone," I told the Bradford County detective. "He said the man didn't know anything useful regarding our case. We were just following up. I'll send you any relevant info from the case files."

"Detective," one of the crime scene techs called from inside Nelson's trailer.

The detective gave me a small salute, my card still in his hand, and went inside.

"Apparently, the killer thinks Nelson does know something," Bradley said. "Maybe something that he doesn't realize he knows."

"I want to know how the hell the killer knew we were coming here."

"Good question. Even *we* didn't know we were coming here until a half hour ago."

"Our phones are encrypted, right?"

"Of course," Bradley said. "But somebody who's technologically savvy might still be able to eavesdrop on us."

"Can our tech geek determine if someone's gotten past the encryption?"

"I don't know, but I'll ask him."

Then he snapped his fingers. "Maybe the killer's not listening in. Maybe he already *knows* who or what might give him away, so he's tying up loose ends."

A chill ran down my spine, even though Foster had said the same thing yesterday.

Who else had this perp killed to cover his tracks? "When we get back, look up every homicide in the area, going back at least two years. See if any of the victims have connections to any of our victims."

"Jacksonville too?"

"Oh yeah."

Bradley whistled softly. "That's a lot of homicides."

"Get Cruthers to help you. He should have a list of possible suspects by now, loner types who fit the profile." Part of it, at least. "Check for connections between them and any of the homicide victims you turn up."

"Profile? I thought we weren't calling in the FBI."

"I have my own personal profiler," I said with a slight smirk.

His eyebrows lifted. "Oh really."

"She's not FBI, but she's good. A psychologist...friend in Baltimore." I tripped over the word *friend* a little.

Cruthers had a list all right, of thirty men. They all either lived near one of the crime scenes or were hanging out there and a uniform had questioned them. Seven of them were on the interview lists for at least two of the murders.

"I was about to grab a couple of uniforms," he said from my office doorway, "and knock on some doors, see if we can narrow things down some."

"Hold off on that." I pointed to Bradley, who was occupying one of my visitors' chairs. "Get with him and cross check your guys against... Well, he'll explain it."

Time to back off some. I was starting to micromanage. It was hard not to go there, with so much at stake in this case.

Bradley and Cruthers went off to the latter's corner of the bullpen, settled at adjoining desks and their fingers began dancing on keyboards.

How did cops solve crimes before computers?

Speaking of which... I checked my email and was delighted to find a message from Councilman Hayes, with the subject line, *Emergency budget approved.*

The body of the email was short:

Hope this helps. Call me when you have a moment.

Mark Hayes

I called him right away. "Councilman, thank you for your support."

"Call me Mark," he said in a soft voice. "And thanks for calling. I wanted to let you know that I voted against the stripped budget that Chief Black submitted. So I was glad for the opportunity to make things right in that respect for your department."

He sounded like a politician, but also sincere. Were those two things even compatible?

"How did you get the mayor to agree?" I asked, not really expecting an honest answer.

He chuckled. "Let's just say I was holding a few of his IOUs."

I gave him my new private-line number. "Only you, the mayor, and a few of my top people will have that number. I'd appreciate it if you kept it to yourself."

"No problem. You went ahead with the phone upgrades before the budget was approved?"

"Only this one upgrade. I have a new assistant now–"

Another soft chuckle cut me off. "So I heard."

"Yes, well, she'll be screening my calls, but you and the mayor should have direct access."

"Call *me* any time, Chief," Hayes said. "Anything you need, I'll do my best to see that you get it."

"Thank you, Councilman."

"Mark."

"Sure. Thanks...Mark." We disconnected.

I headed for the conference room to stare at the murder board and go through the files again.

I found Jacobs in the middle of a video conference with Foster from Jacksonville. I greeted the two men as I sat down.

"Chief," Foster said, "we're going over the victims again. What they do and don't have in common. The two homicides here and the attempted one, Darla Monkton, were all prostitutes, But Pearl Altman doesn't fit that pattern."

"The park she was found in, though," Jacobs said, "it's on the cusp between our red-light district and the old Starlingville section of town. She might have been mistaken for a whore."

"The male victim," Foster said, "seems to be more of a cover-his-tracks killing."

I held up my hand. "We may have a second male victim." I filled Jacobs and Foster in on what we'd found at Nelson's trailer, and that he was now at the Starke hospital under guard.

"So he may or may not be another victim of our perp," Jacobs said. "Couldn't Nelson's condition be due to natural causes?"

"Only if confronting a killer gave him a heart attack," I said. "Bradley definitely saw somebody going out the window, but when he got to it, they were gone."

Jacobs shrugged. "Could've been a burglar broke into the guy's house, and that gave him a heart attack."

"That would be one hell of a coincidence," Foster said.

Before I had a chance to express my opinion of coincidences, he continued, "With our three earlier SAs here in Jacksonville, those victims were all a bit younger, between sixteen and eighteen, and none of them were prostitutes. *And* victim two, Maria Juarez, is Hispanic."

"So the rest of them being white might not mean anything?" I said.

"Maybe not," Foster said. "They just happened to be the women he found when he went hunting."

I nodded. Both teenagers and prostitutes were vulnerable populations for sexual assault. But victims of convenience meant this guy would be *a lot* harder to catch.

"We're bringing in all the males," Foster said, "who are on probation or parole for sexual assault offenses. So far, they have alibis for either Pearl's murder or Darla's."

"We don't have anybody like that in Starling right now," Jacobs said.

That we know of. Someone could have moved here without notifying their probation or parole officer, and we wouldn't know it. Not until they got caught committing some new crime.

"Where exactly was Shelly Trent attacked?" I asked. The report had given a street address, but it meant nothing to me.

"On her way home from a friend's house," Jacobs said. "Not far from her own."

I was impressed that he knew that without consulting her file.

"They were all grabbed off the street," Foster said, his voice turning gloomy, "not far from their homes, and dragged into nearby alleys. All the crime scenes outside, where it's hard to determine what is relevant trace evidence. No fingerprints, next to useless descriptions..." He trailed off.

Jacobs turned his head away from me and coughed into his elbow. "Sorry. Allergies."

"Any luck finding Shelly Trent?" I asked Foster.

He shook his head. "Got a BOLO out and officers talking to friends and family again, but nothing yet."

"Why'd he switch from teenagers to prostitutes?" I asked.

"There was a lot of hoopla around Shelly's case," Foster said, "when the press realized there was a pattern."

Jacobs nodded. "So maybe he figured whores would be safer, less newsworthy."

It was a sad truth.

Jacobs turned away and coughed again.

My cell phone rang. The screen said *Barnes.*

"Anderson," I answered out of habit. But maybe I should be putting *Chief* in front of my name now? I swallowed a sigh.

"The syringe you found must've had epinephrine in it." Barnes's voice was excited.

My heart beat faster. "I'm putting you on speaker." I set the phone on the table. "Detectives Jacobs and Foster are here." Well, more or less here, in Foster's case.

"Nelson has a ton of adrenaline in his bloodstream," Barnes's voice came from the phone. "The doc says it's far more than we naturally produce, and he thinks it triggered a heart attack. They've got him stabilized, but the doc's concerned. Nelson's blood alcohol level is also high, which isn't helping. He's still unconscious."

"Okay, thanks," I said.

"I've called an Uber. Be back shortly." Barnes disconnected.

I called Bradley. "Check on sudden heart attack deaths in the area as well," I said without preamble. "See if any of them are related to our cases in any way."

He groaned.

I disconnected, then sat up straighter in my chair as a thought hit me. *Shelly's uncle.* He'd died of a heart attack shortly after Shelly was assaulted.

But I didn't mention that thought to Jacobs and Foster just yet.

CHAPTER FOURTEEN

I took a walk to clear my head.

Maybe there wasn't a leak that was allowing the killer to stay one jump ahead of us. Maybe Bradley and Foster were on to something and the killer was mopping up. And we happened to have been right behind him a couple of times.

But there were a whole lot of assumptions in that explanation, along with a couple of coincidences.

A leak was a distinct possibility, and I needed to find it, because people were getting killed. On my watch. No, I didn't want to micro-manage, but I needed to control the flow of communication wherever possible.

When I was a good distance from the Municipal Building, I took out my cell and called Foster in Jacksonville. I asked him to talk to me first about anything he found out, before he shared it with my people.

"You trying to root out your leak?" he asked.

"Exactly." I reminded him about Shelly's uncle.

"I'll talk to the aunt again," Foster said, a sad sigh in his voice. "Find out more about the circumstances when he died."

When I got back, Cruthers and Bradley were waiting outside my office, and a woman was measuring its plate-glass walls.

"Blinds company," Cruthers said.

I nodded and motioned the detectives over to Cruthers's desk, out of the woman's earshot.

"We've narrowed things down some," Cruthers said, "to fifteen men, and bumped three names to the top of the list. All loners—two who were interviewed at two different crime scenes and also have connections to other unsolved homicides. And one chap, who lives near the convenience store and the church where Darla Monkton's NA meeting was held. He was interviewed after her death but claimed to know nothing about it, said he'd never met her."

"What puts him near the top?" I asked.

Bradley's mouth quirked up on one end. "His father died of a massive heart attack two years ago, shortly after he and the kid's mom separated. Then a month after Darla's first assault and attempted murder in Jacksonville, he and his mother moved from there to Starling."

Cruthers jumped in, grinning. "*And* in Jax, he went to high school with Shelly Trent. Well, not exactly with her. He was a year behind, a sophomore the year she was assaulted. The *same* year his parents were in the process of breaking up."

"A significant stressor," I nodded, "that could send an already unstable kid over the edge."

Nate Jacobs entered the bullpen and headed our way. "What's going on?"

Damn. No way to compartmentalize this info now. Besides, the first priority was to catch the killer.

I gestured for Cruthers and Bradley to give Nate the rundown.

They repeated what they'd told me. Cruthers handed over the list in his hand.

Nate skimmed it. "I'll take the top five. You each take five," he said to the other detectives. "Grab a uniform to help and start talking to neighbors and coworkers. We won't confront anybody until we're a little surer."

He glanced my way. "You good with that, boss?"

"Yup."

Bradley lingered as the other two trotted away. "I may have found a way to get to the ancestry company's CEO. I asked Pearl's adoptive mom to call him and give permission to release the info. He may or may not do it, though."

"Did the mom know she was looking for her biological parents?"

Bradley shook his head. "But she said she wasn't surprised. Pearl had been asking her a lot of questions lately about the adoption, which was privately arranged. I got the lawyer's name, although I doubt he'll tell me anything without a court order. Oh, and I think I know why she was being so secretive. Her mother told her that there was a caveat in the adoption agreement, that the adoptive parents would never try to track down the biological parents."

"She wanted them to be able to truthfully say they had no part in her search."

He nodded.

"Run down the guys Jacobs assigned to you first. If the ancestry thing leads us anywhere, that'll probably mean that Pearl is *not* one of the serial killer's victims. She was killed by someone else, trying to make it look like the same MO. So we can clean up that loose end after we've gotten this bastard off the streets."

"But if she's not one of the serial killer's victims, why'd he go after Nelson?"

"Nothing's saying he did. Whoever killed Pearl may have gone after Nelson."

"Maybe he saw something. Maybe her killer snatched her right as she was leaving his place."

"Maybe, but then Nelson would've told Jacobs if he'd seen anything suspicious. And why take her all the way to Starling to kill her?"

Bradley shook his head, hard, like a dog shaking off rainwater. "Could this case get any more complicated?"

"Hey," I said, a slight chuckle in my voice, "don't be putting that idea out into the universe."

He laughed and headed out of the bullpen.

When I turned back toward my office, the blinds' woman was gone, and Barnes was back at her desk. "They've got to special order ones that fit," she said.

I grimaced, but she held up a hand. "They're gonna put up some standard-sized ones in the meantime. There'll be overlap and/or gaps, they said, but I figured that was better than nothing."

"You figured right." I went into my office and she followed.

"You're not going out in the field with any of the detectives?" She sounded disappointed.

"Not tonight." I had another chore to take care of.

Barnes nodded and walked back to her desk.

Without sitting, I reached down to my bottom desk drawer to get my briefcase and laptop. My direct line rang.

"Should I get that?" Barnes called out.

"No, only when I'm not here." I picked up the receiver. "Ander...Chief Anderson."

"Good evening, Chief," a mechanical voice said. "I understand you're looking for me."

Ice ran through my veins. My heart stuttered in my chest. "Who are you?" My voice sounded strangled.

"Oh, I'm not going to just *tell* you that."

The voice was too distorted to determine if it was a man or a woman, but I was betting a man.

I whirled around toward my door and the window next to Barnes's desk, a hand waving in the air to get her attention. But she was turned away as she gathered her things to go home.

"Well, then why do you think I'm looking for you?" I said, pulling off a calmer tone a bit better this time. I spun around, scanning the bullpen. It was empty, everyone either catching some rest or out working the case. Searching for *this* guy on the phone.

Because I'd bet my entire savings account, this guy was our killer.

My stomach roiled. The one time I needed someone to be watching me in my fishbowl.

"Well, you'd be pretty stupid if you weren't looking for me. I mean, you being the police chief, and me being the local serial killer."

Thanks for the confirmation, you bastard!

A weird sound in my ear. A laugh, I realized, distorted by the gizmo that was disguising his voice.

I grabbed a pad of paper and hurled it at Barnes's back. It thwapped against the glass separating us.

Barnes jumped and jerked around.

"Now why would I believe that a serial killer would call me up out of the blue?" I said, while frantically gesturing for her to come to me, then holding my finger against my lips in a shhh gesture. If she spoke, I was sure this guy would hang up.

Barnes raced in, and I pointed to the pad. She grabbed it up, put it on the desk in front of me, pulled a pen out of her shirt pocket. I pointed to the phone receiver, then scribbled on the pad—*KILLER.*

Her eyes went wide. She ran out the door, grabbed up her phone receiver and punched buttons.

"Well, I've got nothing better to do right now," the mechanical voice was saying, "so I thought it was time for us to have a chat. We'll meet eventually, but not quite yet."

Anger took over my body, heat rising and pressure building in my chest. But I reined it in. *Oh yeah, buddy, we'll meet some day, real soon.*

"So, convince me that you really are the serial killer. How do I know you're not just some kid?"

A doorbell rang in the background. "Maybe I am a kid." Footsteps on wood, echoing slightly. "Or maybe I'm a sixty-year-old man. Or a woman. Those profilers are full of shit. Oops, now I do have something better to do." The snick of a deadbolt. "Nice chatting with you, Chief."

Silence.

"Hello, are you there?" But I knew he'd disconnected.

Barnes came to the doorway, shaking her head.

"Was he able to get *anything*?" I asked. I couldn't remember the guy's name, our sole tech person.

Barnes shook her head again. "There'll be a record of the incoming number, but Derek said it will probably be a burner. He's working on tracking it down."

I sucked in air, willing my heart to slow back to normal.

Derek, Derek, tech guy is Derek. No clue what his last name was, though.

"He also said to tell you that there are no indicators that anyone's gotten past the encryption on our phones. But he can't be absolutely sure."

Breathing out a quiet sigh, I retrieved my briefcase. "Get your stuff, Barnes. We're walking out together."

I was having trouble concentrating on the gun shop owner's sales pitch. My mind kept going back over the creepy phone conversation.

"How'd he get your private number?" Barnes had asked as we'd walked to the parking lot.

"Good question." I had no answer, but tomorrow I was searching my office for a listening device.

That mechanical voice. A shiver ran down my spine.

I poked my finger against the top of the glass display case. "The Glock."

"It's not new," the shop owner said.

But it's the one I'm familiar with. Today was the first time I'd pulled my weapon since moving to Florida. The department-issued pistol had felt bulky and unfamiliar in my hand.

He glanced sideways at me as he unlocked the case.

I checked the gun over, made sure it wasn't loaded, then quickly broke it down, examined everything for wear, and reassembled it. All the parts went back together smoothly.

His eyebrows were halfway up his forehead. "You a cop or military?" Half statement, half question. He knew I was one or the other.

"Cop," I said, "I'll take this, and some ammo."

I filled out the paperwork for the background check, double-checked that I hadn't missed a page or two. "No application for registration?"

"Guns aren't registered in Florida."

Oh yeah. I'd forgotten that.

"I also need an ankle holster for a five-round, snub-nose revolver."

My Glock in Maryland had belonged to the department, but the small revolver, my backup piece, was mine. I hadn't carried it much, once I'd made lieutenant, but now...

The shop owner's brow furrowed. "You got anything to prove that you're a cop?"

I handed him my badge. He already had my driver's license.

He rubbed a thumb over the words *Chief of Police* on the badge, whistling softly, then handed it and my license back.

"Why'd you need to see my badge?"

"I don't like to sell ankle holsters to people unless they got a concealed carry permit. But if you're a cop, you don't need a permit."

"Out of curiosity, how hard is it to get a concealed-carry permit down here?" It was extremely difficult to get one in Maryland.

"You fill out a form. If you ain't a felon or a crazy person, the permit usually comes through in a few weeks."

I tried to suppress my shudder, but the shop owner picked up on it.

He grinned. "Welcome to Florida, Chief. Land of the free."

At home, I tried out the ankle holster. It was awkward pulling my little revolver out of it. I'd need some time at the range to practice a quick and effective draw and aim.

I put the gun in its holster on my bedside table, next to my phone.

It wasn't all that late, but I hadn't slept very long last night, nor very soundly. I'd had a nightmare—*the* nightmare.

And who knew if I'd get to sleep all the way through the night tonight. I actually hoped that I didn't. I'd told all my detectives to call me with any breakthrough in the case.

Praying for dreamless sleep, I got ready for bed, slipped between the covers, and doused the light.

My mind turned to the creepy caller again and my body tensed. He could be a prankster, but I doubted it. He was our killer.

At this rate, I definitely wouldn't have a nightmare because I wouldn't ever get to sleep.

I reached out and felt around on the table, found the revolver and slipped it under my pillow. I was drifting off in seconds.

It was one of those freaky dreams in which you know you're dreaming.

The woman lay crumpled on the floor.

Here we go again, I thought in the dream.

I walked slowly toward her, trying to convince myself that she was only asleep. But why would she be sleeping on the kitchen floor?

I saw the pill bottle, empty on its side, and my heart raced.

The woman raised her head and stared at me.

Okay, that was new. She'd gotten up before and acted normal, but this penetrating stare was a new development.

Her mouth opened and a mechanical voice came out. "Why didn't you stop me?"

"It wasn't my fault," I said, in a quavering teenager's voice.

"You could have saved them," the mechanical voice said. "You could've saved those–"

A phone rang.

My mother stood up and walked to the kitchen wall phone. It rang again. She picked up the receiver and said, "Hello." But the phone kept ringing.

I jerked awake.

My cell phone was ringing. I sat up in the dark and grabbed the lit-up phone from my bedside table. "Hello?"

"Chief, this is Mark Hayes. I'm sorry to call this late, but..." He sounded odd, kind of choked up.

"Councilman, what's wrong?"

"I...I'm not sure. Maybe it's nothing. I woke up, and my wife wasn't in bed. Her side of the bed isn't even disturbed." His voice caught. He cleared his throat. "I looked all through the house for her. I think... I'm pretty sure she never came home last night."

My heart rate kicked up several notches as my mind conjured up the image of the attractive blonde woman in the news video.

"What if that monster's got her?" Hayes's voice shook.

"Don't jump to conclusions, Councilman. We will–"

"You need to be discreet!" he interrupted. "Can't you..." He trailed off.

It took my still groggy mind a second to process what he was saying. He was upset his wife might be in the hands of a serial killer, but he didn't want the press to know.

He might be the nice guy he seemed to be, but he was still a politician.

I blew out air. "Okay." *For now.* "I'll call in my best people. Meet us in my office in half an hour."

"Thank you, Chief." He disconnected.

I called Barnes, while trying to get dressed one-handed in yesterday's clothes.

"Wha?" Her voice was slurred with sleep.

"We've got an emergency. Call all our detectives. If they're not in the middle of something critical, tell them to come to my office in twenty minutes."

"What's going on?" She now sounded fully awake.

"I'll brief everybody at once. Get moving."

"Yes, ma'am."

I scooped up my blazer off the sofa on my way by. Almost to the door, I froze, then ran back for the snub nose and its holster.

I might not be able to draw quickly yet, but having the revolver was better than not having it.

I was entering the municipal building ten minutes later.

On the third floor, I ran to the bullpen. And screeched to a halt when I saw Bill Walker wiping down the coffee station.

I dropped my snub nose into my jacket pocket, approached him, and asked that he skip the bullpen. "We've got a bit of a situation tonight."

He eyed the holster in my hand. "No problem, ma'am."

He headed out of the bullpen area, almost colliding with Nate, who was coming in. Bradley was right behind him.

"What's going on?" Nate said.

"Hang on. I'll brief everyone at once."

I propped my foot on a desk chair and strapped on the holster, then tucked the small pistol into it. The holster felt weird, weighing down my ankle, but I'd get used to it.

Barnes entered the bullpen. The men's slacks and shirts were rumpled. Like me, they'd grabbed yesterday's clothes—or hadn't been home since yesterday. But Barnes was in a fresh, pressed uniform.

"Cruthers and Patterson didn't pick up," she said. "I left messages."

I waved them to seats at the nearby desks.

"Councilman Hayes's wife is missing," I said without preamble. "He's afraid she's fallen into the hands of our killer."

Wide-eyed expressions of surprise all around.

But Nate's face registered full-blown horror. "My sister?"

CHAPTER FIFTEEN

"Mrs. Hayes is your *sister*?"

Nate nodded, still looking shell-shocked. "Born Karen Ann Jacobs."

Hoo boy!

"This complicates things," I pointed out. "You know you can't work the case if–"

"But I can still help search for her." His tone was desperate.

"Of course."

Mark Hayes rounded the corner from the hallway and hustled across the bullpen.

Nate stood and extended his hand to his brother-in-law. Mark grabbed it and pulled him into a man hug.

Nate pounded his back. "Sorry, man." He choked on the words.

I suspected they were both close to tears.

"Councilman, have a seat." I waved toward an empty desk. "Tell us what happened, from the beginning."

He perched on the edge of the desk, as my people took out their pads.

"She had book club, so we ate dinner early. I told her I had a breakfast meeting tomorrow...today. She said not to wait up. Sometimes, they have a glass of wine and chat for a while, after the discussion of the book."

He coughed, cleared his throat. "I didn't think anything of it, went on to bed when I was tired. But when I got up to go to..." he ducked his head, "the bathroom."

Really, a grown man, embarrassed by a basic bodily function?

"Her side of the bed wasn't even disturbed. I searched the house. Her car wasn't in the garage. Then I called Terri, the woman who hosted the book club meeting. She said Karen never arrived and when she called her cell phone, it went straight to voicemail. She figured something had come up."

"What's Terri's address and full name?" I asked.

"Teresa Adams." He pulled a slip of paper from his pocket and read off the address.

Barnes and the men scribbled on their pads.

"Did anything unusual happen today?"

A slight pause, then he shook his head. Was he hesitating or just thinking, during that pause?

"Did she say anything else before she left?"

"Um, she left a few minutes early, because she had an errand to run on the way."

"She didn't say anything else about what or where the errand was?"

A slight shake of his head.

"Library, dry cleaners, grocery store?"

"Could've been any of those, or the bakery or florist. We're having a big barbeque next week, to kick off my campaign for state senate."

"Do you know the names of those businesses, and their addresses, or general location, at least?"

He stared at the ceiling, this time obviously thinking.

Cruthers and Patterson jogged into the bullpen.

"You're just in time," I called out.

"This has gotta be important if you're calling us in from–" He stopped abruptly when he saw the councilman.

"His wife is missing, so yeah, pretty important. Barnes, call the night sergeant. Tell him we need every uniform he can spare."

She nodded and headed for her desk.

Mark Hayes started listing businesses and locations. I pulled out my pad, since Barnes was otherwise occupied. There were twelve places he thought might be his wife's "errand."

Barnes came back with a sheet of paper in her hand. "Got Mrs. Hayes's car info from the DMV records."

"Good," I said.

Nate snatched the paper from her. "I'll make copies."

"Nobody works alone tonight," I said, in a voice loud enough to carry to the copy machine. "Including you, Nate. This guy is escalating. He called me earlier, disguised his voice. On my private line, a number I've only given out to the councilman here so far."

I scanned the surprised faces around me. "I wouldn't put it past him to try to take out a cop. No heroes tonight, got it? Only good cops doing good police work."

A chorus of "Copy that," and "Got it, Chief."

Nate came back and distributed copies of the car info.

I assigned each detective two of the locations. "You each take a uniform and check out your locations. And the route from it to the councilman's house, and from it to Ms. Adams's house. When you're done, check in with me and I'll assign one of the remaining locations."

To Nate, I said, "Sorry." It should be him they were checking in with, but not when his sister was the potential victim.

He nodded, his expression grim.

Hayes stood up. "I can help."

"Sir, I need you here, where I know you're safe and I can reach you if we have any questions. Barnes, get a uniform to keep the councilman company." I gave her a meaningful look.

The kidnapping of the council chair's wife, and the sister of a cop to boot, felt an awful lot like the killer was thumbing his nose at us. Thus the lecture about how he might try to take out a cop. And the councilman stumbling around in the dark would be a very tempting target indeed.

Barnes went to her desk to call the night sergeant again.

"The officer will get you anything you need," I said to Hayes.

He pursed his lips. "If I'm too important to search for my own wife, then why are you going out?"

I raised my eyebrows at him. "Because it's my job, and I'm trained to do it. Barnes, you're with me. Everybody else, go!"

"Sarge said the uniforms will be out front," Barnes called after the detectives as they raced across the bullpen.

A slightly overweight uniform, one of the officers first on the scene the night Darla died, hustled around the corner.

"You've been briefed?" I asked as he approached.

"Yes, ma'am." He gave me a small nod.

Barnes and I power-walked to the elevators. "Officer Jessups will do his best to keep the councilman here," she said. "And if he can't, he'll call me."

Jessups. I repeated the name in my head several times, visualizing his face.

"Damn." I said, as the elevator reached the ground floor. "I should've gotten a photo of the woman for everyone." My brain was way too sleep-deprived. If I didn't get some decent rest soon...

"They all know her face," Barnes said.

I tilted my head toward her as we exited the elevator.

"She's on the local news a lot. Social events, charities and such."

"So she's Starling's version of a socialite?"

"More like ambassador for her husband."

"He's pretty ambitious then," I said, "if he's running for state senate."

Barnes shrugged. "I'd say she's more ambitious than he is. He tried for the state senate last time and lost. He's got a good shot this time, though. The incumbent's retiring."

The night air had cooled slightly, but the humidity had risen, leaving one's skin clammy. We—my people, Barnes and I—walked the routes from each location to the friend's house, and from each to the councilman's house. Shining flashlights in alleys and driveways, around people's yards.

Hoping to find Karen Hayes, praying we didn't. If she was lying out here in the dark, the likelihood that she was alive was slim to none.

At some point a few lights came on in the Hayes's home. A tall, male silhouette stood in the large, front window.

Barnes called Jessups. The councilman was still at 3MB.

"Their eldest boy, Brian," Barnes said softly.

I vaguely remembered him from the press conference on TV.

"He's nineteen, I think. Goes to UNF," Barnes informed me.

Despite being tired, my brain made a connection. Hayes's wife, at the news conference—that's why she'd looked familiar. Her facial features were like Nate's, only finer, more feminine.

My throat tightened.

Two hours later, a faint lightening of the sky heralded morning.

We'd scoured the routes to and from all the locations, and knocked on doors. Without using her name, we'd asked if anyone had seen a woman matching Karen Hayes's description, or had seen her car, or had heard anything unusual.

The detectives and uniforms were now expanding the search outward.

Barnes and I returned to 3MB.

Officer Jessups nodded a greeting from his perch on the edge of a desk in the bullpen.

Hayes was sitting at another desk, arms folded in front of him, head resting on them. He might have been asleep, but he jolted up as we approached.

I shook my head slightly. His head fell back onto his arms.

"Councilman...Mark," I said gently, "come into my office, please."

He slowly stood and shuffled after us.

I signaled for Barnes to stay back. She closed my office door and went to her desk. Jessups headed down the hall toward the restrooms.

"Is there anything else you can tell us that might help us find her?" I asked.

Mark Hayes slumped into one of my visitors' chairs, turned his head slightly away from me. "Maybe she left."

"What do you mean?"

He cleared his throat. "She might have left me."

Shit! Would've been nice to know that up front.

With anyone else, I would have said that out loud, but this guy was the city council chair.

"Were any of her clothes gone? Jewelry?"

He shook his head. "She has a fistful of credit cards. She could replace it all. She knows I won't cancel them."

"Why do you think she might have left you?" I asked in a soft voice.

"We had an argument. Yesterday...I guess day before yesterday now. She hadn't spoken to me since."

"But you said she told you–"

"She writes me notes, when she's mad."

I thought of Barnes's comment that his wife was ambitious for him. Would she really leave?

"What did you argue about?"

He ducked his head. "The usual."

"Which was?"

"That I didn't really care about Starling or I'd want to represent it in the state legislature." He looked up, made eye contact. "I keep trying to tell her, I *do* care about this city, but I want to fix its problems, reduce crime, create jobs. I'm not sure the state legislature is the best place to accomplish that."

"But you were about to declare your candidacy?"

He nodded. "To keep Karen happy. I doubt that I would've won."

I noted that his statement was in the past tense.

Without his wife around, apparently his candidacy would be past tense as well.

Would this seemingly mild-mannered man kill his wife to keep her from pushing him where he didn't want to go?

Bradley found Karen Jacobs Hayes at seven-fifteen a.m., in an alley ten blocks from her florist. Not wanting to draw the press's attention to what was going on, I did not go to the crime scene.

He snapped a picture of her and sent it to me. She looked downright peaceful, posed with her hands on her thighs, eyes closed, face slack.

The Jacksonville ME put the autopsy at the head of the line.

By two-thirty, I had the preliminary report. Karen Hayes had been garroted with a smooth, soft object, consistent with a woman's stocking or scarf. And micro-abrasions in her vagina indicated she'd been penetrated with an object—most likely an old-fashioned soda bottle, the report had said.

Like Pearl Altman.

Karen Hayes's car was nowhere to be found. I hadn't put out an official BOLO, but all the uniforms on patrol were watching for it. If it had been parked on some side street or in an alley, we would've found it by now.

At four, the three detectives who were exclusively working the serial killer case—I refused to call him the Midnight Killer—were gathered in my office, along with Barnes. Foster was on my computer screen, via Zoom.

I had managed to find time this morning to do a quick search. I'd found no listening device. The new soundproof door had arrived yesterday, so I felt relatively comfortable meeting in my office.

When we had the time, Barnes and/or I would search the small conference room, where we had the murder board and had discussed the cases many times.

Barnes lowered my new, makeshift blinds, installed under her supervision earlier this afternoon. Sure enough, there were three one-inch gaps, the glass walls showing behind them, and one spot where the blinds overlapped and caught on each other when you opened or closed them.

Bradley gave a summary of what we had so far on Karen Hayes's homicide.

"You all are searching for her car," I asked Foster, "over there in Jacksonville?"

"Yes," he said, "but it's a much bigger city than Starling."

"Guys," I said to my detectives, "you have CIs?"

They all nodded, as I figured they would. Most detectives tried to cultivate at least one confidential informant.

"Put out the word that we're interested in any chop shop that's had a late model silver Audi come through in the last twenty-four hours. We're not out to bust the chop shops, but we need to know when and by whom it was delivered."

More nods all around.

"We need to nail this bastard," I said. "Today!"

They filed out, shoulders sagging from fatigue. Especially Jacobs. But I wasn't about to suggest he get some rest. He'd ignore the suggestion anyway.

I slumped back in my desk chair and gestured for Barnes to sit down.

"What rock have we failed to turn over here?" I muttered, more to myself than to her.

"I can't think of any," Foster said, making me jump a little. I was so tired, I'd forgotten he was still there.

"Thanks for all your help, Detective," I said.

"No problem. We're invested in this too. If...*when* we get this bastard, we'll be able to clear four SAs and two murders. Talk soon." He ended the connection.

My desk phone rang. The private line. The incoming number was blocked. I stared at the ringing phone. I was not up for jousting with our killer right now.

Bracing myself, I picked up the receiver.

"Any news?" Mark Hayes said without preamble.

I quietly blew out the breath I'd been holding.

"Afraid not, sir." I wasn't about to tell him the details from the autopsy.

He'd tried to go to the crime scene, but I'd managed to talk him out of it. His oldest son had come to take him home. The kid had looked familiar, and not just because of a family resemblance. I'd seen him somewhere before.

"Did you get any rest?"

"Some. What are you doing to find this son of a bitch?"

It was the first time I'd heard Mark Hayes swear.

"Everything possible. We're working the case twenty-four-seven. We *will* get him."

Or drop from exhaustion trying.

"Look," Hayes said, "the media's gonna catch on to what's happening soon, and I...I can't face that right now. Can you hold a news conference or something, control the message. And tell them to leave us alone. My kids–" He choked on his words. "My kids and I need privacy, to grieve."

"Of course, sir." But I was talking to dead air. He'd already disconnected.

I glanced at the time on my computer. Four-thirty.

"Can you pull together a news conference by five-thirty?" I said to Barnes, still slumped in my visitor's chair. I wanted to make it onto the six o'clock news.

She nodded.

"Good. No hints as to what it's about, no matter how much they beg or try to trick you into saying something you shouldn't." I doubted the press would respect the councilman's privacy, but I would do my best to shame them into doing so.

"Of course." She looked slightly offended.

"I'm going to freshen up." I tilted my head toward the tiny bathroom off of my office. It had a minuscule shower, and I kept a fresh white shirt hanging on the back of the door.

Fifteen minutes later, I exited the bathroom, the hinges squeaking as I nudged the door closed.

I felt somewhat refreshed, and I didn't smell bad anymore. But I still wasn't ready to face the press.

Comes with the job. I sighed. A lot of things came with this job, some of which really sucked.

I tried to review some reports, without much success. My mind kept wandering.

Barnes bustled in, her face grim.

"You get all the major news outlets on board?" I asked.

"All but Marly Davis. I was told she was unavailable." Her voice was tight. "That she was about to go on the air with a special report."

A knot of dread formed in my stomach.

She grabbed the remote for the tiny TV perched on the bookcase across from my desk. She aimed it at the TV like it was a laser gun and hit the *on* button with considerable force.

Marly Davis's face filled the small screen. A banner proclaiming *Special Report* streamed along the bottom.

"...did not come to work today. His son called in for him, saying he had a cold. But this reporter just found out the real reason for his absence." She paused, took a deep breath, and belatedly adjusted her expression from gleeful to somber.

"Councilman Hayes's wife, Karen Jacobs Hayes, was the latest victim of the Midnight Killer."

CHAPTER SIXTEEN

I banged my fists on the desk and cursed, calling the reporter every nasty word I knew.

When I wound down, Barnes said, "Do you want me to call Jacobs in to stand with you at the podium?"

"Hell no. I'd never ask him to go through that." I thought for a couple of seconds. "Which sergeant is on duty?"

"Collins."

"Good, get him over here, and another uniform if there's one handy. I need to work on my statement."

I turned to my computer and started typing.

I don't usually wear much makeup. But I went into the bathroom—wincing at the squeak from the hinges—and dabbed some concealer on the dark circles under my eyes, then applied lip gloss.

Meanwhile, Phyl Gladstone took a quick look at what I'd written. She suggested a few changes. They were good changes.

At five-thirty on the dot, I entered the conference room, Barnes behind me. Sergeant Collins and Officer Armstrong stood at the far end of the table, a few feet back from the podium.

Every seat at the table was taken and reporters stood along the walls, some from news channels in Jacksonville and one from Gainesville.

Those lining the right side pulled back against the wall to let me pass. I nodded to each of them as I went by.

At the end of the table, I stepped in front of my officers, facing them. They maintained neutral expressions, but their eyes were sympathetic.

Armstrong whispered, "Go get 'em, Chief," somehow without moving his lips.

I turned and nodded to Barnes, who closed the door.

My badge was clipped to the breast pocket of my black jacket, my fresh shirt crisp, and my rumpled slacks hidden behind the podium. I took a deep breath.

Silence reigned, all eyes watching me expectantly.

"There will be no questions, ladies and gentlemen." I scanned the room, giving them my best don't-mess-with-me look.

There were a few nods, but nobody said anything. My guess was, they'd all seen or heard about Marly's special report. They knew what was coming.

I took another deep breath to continue, and the door burst open.

The devil herself barged in, cameraman in tow. She tried to push past the others on one side of the table, but they closed ranks and wouldn't let her through.

I hid a smile and glanced at her cameraman.

His face was beet red. He quickly lifted his videocam and covered his face with it.

Poor guy. I'd be ashamed to be seen with her too.

"As I said, *no* questions." I proceeded to read my statement, with the bare-bone facts regarding Karen Hayes's disappearance last night and the discovery of her body this morning.

There were no gasps, since this was not new news.

I ended with the request from Hayes that the press and the public respect his family's privacy as they grieved the loss of a beloved wife and mother.

I gave them another stern look. "I hope you all will honor his request. That's all for now. We'll keep you posted."

Marly immediately waved her hand in the air. "What about Detective Jacobs? Why isn't he here? He's her brother, isn't he?"

Now, a gasp rippled through the room. Apparently, there was a line that even reporters weren't supposed to cross.

Ignoring her, I started along the side of the table. The reporters again made way for me.

"Well, where is he?" she demanded. "Is he out in the field, working the case?"

Out of the corner of my eye, I saw Armstrong elbowing his way along the other side of the table.

"Ms. Davis," Collins's voice from the podium behind me. "The Chief said no questions. It's best you leave." Barnes opened the door behind the reporter.

Marly looked at me, at Collins and finally at Armstrong who was almost to her. She whirled around and left.

A couple of the local reporters clapped softly. The out-of-town ones looked confused.

I had trouble keeping a straight face as Barnes and I swept from the room, Armstrong as our rear guard.

"*That* woman and some of the other reporters are still out front," Barnes reported to me an hour later. "You might want to leave out the back."

"I'm not leaving until we have an arrest to tell those reporters about." I leaned back in my desk chair and sighed. "But, unfortunately, I can't go out into the field right now, for fear I'll draw some of them with me. Which wouldn't exactly make the detectives' jobs easier."

Barnes nodded. I gestured her into one of my chairs. She perched on the edge.

"Sit back and get comfortable. It's gonna be a long night."

"Uh, Chief, these chairs aren't very comfortable. I think the former chief did that on purpose so people wouldn't linger."

I snorted. "Put that on the list of things to order when we get through this. But just get one that's comfy. We'll keep it over there." I pointed to the corner near the bookcase and TV. "And only offer it to people we like."

Barnes chuckled.

"You should go home, get some sleep," I said.

She shook her head. "If you don't need me right now, I'd rather be out on the street, helping with the investigation."

I nodded. "Put on your vest before you go out there." Then a thought had me sitting up straighter in my chair.

"And on your way out, get Marly Davis aside and tell her I want to see her, *alone*."

"You want me to stick around then?"

"No, I don't want any witnesses."

"Hmm, that sounds interesting." She chuckled again. "You gonna rubber-hose her?"

"Oh, if only I could get away with that."

Marly Davis entered the bullpen a few minutes later. She seemed to know her way around, making a beeline for my office.

I stood up behind my desk. "Come in. Have a seat." I gestured toward a visitor's chair, glad that they were uncomfortable.

She looked at me as if I were a teacher who'd asked a trick question.

I forced a smile. "Honest, I don't bite."

Her return smile was about as genuine as mine. "Thanks." She sat.

"Coffee?"

"No, thanks. It's too late in the evening for me. It'll keep me up."

I poured myself a cup. "That's the idea." I took a sip, still standing.

She blinked. "What's the idea?"

"I need it to keep me up. I doubt I'll get any sleep tonight."

She blinked again, didn't say anything.

I sat in my desk chair. "Look, I know this is a highly irregular request, but we've got a serial killer on our hands here. People are dying. *I* need to know how *you* know things that haven't yet been released to the public."

Her mouth twitched. I suspected she was trying to hide a smirk. "That's my job. To find out things and tell the public about them."

"But you're finding out things that only a few people know." I was choosing my words carefully, not wanting to say directly that I thought my department had sprung a leak. *That* would then be tomorrow's headline!

She shrugged. "It's hard to keep secrets in this town."

"These aren't secrets. They are confidential pieces of information in a highly sensitive case. You're potentially helping a serial killer, or at the very least creating a distraction that makes it harder for us to do our jobs and catch him."

She bristled some. "So sorry if doing my job distracts you from yours."

I slowly sucked in air. "It's important that I know how you are getting that information."

She gave me a smug look, sat back in her chair, and grimaced. She moved to the front edge again. "I do not reveal my sources."

I knew that was what she was going to say, but it was worth a shot. Then I delivered my message—the real reason I'd wanted to see her. "Okay, but if you step over the line and obstruct the investigation, or withhold critical information, I *will* have you arrested."

She stood. "Duly noted, Chief."

As she flounced toward the door, I said, "You should know that this killer cleans up after himself. He doesn't leave loose ends. For all you know, your source may *be* the killer."

She whirled around in the doorway. "I can assure you that my source is not the killer." She laughed.

"Just watch your back, Marly."

"You watch yours," she said in a middle-school, mean-girl voice. She stormed across the bullpen. As exit lines went, it was pretty lame.

I checked the time—seven-thirty—and pulled out my cell phone.

Kate answered on the third ring. "Hi, Judith."

"Is this a bad time? The kids' bedtime maybe?"

"No, it's good. They pretty much put themselves to bed these days, and not for several hours yet."

I squirmed a little in my desk chair. What the hell did I know about teenagers' bedtimes?

"What's up?" Kate asked in my ear.

"We've got another victim." I told her about Karen Hayes, and the fact that her case's details matched Pearl's more than the others.

"That's really odd," she said. "When was the last attack in Jacksonville?"

"A year and a half ago."

"Then you have Pearl," Kate said. "Somewhat different MO. Then Darla, almost the same MO as before. And now another victim with an MO that matches Pearl's. I'd say you have a copycat who's responsible for Pearl, and maybe Karen. They've stirred up the original killer, and he went after Darla, the one who got away. But he's trying to make it look like it's the same person who killed Pearl."

"Why did he stop before, when Darla got away?" I asked. "Was it only fear of getting caught?"

"Maybe, but I can think of a couple other possibilities. He may have gotten enough of his anger out of his system—over whatever crap in his past helped set him up to be a killer. And/or he may have matured some, now has enough good things going on in his life that the stakes are higher. He's got a successful career, maybe a family, children he cares about."

"If they're psychopaths, do they really care about anybody?"

"Well first of all, like all disorders, antisocial personality disorder is on a continuum, from mild to severe–"

"It's genetically based, correct?" I was hoping to move things along. She was going into professor mode, telling me things I already knew.

It didn't work, at first.

"Yes, their brains are wired differently. They don't feel empathy or remorse. Indeed, they don't feel most human emotions the same way that we do, but the smart ones learn how to fake them. Getting back to 'can they feel love'..."

Please, I thought.

"Their version of love is very self-centered. It's all about their needs. In the case of kids, it's about how the child reflects well on them, makes them proud, adores them, which feeds their egos. This guy started out as a serial rapist. They're full of anger, usually combined with distorted sexuality from childhood sexual abuse. But rape wasn't enough after a while.

"Psychopaths get off on power over others. He had to kill to get that sense of power again. But maybe after a couple of kills, the rage has dissipated some. He tries to escalate with Darla, to get the thrill back, but she escapes. If he's married by this point, has kids, that could've mellowed him some. And he has more than his freedom to lose if he gets caught."

"Then someone kills Pearl, using an MO similar to his." I sat up straighter in my desk chair. "And maybe that pisses him off."

"And he somehow figures out where the one who got away lives–"

"That's a good point. We need to look into Darla's life more. How did she end up on his radar again, after moving from Jacksonville to Starling?"

My head was spinning some, but that was partly fatigue. Who was supposed to be following up on Darla's movements? Panic set in. I was losing control of this investigation.

Wait, it wasn't my job alone to oversee the investigation. Nate was my lieutenant, and I was pretty sure he was the one who was following up on Darla.

I took a calming breath. "We're looking into the loners' angle," I said. "Any ideas on how to narrow down the suspect pool if he's an upstanding family man?"

"Actually, I've been giving that some thought. Juvenile records. The antisocial behaviors start young. But in kids, it's called conduct disorder. He'll have a history of aggression, stealing, lying, cruelty to animals."

I perked up, then deflated again. "We can't get juvie files if they're sealed, not without probable cause."

"But can you at least find out if they *have* a juvenile record?"

I wasn't sure how that worked in Florida. "I'll check that out. Hey, we've had another development as well." I told her about the attack on Nelson and how he might be connected to Pearl's case.

"More evidence that you have two killers," Kate said. "And the original one wants all the murders blamed on Pearl's killer."

During our entire conversation, I'd been debating whether to tell her about the call from the killer. It would be good to get her take on it—did she think it was genuine, not some prank?

But I couldn't make myself bring it up, and I wasn't sure why that was.

I was down to the wire, and I just couldn't do it.

"Thanks for all your help, Kate."

"Happy to help. Now I'd better go check on the teenagers, make sure they're not plotting to take over the world, when they're supposed to be doing their homework."

I chuckled. "Whenever I momentarily regret not having kids, I just talk to you for a little while."

Kate laughed. "Sadly, I totally get that. Take care, Judith."

I disconnected and sat back in my desk chair, realized I was smiling.

And suddenly I knew why I hadn't mentioned the killer's call. One, I knew in my gut that it was genuine, not a prank.

But two, I hadn't wanted to worry my *friend*.

And that *would* have worried her. She would've seen it as a personal threat against me?

Was it? Should I be worried?

I shook my head, turned my thoughts back to processing all that Kate had said.

But I was so tired. I was getting drifty.

My cell phone rang. I jerked forward and grabbed it up off the desk. "Anderson."

"Armstrong here, Chief. There's been another attack–"

"Where?" I jumped out of my chair.

The sound of air being sucked in. "It's Barnes. She's on her way to the hospital."

My heart plummeted into my stomach. "How bad?" I demanded, swallowing hard.

"The EMTs weren't sure," Armstrong said. "She was unconscious."

"I'm on my way."

CHAPTER SEVENTEEN

I ran across the dark municipal parking lot, one hand on my gun at the small of my back.

Come on, you bastard, come after me*!*

The son of a bitch did not comply.

Breaking every speed limit—which wasn't a big deal, since the roads were pretty much deserted—I made it to UF Shands-Starling, our only hospital, in record time.

When I asked at the main desk where Officer Gloria Barnes was, the person manning the desk asked questions in return, such as, was I a relative.

I flashed my badge and she instantly became more cooperative. Good thing, because my next tactic would've been to grab her by the front of her blouse and lift her off her feet.

Following her directions, I raced down corridors to the ER.

Bradley and Armstrong were there, hovering outside a curtained-off cubicle.

I skidded to a stop. "How is she?"

"She'll live," Bradley said, his expression thunderous.

I couldn't blame him. "Tell me what happened."

"She was paired with Detective Jacobs," Armstrong said, "and–"

"He went into a house," Bradley cut him off, his voice angry. "Leaving her out on the sidewalk. I was talking to somebody down the street." He paused, shuddered. "I heard her scream."

Armstrong put a hand on the detective's arm.

Bradley sucked in air. "I shouted and the guy ran off."

The curtain was peeled back by a white-coated kid. "Would y'all keep it down, please?"

It took a moment to register that he was the doctor.

"How is she, Doc?" I asked.

"Contusions and abrasions on her face and neck," he said, "and on her left side, where her Kevlar vest was jammed against her ribs, but mostly she's shaken up."

"I am *not* shaken up!" Barnes's voice, from behind him.

Jacobs jogged up at that moment. "How is she?"

Both Armstrong and Bradley gave him dirty looks and didn't answer.

I pushed past the young doctor, who shrugged and walked away.

Jacobs and Bradley followed me into the cubicle. Armstrong stayed outside. Before the curtains flapped shut, I noted he was scanning the room, as if our perp might try to attack again right here in a crowded ER.

I struggled not to react to the "contusions and abrasions." Barnes sat on the side of a gurney in a hospital gown, her dark hair down, hanging lank beside cheeks that were scratched and battered. One eye was swollen shut, the other bruised. More scratches on her neck, probably from her own fingernails.

I winced.

Shiny ointment had been applied to the scratches.

"Wish I could say you should see the other guy," she quipped.

Nobody laughed.

"Tell us what happened," I said.

"Most people weren't answering our knocks. Everybody's scared now. So Detective Jacobs asked me to stand out on the sidewalk, where people could see me, in uniform, from their windows. It worked at the second house where we tried it. The door opened. He gave me a discreet thumbs up and stepped inside."

She swallowed hard. "He was in there for a while. I, um, must've let my guard down. Suddenly, this *thing* is around my neck. I kicked back and twisted, ducked down, trying to loosen his hold. He started punching me with one hand from behind me, while keeping the pressure on that cloth around my neck with the other." Her hand moved toward her throat, then fell back into her lap.

"When I kept fighting him, he tried to jab me with a knife, up under my vest, but it must've caught in the Kevlar. I heard someone yell, and the guy jerked away from me and ran off."

She took a deep breath. "I must've passed out for a few seconds. Next thing I know, I'm on the sidewalk and Danny...Detective Bradley's hovering over me."

"Can you give us a description?" I asked gently. "Take your time."

Bradley was breathing hard, eyes red-rimmed. He was going to lose it any second.

I caught a small smirk on Jacobs's face, before he wiped it clean. You'd think he'd have more sympathy for Bradley, since he'd just lost his own sister to this monster. But the animosity between them ran deep apparently.

I shot Bradley a look, mimicked taking notes on a pad. It was as much to ground him as to have the record.

Barnes visibly collected herself. "Medium height and build, I think. I only got a glimpse of his face. He had that stocking over it. I couldn't see his features clearly, but I think he's white. Black hoodie with the hood pulled up, so no idea of hair color. Not sure about eye color either."

"What else was he wearing?"

She closed her eyes, winced. "Dark pants, might've been jeans or sweats, I don't know. Black shoes, sneakers maybe?"

"Did you get a look at the perp?" I asked Bradley.

He shook his head. "Too far away. When I yelled, he took off, just a dark figure, running. I'm pretty sure he was medium build, for what that's worth."

We all knew that wasn't much help. A lot of people were medium build. That's why it's called medium.

"I couldn't really say how tall he was." Bradley seemed calmer. "He was hunched over as he ran."

It was getting claustrophobic in here. "Nate, how about finding a chair somewhere and writing down what Barnes told us? Then she can look it over."

"Find a chair where?" His gaze darted around the tiny cubicle.

A surge of annoyance. I reined it in. We were all sleep deprived and flustered by an attack on one of our own.

"Out there." I gestured toward the slight gap in the curtain around the cubicle.

He ducked through the gap.

I glanced out. He'd taken a chair about fifteen feet away.

I nodded to Armstrong. "Take a break, Officer."

He walked away slowly, looking back over his shoulder.

I turned back to my assistant. "Barnes...Gloria." I put a hand on her shoulder. "You need to take a few days off, longer if you need it."

She started shaking her head.

"And I'm putting a guard on your house."

She shook her head more vigorously, grimacing, her loose hair flapping against my wrist.

"You need everybody on the streets," she said.

I bent my knees so I was eye level with her. "You are at *risk*," I said emphatically. "If he thinks you can identify him, he'll come after you again."

"I'm between apartments, staying with my parents temporarily. This will totally freak them out."

I glanced up at Bradley, a question in my eyes. He nodded.

"How about you stay with your brother? And we'll discreetly put a guard on the place. Maybe we'll catch him that way. But you don't go anywhere alone, understand?"

Her expression morphed from defiant to defeated. "Understood." Then a light came on behind her eyes again. "Maybe we should tell the press where I'm staying, use me as bait."

"I don't think so!" Bradley and I said in unison. It would have been funny under different circumstances.

"Do we have the knife?" I asked Bradley.

He shook his head.

"Her vest?"

"It's on top of my uniform over there." Barnes pointed to a chair.

Bradley crouched down and looked at the vest without touching it. "It's got a slit in the back, near the bottom."

"Bag it," I said, "and find her something else to wear."

He nodded again, but didn't move.

"Go do that now, and find the doc to see about getting her discharged."

He left the cubicle.

I used my phone to take photos of her face from several angles. "Can you lift your gown up some," I said gently, "so I can get the other injuries?"

Red crept up Barnes's neck. She moved stiffly, wincing as she raised one side of the hospital gown.

My stomach churning, I photographed the abrasions and red marks on her side. They would be nasty bruises by tomorrow.

Bradley returned with evidence bags and a set of clean scrubs. He handed the latter to me and, with gloved hands, slid the uniform and vest into the bags.

I waited for him to label them and leave, then shook out the scrubs top.

"I can get dressed myself." She reached for the top and grimaced, her other hand grabbing her side.

"Sure you can." Trying to protect her modesty as much as possible, I helped her get dressed.

"At least he didn't break my nose." She touched its tip with her finger.

"Yeah, that would've been a shame," I said without thinking. "It's a cute nose."

She ducked her head.

And I felt that weird feeling again, the one I couldn't identify the other night—a strong tugging sensation in my chest. My throat tightened.

Maternal? Damn, is that what I'm feeling?

A fierce rage consumed me, heating my entire body. I wanted to take Barnes home and lock her in my spare bedroom, with ten uniforms standing guard. Damn, how had I gotten so attached to this young woman in such a short time?

It had taken years of knowing Kate before I'd felt anything akin to caring. Dolph had gotten in easier, but then I'd ridden with him every workday for ten years.

"I need a cat," I muttered.

"Chief?" Barnes said.

"Never mind. You ready to go?"

"Most definitely."

The doctor intercepted us outside the cubicle. "We really should keep her overnight, for observation. She's moderately concussed."

Barnes shook her head and winced.

"I think that's a big no, Doc," Bradley said from behind him.

Jacobs joined us as the doc huffed off.

He handed his pad to Barnes. I read over her shoulder. It looked like he'd gotten everything, even the description that Bradley had already written down.

"I'm not at all sure about the shoes," she said. "I really didn't see his feet that well, just a flash as he ran away."

"Oh," Jacobs said. He stilled for a moment. "Okay." He scratched the word *sneakers* off the bottom.

Bradley slowly led Barnes away. I followed.

Armstrong trailed behind. "I'd like to volunteer to be her bodyguard, Chief," he whispered. "I can do it twenty-four-seven, so you don't have to pull anybody else off the case."

I slowed my steps, letting Barnes and Bradley get ahead of us. "Why?" I asked him.

"I, um... Maybe she was too green to be out on the street during all this, without a training officer."

I resisted the urge to point out that she'd been out on the streets for the last three months on her own, on evening shift.

Guilt is rarely logical.

Instead, I said, "She was with a detective. You're not responsible, Officer." I glanced at the wedding band on his left hand. "And how would your wife feel about you being gone for days?"

"She'll understand." Armstrong tilted his head toward where Barnes was shuffling through the opening between the double sliding-glass doors of the ER. "The girl reminds me of our eldest daughter. Cussedly independent, among other things."

I stifled a chuckle. Apparently, Barnes had wormed her way into more than one hard-ass cop's heart. I didn't feel so bad.

I nodded.

"Thanks, Chief. I won't put in for the overtime."

"You sure as hell will," I said, "and when all this is over, you're taking your wife on a nice vacation with the money."

Armstrong flashed me a grin. "That will definitely sweeten the deal for her."

I let him follow Barnes and Bradley out of the ER and turned to look around for Jacobs.

He was standing nearby, waiting for Armstrong and me to finish our conversation.

"Any follow-up info on Darla Monkton's movements yet?" I asked him.

He shook his head. "I haven't had time to talk to the sister again."

"There are way too many loose threads hanging in this investigation."

"Tell me about it," Jacobs said with a slight chuckle.

I'd meant it as veiled criticism, but he hadn't taken it that way. I let it go. Not the right time to pick a fight with him.

"I'll go talk to her now," I said.

Jacobs nodded, turned away.

"And I got another lead from my psychological consultant."

He turned back toward me, his expression neutral. "What's that?"

"Our perp is most likely a psychopath, and they start young. She said to look at juvie records for signs of 'conduct disorder.'" I made air quotes, then told him the list of not-so-nice behaviors Kate had given me.

"In other words, they're miniature thugs," Jacobs said.

"Yup, pretty much."

"I'll have somebody start pulling the records of our suspects."

"Not the ones on our list. I want to check for juvie records for every male who lives in that part of town, between the ages of eighteen and forty."

He whistled, drawing glares from a couple of nurses and the teeny-bopper doc.

I moved us toward the doors. They slid open automatically. "There's no guarantee that our guy is a loner. My consultant says he could seem like an upstanding citizen on the outside, but it's very likely he'll have those behaviors in his history."

Jacobs sighed. "Okay, I'll pull Cruthers in, put him on it. He's good at skimming through stuff like that."

"Sounds good."

He made a gesture, half wave, half salute, and walked toward his car.

I got in mine and headed for Arliss Monkton's apartment.

Arliss opened her door to my knock. "Did you get him yet?"

I shook my head. "No, but I think we're getting closer. I wanted to double check something with you."

She opened the door wider. I stepped inside.

Perched on the edge of her sofa, I asked, "Did Darla go out much?"

"Only to work and NA meetings."

"Can you be sure she didn't go out during the day, when you were at work?"

She shook her head. "I work from here." The slightest of pauses. Her cheeks flushed. "I make cold calls for a vehicle warranty company."

It took my brain a couple of seconds to understand the blush. She was a telemarketer, something she apparently wasn't proud of.

"Where did Darla work?"

"At the dry cleaners, two doors down from the convenience store. Her sponsor helped her get the job. It was only part time. What are you getting at?"

I suppressed a sigh. "You realize we have to look at all angles. We're trying to figure out how this guy found her, and..." I trailed off.

"And you're wondering if she was hooking and doing drugs again."

I nodded.

Arliss blew out air. "Part of me wants to get offended, but of course you'd wonder that. No, I don't think she was doing either. She did slip a couple of months ago, but it was short-lived. She bought some uppers on the street, got high for a couple of days, but ended up flushing half of them. Then she checked herself into rehab again."

My chest ached. Darla had been trying so hard to get herself straightened out. Only to end up on an autopsy table.

"Did anything happen, during the days just before...?"

Arliss began to shake her head, then stopped. "Wait, she said she had this weird feeling someone was following her. But when she'd turn around, nobody was there."

"When did this start?"

She thought for a second. "Shortly after when y'all came to talk to her. She said it happened a couple of times."

"Did she have any idea who might be following her?"

"She wondered if it was that guy at the convenience store, the daytime clerk. She thought he was sweet on her."

Hmmm...

"Any idea where she got the uppers?"

Arliss's face pinched. "She wouldn't say, but I have a pretty good idea." Her tone was sharp. "I think the guy who owned that store was pushing pills on the side."

"Tremont?"

That would explain his nervous behavior, when Jacobs and I talked to him.

"Yeah, the one who got robbed and stabbed. I'm thinking about moving. This neighborhood is going downhill."

I thanked her and made my exit.

Outside her apartment building, I looked around trying to remember where I'd parked my car.

Damn, I'm tired.

The back of my neck tingled. A hand on my gun under my jacket, I did a slow 360, scanning the dark street. Nobody was around. Still, the hair on the back of my neck was standing at attention.

I shook my head. I was letting my imagination take over.

I spotted my car and hustled over to it, jumped in and, imagination or no, quickly hit the lock button.

I'd intended to sit there for a moment, writing notes from my meeting with Arliss Monkton. But my neck was still tingling.

I drove to the municipal parking lot, then sat in the car and jotted down my notes.

CHAPTER EIGHTEEN

My cell ringing jolted me awake. I'd fallen asleep with my head resting on my arms on my desk.

I grabbed the phone up without checking caller ID. "Anderson."

Crap, I forgot the *Chief* again. Hell with it, I'd been just plain *Anderson* for too many years to change the habit now.

"We think we got him, Chief," Bradley said, as excited as I'd ever heard him.

"Tell me." I wasn't getting worked up until I knew there was something to be excited about.

"Guy's name is Douglas Cleaver, as in *Leave It to Beaver*."

Was Bradley even old enough to remember *the Beave*? I barely was, from reruns.

"He's the guy that went to high school with Shelly Trent. We're sitting on his house, waiting on the warrant. My CI lives near him, said he was in his room a few times. They were probably doing drugs together. Anyway, one time he saw a woman's jewelry box on the guy's dresser. He went to pick it up and Cleaver went ballistic, told him not to touch it. He said—get this—it was full of, quote, 'special souvenirs.'"

"Where's your sister?" I asked.

"At my place, with Armstrong. She insisted I come back out."

"Who's working on getting the paper?"

"Jacobs. He said he had a pet judge."

Note to self, tell Nate to never, ever say that out loud to anyone ever again.

Especially with reporters like Marly Davis poking around.

"You need any help?"

"Got some uniforms with me, and a SWAT team is on the way. You coming out?"

I was dying to do just that, but the reporters... Surely, Marly and the crew had gone home. My computer screen said it was four-ten a.m. She'd be tucked in bed by now, while we were all working our butts off, or in my case, anxiously waiting.

"Yes, give me the address."

I went out the back of the building, in case reporters were out front. I was almost to my car when a siren bleeped behind me, making me jump.

I whirled around. Collins was stepping out of a cruiser.

"Good lord, Sarge, you almost gave me a heart attack."

"Sorry, Chief. Um, I thought you told us not to go anywhere alone."

"Yeah, well, my shadow's out of commission at the moment. And what about you?"

"Lewis took over as watch commander. So I'm glorified patrol right now. I was headed to the suspect's house. You want a ride?"

Hmm, another cop car among many wouldn't be that noticeable, whereas Marly and a few others of her ilk now knew what my car looked like. "Sure, thanks."

A few minutes later, Collins pulled up behind another cruiser on a side street.

Despite it being the wee hours of the morning, a small group of neighbors had congregated on the sidewalk across the street. Two officers stood in front of them, keeping them back.

I opened my door and stood up, but didn't move away from the car. I scanned the crowd. No reporters that I could see. I spotted one face that looked familiar, although I couldn't place him.

Everyone, including the bystanders, were keeping their voices down. With any kind of luck, the occupants of the house were still asleep and wouldn't have time to hide evidence.

Nate pulled up behind us. He jumped out of his car without even turning off the engine, waving papers in his hand.

Bradley stood off to the side, at the bottom of the steps leading to the house's wooden porch. He'd ditched his suit jacket and had a Kevlar vest on over his dress shirt.

The four-person SWAT team bracketed the house's door. One held a ram.

Nate, standing beside me, spoke softly into his radio. "Any action in the back?"

"No, sir," came the staticky answer.

Bradley looked over at me.

I nodded.

Collins had taken up a position on the other side of the porch steps. Both had their weapons drawn, but down by their legs.

One of the SWAT team members pounded on the door. "Police, open up." They waited a beat, then the one with the ram swung into position.

The door cracked open and a plump middle-aged woman stuck her head out. "Why in the devil are y'all bangin' on my door in the middle of the night?"

She showed no surprise at the sight of the police cars in the street. She'd already been awake—most likely, watching out a window.

A SWAT officer grabbed her arm and handed her off to a female officer standing by. She hustled the woman down the porch steps.

The SWAT team disappeared inside.

The woman and her police escort had reached us by the cars. "We have a search warrant, ma'am," Jacobs said. "Is your son at home?"

"Well I expect so. Lemme see this search warrant."

"You don't know for sure, ma'am?" Jacobs said as he handed it to her.

"He's a grown man. I don't monitor his comin's and goin's."

Shelly Trent had just turned nineteen, and Cleaver'd been a year behind her in school—making him eighteen. Technically grown but...

I didn't know a lot about parenting teenagers, but I suspected most parents wouldn't consider eighteen "a grown man."

The SWAT team leader appeared in the house's open doorway. "All secured," he called out. "You're gonna want to see this."

Bradley bounded up the steps.

Nate and I left the mother with her keeper and jogged after him.

Halfway down a hallway off the living room, Bradley had stopped in a doorway that was flanked by two SWAT officers. He snorted, then grinned.

He made way for Nate and me to look into the room.

The fourth SWAT officer stood next to a twin bed, his gun aimed at its occupant.

But the suspect appeared to be no threat at the moment. He was snoring loudly.

Bradley rolled his eyes and I snickered.

I watched for a few minutes, while two uniforms stood guard over a glassy-eyed Douglas Cleaver, and Bradley and Nate searched his room.

With the adrenaline draining away, my body was beyond exhausted. And I wasn't needed here.

Outside, I found Collins and he instructed a uniform to take me back to 3MB. I didn't bother going inside, just had the officer drop me at my car in the lot.

It was only a twelve-minute drive to my apartment, but I had the AC going full blast, the vents all turned toward my face.

Halfway home, my phone rang. *Bradley* flashed on the dashboard screen. I answered, "Ander–"

"We found the jewelry box." his voice was excited. "It wasn't on his dresser. He'd hidden it behind some books on a shelf."

That kid had *books*.

"I only glanced in the jewelry box," Bradley continued, "didn't want to contaminate it. Buttons and a few other things. Sure look like trophies to me. I'm headed to the FDLE lab with it now. And Cleaver is in custody and headed for a holding cell. The uniforms and Collins are going through his room again, to make sure we didn't miss anything."

"Good work, Detective. Drop off the box and then go home and sleep."

"I wanted to interrogate Cleaver when I got back."

"He's stoned out of his mind. You let him be for tonight. We don't want his attorney saying we questioned him when he was incapable of understanding his rights."

"Okay. Got it." He chuckled. "Bed, what a lovely three-letter word."

"Oh, did you get anything out of the mother?"

"Nope. She knows nothin' about nothin'."

I was not surprised. She might indeed know something but I doubted she would share it willingly.

"Sleep in tomorrow," I said. "You deserve it, and Cleaver will keep."

We both snickered.

"I wonder how much he was teased as a kid?" Bradley said.

"Probably not that much. His generation's too young to know about *Leave It to Beaver*. How come you even know about the show?"

"My mother loves it. She watches the reruns all the time."

I chuckled. "Sleep tight, Bradley. I'll see you tomorrow when we both come up for air. Oh, wait! I talked to Darla's sister this evening...umm, last night now. She said Darla didn't go out and swears she wasn't using drugs or hooking again, despite a small slip recently. Darla worked at a dry cleaners near the convenience store. Talk to the people there, and the clerk at the store again. Maybe Cleaver hung around there and that's how he spotted Darla. That would put another nail in his coffin." I told him about the creepy feeling that Darla had mentioned to her sister. "She thought the clerk at the store was sweet on her, but it might have been Cleaver following her."

"Got it. I'll try to find out as much as I can before I interview him. Good night, Chief."

I pulled up in front of my apartment building with a smile on my face.

My head hit the pillow at five-fourteen. I was out cold.

My phone rang, it felt like no more than ten minutes later. I squinted at my bedside clock. Six-fifty.

"Anderson," I mumbled into the phone. "This better be good."

"Um, Chief," a young female voice said hesitantly, "do you still want to hear about missing person calls?"

"No, cancel that order." *We have our killer.* "Wait, who's missing?"

"The reporter, Marly Davis."

My stomach clenched. *Shit!* "Who's on duty?"

"Sergeant Lewis and some uniforms. The detectives all went home. Do you want me to call one of them in? We've completely lost track of who's up next. Or should I give it to the sarge?"

The detectives' normal rotation had gone out the window several days ago, and they all deserved some rest. But I wasn't about to trust a missing reporter case, full of potential land mines, to Lewis.

"I'll take it. What's the address?"

Forty minutes later, I was sitting in the Davis's living room. I'd hit a coffee shop's drive-thru on my way over, but I gratefully accepted when Mr. Davis interrupted his crying and gnashing of teeth to offer me more coffee.

He'd expected his wife home by ten last night. "And she always calls when she's going to be late," he sobbed out.

He was laying it on a bit thick, even after I'd tried to reassure him that there was most likely another explanation for Marly's absence, other than her falling prey to the serial killer. But I couldn't tell him we had a suspect in jail for that case.

Assuming Marly eventually came home unscathed, hubs no doubt would tell her everything I'd said.

And then it would be all over the news.

Hands wrapped around the mug of lovely liquid caffeine, I asked him the usual questions, repeating the crucial one—where she might possibly be?

"I don't know," he wailed. "Just find her. She's my life."

I left him with another vague reassurance and headed for 3MB.

And found Barnes sitting at her desk, her uniform clean and crisp, her face a mess.

The sight of it made my stomach roil. Pressure built in my chest.

"What are you doing here?" I said, more crisply than I'd meant to. I wasn't angry at her.

"I was going stir-crazy," she said, "just sitting around. And the danger's gone now, right?"

I blew out air. She'd been "sitting around" for one whole evening and night, and today was Sunday. I was about to tell her to go home, but she was giving me puppy-dog eyes.

And I really could use her help today. There would be a lot of loose ends to tie up. Plus, there was Marly.

I sighed. "Yeah, okay. Did you hear who is missing?"

"Yes."

Of course she had. Why did I even ask?

"Have we heard from the lieutenant yet this morning?"

"No, but Patterson's around here somewhere."

She'd no sooner said the words than he walked into the bullpen.

I called the detective over. Fortyish and dark-haired, he wore jeans and a polo shirt—a little casual if he was on duty today.

I gave him the rundown on Marly Davis.

"Uh, Chief, I'm supposed to be on leave. I'm taking my daughter tomorrow, to check out a college in Georgia. I only came in today to finish the paperwork on a case I closed last week." His voice was neutral but his eyes were worried. "I figured since we have an arrest in the serial killer case, it would be okay for me to still go."

I thought for a moment. "Get started on the Davis case, contacting friends and coworkers, other family members. We'll have somebody else take the case over by the end of the day, if at all possible, so you don't have to cancel your trip."

He nodded, relief on his rugged face, and headed for his desk.

I'd barely settled behind my own desk, with my third cup of coffee, when Bradley showed up.

"I thought I told you to come in late?"

He shrugged. "I don't need a whole lot of sleep. I'm about to tackle Cleaver. You wanna sit in?"

My eyebrows shot up. "You already talked to all those people we discussed last night?"

"Yes and no. I tried, but struck out all over. Dry cleaner's closed on Sundays. The clerk at the convenience store is a part-timer. He said that regular guy, Ronnie Malcolm, was also working today but wasn't in yet. He recognized Cleaver's picture but not

Darla's. I even called the folks in her NA group again, to see if they'd thought of anything. Got voicemail all the way around."

They'd probably turned their phones off to sleep in on a Sunday morning. If only I'd had that luxury.

"I'm going to tackle him now," Bradley said, "then come back at him when I have more input. If he lies about anything this first time through, I'll catch him in the lie later."

"If he doesn't scream for a lawyer." I pushed up out of my desk chair. "He's got issues with women, obviously, so maybe it's best if I don't sit in, this first time. I'll watch via the video."

As we walked to the interrogation room, I filled Bradley in on my interview with Marly Davis's husband, finishing with, "I'm not usually one who automatically assumes the spouse did it, but this time... I think he doth protest too much."

"Still," Bradley said, "I'll check Cleaver's alibi for last night."

I grunted. "If he took her, she may still be alive somewhere, and if that's the case, we need to find her asap."

He chuckled. "Ya wanna bet she's found some juicy story and she's staking out some poor schmuck's house?"

"Nope, not taking that bet."

Bradley gave me a half grin, pushed the door to the interrogation room partway open, took a deep breath and plunged in.

I went to the video screen on the wall and found the right buttons to push to get it working.

Douglas Cleaver looked awful, huddled shivering in yesterday's clothes, which he'd been sleeping in when he'd been arrested. They hung loosely on his scrawny frame.

Hmm... What few descriptions we did have indicated medium build. But the hoodie he'd worn could have given the impression he was heavier.

His hair was long, dirty blond, pulled back in a straggly ponytail. And his hazel eyes were no longer glassy. Instead, they were filled with terror.

Guess he never thought he'd get caught.

Bradley went through the preliminaries—date, time, location, identifying the suspect and himself, Mirandizing the kid again.

Cleaver mumbled his answers when Bradley asked him a question.

"Speak up for the recording, please." Bradley said.

But the guy didn't have much to say, only continued denials that he'd done anything wrong. He also denied any knowledge of Marly Davis. Said he'd never heard of her, that he never watched the news.

That last part I could believe.

"You remember Shelly Trent?" Bradley said, switching gears.

"Who?"

"Shelly Trent, from high school."

Cleaver's brow furrowed. He seemed genuinely confused.

"In Jacksonville. She was a year ahead of you."

His eyebrows went up slightly, but he shook his head.

Bradley handed him a recent photo we'd gotten from the aunt.

Cleaver tilted his head slightly as he examined it. "She looks vaguely familiar."

"She was the girl who was sexually assaulted."

His eyes went wide. "Oh, her. Yeah, I remember that. But I didn't know her. She was a junior and *way* outta my league." He shoved a stray hank of hair out of his face.

Bradley gave a slight nod. "Where were you last evening *exactly*?" His voice was sharper. When he'd asked the question before, Cleaver had said he didn't remember, that he had a really bad memory.

Not surprising, if you're stoned most of the time.

The kid started to shake his head, then sat up straighter in his chair. "Oh yeah, I was hangin' with Ronnie earlier, at Pronto's."

I sat up straighter as well. He knew Ronnie Malcolm, hung out at that store. He had to have seen Darla there.

Something else clicked in my brain *Aha! That's* who that guy was in the crowd last night—Ronnie, the clerk from the convenience store.

Bradley was trying to pin Cleaver down on where he went after he'd left Pronto's "somewhere around ten-thirty."

The kid was back to saying he didn't remember. Had he been doing drugs, or was he kidnapping Marly?

I texted Bradley's phone. *Ask him about Darla. I'll go talk to Ronnie again.*

Bradley glanced at his phone, gave a small nod meant for me.

I power-walked to my office to get my gun and tell Barnes where I was going.

She stood, to go with me.

I opened my mouth, about to say she looked kind of scary, then thought better of it. Wouldn't hurt for Ronnie boy to be a bit nervous.

CHAPTER NINETEEN

Ronnie Malcolm gave Barnes a quick, trying-not-to-stare look, as I informed him we needed to ask a few questions.

He turned the counter over to his helper and we walked toward the coolers. I asked him about Cleaver.

"Yeah, Doug was in here most of the evening, from about seven on." He gestured toward a pinball game in the corner of the store. "He hangs around a lot on Friday and Saturday nights, when he doesn't have to get up the next morning for work."

"What does he do for a living?" I asked, even though I knew the answer.

"Drives a delivery truck for a furniture company. He's a good worker, makes a point of being..." He trailed off.

"Being what?"

"Uh, on time."

"Hmm, I have a weird little feeling that you were about to say *sober*."

He winced. "He drinks some, but mostly he smokes weed and pops pills."

Again, I knew this. The uniforms had found both marijuana and an assortment of pills in his room. It was a good test of whether Ronnie was being straight with us.

"How else do you know him," I asked, "besides him coming into the store?"

"He lives down the street from me."

"So he's an old friend?"

He quickly shook his head. "More like an old acquaintance."

"Why were you working the night shift last night?"

"I've been working double shifts most days lately. We've only got a couple of part-timers, besides me. Mrs. T made me the manager and said to hire someone for the night shift." His eyes brightened. "Say, do you know any cops who'd like to pick up some extra money. Nobody'd mess with a cop working the evening shift."

"I don't know. We'll ask around."

Barnes was dutifully scribbling notes in her little pad. I gave her a meaningful look, hoping she'd take the hint and ask something, draw Ronnie's attention.

She did. "Exactly what time did Doug Cleaver leave last night?" she asked.

He made eye contact with her for the first time, no nervousness in his body language. Apparently, he'd gotten used to her battered appearance. "Around ten-forty. I remember 'cause I'd just started my close-up routine. It takes me about twenty minutes, more if I get a lot of late customers."

"Did you get any late customers last night," I asked, "while Doug was still here?"

"Only a few."

"Any regulars?"

He shook his head.

Damn, I'd been hoping for somebody who could verify when Cleaver left.

"Did Doug leave at any time during the evening?" I asked.

Ronnie thought for a moment. "Nope."

I glanced around the store. There were video cameras in the corners of the ceiling. I pointed to one of them. "We need to see the footage."

Ronnie sighed. "The system's been glitchy for a while now. Some days it works, some it doesn't. Yesterday..." He shook his head.

Handy, if you're dealing drugs from under the counter.

"The outside cameras?"

He sighed again. "Somebody kept bashing them up. Kids, throwing stones, most likely. Mr. T finally took them down."

I held out Darla's picture. "You knew her, right?"

He nodded. "I didn't know her name though, but she was a regular customer."

"So Doug would've crossed paths with her."

"Yeah, I guess, but I never saw them talking or anything."

I paused for a moment, trying to think if I'd forgotten anything. I was still seriously sleep deprived, and it would probably be a while before my back forgave me for sleeping with my head on my desk part of last night.

Ah, the supposed crush.

I waved the photo a little. "You say you didn't know her name. Did you find her attractive?"

He looked at me as if I were a brick short of a load. "Uh, no."

"Did Doug say anything about finding her attractive?"

He shook his head. "I guess he might have. They were both... But he never said anything about that to me."

I suspected he'd been about to say that they were both druggies.

A beat of silence as I asked myself again if I'd forgotten anything.

Duh, the drugs.

But I opted not to get into that right now. Arliss's suspicions might or might not be valid. And Ronnie might or might not be involved. If he was, he'd clam up. And if he wasn't, he'd be offended that we were accusing his boss, whom he'd liked. Either way, we'd lose his cooperation.

At this point, the serial killer case was all important.

"Is it always this quiet this time of the morning?" Barnes asked. There hadn't been a customer for at least ten minutes.

"Yeah, there's a big rush first thing, people getting coffee and breakfast. It settles down about nine, then just a trickle, until the early lunch crowd."

My stomach rumbled. *Speaking of breakfast...* I hadn't had any this morning.

Barnes gave me a small, lopsided grin.

I thanked Ronnie and we exited the store.

In my car, Barnes said, "Kinda convenient that the cameras are mostly nonfunctional."

"The inside ones were working Tuesday. Jacobs reviewed the video from that night."

I put the car in gear and headed for a fast-food place down the street. "Tremont may have turned off the inside cameras himself at times." I told her about Arliss Monkton's suspicions and the fact that Tremont had been acting "squirrely," as Nate had put it, when we'd first interviewed him.

I wondered if whatever he'd been groping for under the counter that day had been drugs he was trying to shove farther out of sight.

But Tremont wasn't around now, so why were the cameras off last night?

I pulled into the fast-food joint's drive-thru. Barnes asked for a vanilla milkshake and I ordered an egg and cheese sandwich.

Once we got our order, I pulled into a parking space.

Barnes winced a little as she sucked on her straw.

Again, that weird tugging sensation in my chest, when I realized she was drinking her breakfast because it hurt to chew.

While I ate, I pulled out my pad and reviewed my notes from the interview with Arliss, to make sure I hadn't missed anything.

I was swallowing the last bite of my sandwich when my phone rang. *Cruthers* flashed on the dashboard screen.

"Anderson," I said. "You're on speaker. Barnes is with me."

"Chief, I was looking over the canvassing reports for the Tremont case again, to see if anyone mentioned somebody matching Cleaver's description. There's a couple reports from neighbors around the Tremont home that mention a younger man coming around some, at times when Tremont wasn't there. But it's not Cleaver. This guy's about six-one, well built, medium-length brown hair with blond streaks, boyish face."

Barnes and I made eye contact. "Ronnie," she mouthed.

"Want me to follow up?" Cruthers said. The dashboard speaker let out an annoying little screech.

It had been doing that off and on lately. I really needed to get it looked at.

"No," I said, ignoring a slight echo from the speaker. "I'll go talk to her. She might open up more to a woman. Did you see if Cleaver has a juvie record?"

Bradley had already checked for more recent offenses. There weren't any. Ronnie was right. The kid knew when to stay straight and when it was relatively safe to use his recreational drugs.

"None here in Starling," Cruthers said. "I've got a call in to Foster to see if he has one in Jax, since he lived there until a year and a half ago."

"Good. Did you hear about the new missing person's case?"

"Yes." Another small squeak. "You want me to work on that?"

I hesitated. I still hadn't heard from Nate. Was he taking the day off, since it *was* Sunday and we had a suspect in custody?

"Yeah, take over that case from Patterson. He's trying to get things tied up so he can go on vacation tomorrow."

"Got it." Cruthers disconnected.

Barnes's straw gurgled as she hit the bottom of her milkshake. She let out a soft "Aaaahh," of satisfaction.

I smiled at her. "Let's pay Mrs. Tremont a little visit, shall we?"

Bradley, Cruthers, Barnes and I gathered in my office. Still no word from Nate Jacobs, but it wasn't quite noon yet.

I debated internally about keeping the information regarding the various cases partitioned, but I was too damn tired to deal with all that. I still wanted to find the leak, but it seemed less pressing now.

First, I had Barnes report that Ronnie confirmed Cleaver's alibi for the previous evening, until ten-forty at least. Then I filled them in on Mrs. Tremont, who'd sworn that no young man had been coming to her house on a regular basis, and Ronnie Malcolm had only done so a couple of times since her husband's death. But she'd given off multiple tells that she might not be telling the truth, the whole truth and nothing but the truth—not making eye contact, blushing. She even bit her lower lip one time, right after protesting that she would never, ever cheat on her husband.

I nodded at Cruthers. "What have you got on Marly Davis?"

He handed me a sheet of paper and read the same info out loud from his own copy. "Marlene Ann Jones, born 1968, in Miami. Married Joseph Snyder in 1992, one son born in '95, divorced in '97. Six domestic violence calls during that marriage. She finally testified against him, and he went to prison for assault for two years. It wasn't his first offense. She got full custody of the kid, who is now grown.

"Moved to Starling and remarried in 1998 to her current husband, James Davis. He's thirteen years older than her. Daughter's born a year later. Marly was a stay-at-home mom until seven years ago when she started part-time with the paper. Became full-time after her daughter left for college, and began doing some reporting for the TV station, owned by the same corporation."

"What's the husband do?" I asked.

"He retired six months ago, from..." Cruthers paused, ruffling through additional pages on his lap. He was an odd combination of tech-savvy and old school.

"Well, damn, I missed that before. He was an executive in the parent company that owns the newspaper and our fledgling local TV station."

"Can we say *nepotism*, boys and girls?" Bradley said.

Seriously, he's a Mr. Rogers' fan as well? I caught myself in mid eye roll.

One side of Bradley's mouth quirked up.

"I'm working on tracking down the first husband's current whereabouts," Cruthers was saying. "Marly was last seen at a charity function last night. She stuck her microphone in the mayor's face and asked for a comment on the suspect the police were pursuing for the Midnight Killer murders."

"Say what?" I half-shouted. "How'd she know about that at... What time was that, Cruthers?"

"Around nine-thirty."

"She might've been making it up," Bradley said, "just to see what Mr. Mayor would say."

I tapped a pen on my desk, willing my teeth to unclench. "She was due home at ten, and her husband said she always calls if she's going to be late. If somebody snatched her, it was most likely during that half hour, between nine-thirty and ten. Where was the charity event held?"

"The community center in Starlingville."

"Right smack in the middle of our killer's comfort zone," Bradley said.

I turned to him. "And what does Mr. Cleaver have to say for himself?"

"Other than offering his alibi for last night and repeatedly denying he's our killer, not much. For every other time period, from when a victim was last seen 'til their body was found, he had no clue where he was, because..."

"He has a really bad memory," we said in unison.

Bradley's half-smile was more of a smirk this time. "He also said at first that he didn't know Darla Monkton, but then admitted to seeing her at Pronto's occasionally. Never knew her name."

"He claims," Cruthers threw in.

"How bright would you say he is?" I asked.

Bradley shrugged, frowning. "Not very. He might have been smart once upon a time, but he's fried his brain with drugs."

I nodded. That was my impression as well.

"He's got an alibi until ten-forty last night," I said, "so it's unlikely he made Marly disappear. But we can't rule him out completely. There could've been some reason she didn't call her husband to say she was running late—phone battery crapped out or she lost it, maybe—and Cleaver grabbed her after he left Pronto's." I leaned forward in my chair. "But–"

A knock on my door.

"Come."

Phyl Gladstone stuck her head in the office. "Chief, sorry to interrupt, but I'm getting a lot of inquiries from the press about a possible suspect we supposedly have in custody."

Thanks a lot, Marly.

I motioned for her to come in and close the door behind her.

To all of them, I said, "I'm not willing to tell the press we have our man. Phyl, send out a press release. Say we have a person of interest we are questioning, but the public should not let down their guard yet. Then resist all attempts to get more out of you."

"Got it." Phyl opened the door, and Jacobs plowed past her.

"Chief," he said, excitement in his voice, "got the prelim results from the state lab. The items in that box are linked to five of the victims. They *are* his trophies."

Phyl hovered in the doorway, looking uncertain.

"Your orders stand," I told her.

She nodded and left.

"One of the things in that box was a lock of hair." Jacobs's face sagged into a sad expression. "The lab said it probably belongs to Shelly Trent. They're working on the DNA analysis."

My throat tightened. Poor Shelly. We needed to find her, even though I doubted she was still alive. And Marly Davis. Her disappearance muddied the water.

I scanned the faces in the room. "Nothing of this discussion better make it into the press or I'll know who to come after. I want more evidence before we tell the world that we've got the killer."

Jacobs shook his head. "But the trophies–"

"Are a strong piece of evidence. All a defense attorney needs to do, however, is put Cleaver on the stand. In two minutes, the jury will know he's not bright enough to pull all this off. So, either he has a partner or there's more to him than meets the eye. Talk to his coworkers and family. How does he behave when he's not high?"

"Maybe he's got those split personalities you hear about sometimes?" Jacobs said.

"I doubt that." But I made a mental note to run the possibility past Kate. "Bottom line. We don't have the whole story yet."

Jacobs left, his body language grumpy. I knew he wanted this case solved. We all did. But we also wanted the *right* guy behind bars.

Cruthers rose. "I was with JSO until five years ago. Still got a couple of CIs over there. Want me to see if they know anything about Shelly Trent?"

"Yes, thank you. Have we told the public that Marly's missing yet?"

Cruthers checked his watch. "About to. It'll be on the noon news."

I nodded and he left.

Barnes walked over to the door after him. I thought she was leaving as well, but she closed it, then turned back toward her brother and me. "What if Ronnie Malcolm and Doug Cleaver are in on it together?"

A few beats of silence, broken by Bradley. "That would explain the differences in the MOs."

"And blow up both of their alibis," I said. "Might be worth looking into."

At one-thirty, I was chowing down on a sandwich from a nearby deli and trying valiantly to catch up on reviewing reports, when I had a *déjà vu* moment.

I'd spent twenty plus years protecting and serving in Baltimore County, which surrounded the city by the same name. Baltimore was one of the most violent cities in the U.S. In the county, we'd dealt with the spillover from that violence on a daily basis.

And now my new "protect and serve" territory was on the outskirts of Jacksonville, another violent city. We had a small rural buffer, what was once the original Duval County, before the consolidation in the sixties.

But still we had more than our share, based on our size, of city-type violence. And this morning we'd had one of the worst kinds of big-city crimes—a drive-by. In the red-light district. One fatality and one critically injured, but thank heavens no children had been hit by stray bullets.

My desk phone rang. Not my private line. I let Barnes intercept the call.

I scrolled on to the next report, a disorderly conduct call regarding a guy in a clown suit who was annoying breakfast customers at a local diner.

I was chuckling over that one when Barnes stuck her head into my office.

"The FDLE lab's on the line. They've got something important, and they can't get ahold of Jacobs."

"I'll take it." I picked up my receiver. "Chief Anderson." I remembered the *Chief* this time.

"Hi, Chief, nice to meet ya." A male voice I didn't recognize.

My stomach clenched. *Is this our killer, playing games again?*

"Wish it was under better circumstances," the voice continued. "I'm Joe Phelps, from the FDLE lab. I've got some more details on the stuff you sent over."

I quietly blew out air. "Good to meet you too. Again, would be better under other circumstances. Thanks for processing the evidence on a Sunday."

"No thanks necessary. That's what we're here for."

"What have you got for us?"

"Well, all the little goodies in this box do match up, one way or another, with one of your victims and four of Jacksonville's. Three buttons, one from Darla Monkton's jeans, a small strip of cloth torn from a blouse, and a lock of hair. But there's two strange things. One, there aren't any fingerprints, not even smudged partials, on any of the buttons. Killers who take trophies, they like to fondle them, ya know what I mean?"

"Yes." I shoved away the thought of what else they might do while fondling the trophies.

"And how did the buttons get into the box with no fingerprints?" Phelps was saying. "Bad guys don't usually wear gloves when they're stashin' their keepsakes in their trophy box."

"Definitely strange. And the other thing?"

"The lock of hair's from the missing person case here in Jacksonville, Shelly Trent. But these hairs, they're real dry and brittle. Either they were cut off the victim a long time ago or..."

"Or what?"

"Or they've been frozen."

"You said cut, not torn. How old would the sample have to be if it wasn't frozen?"

"Yup, definitely cleanly cut. And I'd say about four or five years, at least, to get this dry, longer if it was in this box the whole time."

"Then they couldn't be from the earlier assault of that victim. That was only two years ago."

"Most likely frozen then."

"Okay, thanks for getting back to us so quickly."

"No problem. I know y'all have a guy in custody, and since you hadn't announced about the case being solved, I figured you had some doubts."

"You figured right."

"Sorry I had to add to those doubts instead of makin' them go away."

"That's okay. It is what it is." I thanked him again and disconnected.

A chill ran through me.

The odds of Shelly being alive just went way down. But where had Cleaver stashed the body? And how had his trophy lock of hair ended up frozen at some point?

And no fingerprints on the buttons? Had the trophy box been planted?

Nate Jacobs stuck his head into my office.

I'd opened my mouth to tell him about the call from the lab, when he said, "Cruthers's got a lead on Marly Davis. Some kid saw her stumbling along the side of the road, out in the countryside north of here, in Clover County."

CHAPTER TWENTY

In the front yard of a house in Clover County, a thirtyish woman kept her hand on the shoulder of a six-year-old boy whom Cruthers was questioning, apparently for the second time.

"You told me before," the detective said from his crouched position in front of the child, "that you saw a man with the woman, but you didn't see his face. Can you tell me anything more about him?"

Jacobs took sunglasses from his suit jacket pocket and put them on, distracting me for a moment from the boy's answer.

He must have sensitive eyes. The sun was behind a cloud.

"Was he taller than your mom?" Cruthers was asking when I tuned back in.

The boy, slim and dark-haired like his mother, nodded.

"Was he as tall as your dad?"

The boy shrugged. "Maybe."

"I'm five-seven," the woman said in a quiet voice. "My husband's six-foot even."

"Five-nine to maybe six-foot," Barnes muttered from beside me, scribbling on her pad. She kept her head down, hat brim hiding her battered face, so she wouldn't freak out the little boy.

"But you saw the lady's face and it was the one on the TV?" Cruthers asked.

The boy nodded again.

"I've been checking the news a lot," the mom said. "You know, to keep track of things." She shot me a nervous glance. "To know when it's safe."

"Safe from what, Mom?" The boy looked up at her with curiosity on his face, but no fear.

"Nothing you need to worry about."

"How close to these two people were you, Jamie?" Cruthers asked.

"I told you, I was right about here." His voice was a bit impatient. "Lyin' in the grass, and they was over there." He pointed to the road, about twelve feet away.

Cruthers gave him a small smile. "Sorry, but police officers sometimes have to ask questions again, to make sure they heard the answer correctly the first time."

Good save, Cruthers. The re-questioning was partly for our benefit, but also to see if the kid's story changed in any significant way or sounded too rote.

The boy seemed to buy the explanation. He nodded sagely, as if thinking that adults never listen half the time anyway.

"Tell me again why you were outside."

"To count the stars," the boy said. "I couldn't sleep."

His mother's hand tightened on his shoulder. He looked up at her, now with some fear in his eyes. He knew he was going to get it later.

"My dad and I do that sometimes at night, when he's home. But the moon was too bright, or there were clouds or something. I couldn't see many stars. So I was just lyin' there and wishin' Dad would come home sooner than Sunday."

"That's when he's due back from his run," the mom said, again in a low voice.

I assumed the father was a trucker, another clue coming from the very large tire leaning against the side of a nearby garage.

"What was the man wearing?" Cruthers asked.

"A hoodie, with the thing up over his head." The boy mimicked pulling up a hood. "That's why I couldn't see his face."

"And nobody said anything?"

The boy shook his head.

"Are you sure?"

"Yeah. I was prayin' they wouldn't see me in the grass and say somethin' to me, 'cause my mom has real good ears."

He gave her a feeble smile.

She patted his shoulder. "Just don't ever go out of the house after dark without tellin' me again," she said in a stern voice.

"And was he a big guy like me?" Cruthers stood up. "Or thin, like your mom?"

The boy tilted his head to one side. "Closer to my mom, I guess."

Cruthers looked at me and Jacobs. I nodded, signaling that I had no questions.

I stepped forward and handed my card to the mom but spoke to the boy. "If you ever want to see the inside of a police station, Jamie, ask your mom to call me. We'll set up a time and I'll give you a tour myself."

"Who are you?" the boy asked matter-of-factly.

"Jamie, don't be rude," his mom said.

"It's a totally fair question." I stooped down to his level. "I'm Chief of Police in Starling." I held out my hand.

He shook it tentatively, staring at my face. "Wow, they let girls do that?"

I chuckled as I stood. "They let girls do a lot of things these days."

His mom and I exchanged a smile.

Cruthers, Nate and I walked away. "Those were the same answers he gave earlier," Cruthers said.

"Rehearsed?" Nate said.

"No, not exactly the same. And the stuff about counting stars with his dad and missing him, that was a new piece. First time through, he only said he couldn't sleep."

"Do we have access to a search-and-rescue dog and/or a cadaver dog?" I asked.

Nate was shaking his head, but Cruthers said, "Both. I know a guy, south of Jacksonville, who trains them."

"See if you can get him here asap," I said.

A burgundy sedan pulled up—Bradley's car. He stepped out of it.

Two Starling cruisers were right behind him. Four of our uniforms piled out.

I jogged over and told them to report to Detective Jacobs for assigned areas to search.

Bradley motioned me to his car. Barnes tagged along.

Nate and Cruthers were now talking to the uniforms.

"You hear about that drive-by earlier, Chief?" Bradley asked in a low voice.

I nodded.

"One of the victims is my CI."

"Is he okay?"

He wobbled his hand in a *maybe* gesture. "He's in surgery at the moment, but he told me before they wheeled him away that the other guy set up the meet this morning. He didn't know why. He confessed that he hadn't seen the trophy box himself in Cleaver's room. It was this other guy who told him about it. He was hoping to get something else on Cleaver today, to pass on to me."

"Who's the other guy?"

"Name was Reggie Diaz. He's dead."

"Damn," I said.

"Yeah, my sentiments exactly."

"Awful big coincidence," I said, "that they get gunned down right after passing on that info to us about Cleaver."

Bradley shrugged. "They were both lowlifes. One or the other of them probably got crosswise with a drug dealer."

"But the chief doesn't like coincidences," Barnes piped up. "She's allergic to them."

Her brother gave her a quelling look.

Then he took a deep breath. "And, we might have another missing woman."

My stomach did an unpleasant somersault as I digested Bradley's report. He'd tried to track down the NA meeting attendees again, to see if any of them knew Cleaver or had seen him hanging around Darla. One of the women from the meeting—who'd given her name as Stormy—hadn't been home since yesterday morning, according to her mother with whom she lived. The mother hadn't been overly concerned, saying that her daughter sometimes stayed with friends.

"Put a BOLO out on her anyway," I said. "You have her last name and description?"

"Yes. Stormy's a nickname. Her real name is Cynthia Price. I'll call that in and then join the search."

"No, go back and start canvassing around the area of the drive-by, see if you can find any witnesses."

He snorted.

"I know, not exactly a section of town where cooperation with the police is high, but try. And keep the fact that one of the victims was your CI to yourself for now."

I'd no sooner sent Bradley on his way when two white cruisers, with dark green markings and Clover County written on their sides, pulled to the side of the road.

A rotund man in a khaki uniform and matching Stetson stepped out of the driver's side of the lead car. He hustled toward us—a stereotypical rural sheriff with graying hair and a bushy mustache.

"This here's county jurisdiction," he said as he approached where Barnes and I stood.

"I know that. That's why I called your department." I'd already explained the situation to the deputy who'd answered the phone, so I wasn't inclined to say more.

The man opened his mouth, but another voice interrupted. "I'll take it from here, Deputy. Why don't you join in the search?"

"Harumph." The rotund man huffed away.

A slimmer, taller man, mid-forties—also in a khaki uniform—stepped forward, hand extended. "Sheriff Sam Pierson, ma'am. You must be Chief Anderson." His voice was a pleasant baritone.

I shook the hand, trying to hide my surprise. *I* should know better than to make assumptions based on stereotypes. "Good to meet you, Sheriff."

"Call me Sam." He gave my hand a slight squeeze and let it go.

I hesitated, then said, "Judith."

He raised an eyebrow, and I figured it wouldn't be long before he tried to call me Judy.

He looked around, slowly shaking his head. "A serial killer's one hell of a welcome to Florida for you."

"We appreciate your cooperation."

"And you'll always get it. Any of my people ever give you a problem, you call me direct." He made eye contact as he handed me his card. His eyes were a piercing blue.

I put the card in my pants pocket and headed for my car, gesturing for him to follow. My cards were in my jacket, lying on the backseat.

He strolled along beside me. "What makes you so sure your missing person is one of this guy's victims?"

"I'm not, but the odds are..." I'd been about to say *high*, which told me I'd already unconsciously accepted that Douglas Cleaver was not our killer.

We reached my car and I got out one of my cards to give to the man. But first I wrote an additional number on the back.

I handed the card to him, that side up. "Private line. You're only the second person I've given it to."

Perhaps it was premature to trust this guy with it, but I might have to get the number changed anyway, thanks to the killer.

He flashed a smile, his teeth a bit dazzling in the sunshine. "Thanks, Judith. Now where can I be the most help?"

I filled him in on what the boy had said, my eyes scanning the surrounding fields, bordered by strips of piney woods. I concluded with, "If you were a serial killer, with a body you *didn't* want tied to you, where would you hide it out here?"

"Why wouldn't he want this one tied to him?"

I sighed. "Keep this under your hat, please."

He tipped said hat, a Stetson that matched his uniform. Beneath it was a thatch of sandy hair, a few sprinkles of gray here and there. "Consider it kept there."

"One, the missing woman is a reporter who knew things that only my people and the killer would know. She may have been getting that info from the killer–"

"So this time, he's cleaning up loose ends rather than satisfying his sick needs."

I noted that Sheriff Sam was not dropping his g's. His voice sounded more like mine. Another Northern transplant? Apparently, there were a lot of them...us, in this part of Florida.

I nodded. "Two, she went missing during a time for which the kid we've got in custody has a partial alibi."

He arched an eyebrow again. "You've got someone in custody?"

"Yes, but it's starting to look like he was set up."

The sheriff nodded, then pointed toward the horizon. "That row of trees there, that's the edge of a swampy area. If I were hiding a body around here, it would be there." He paused. "So the gators would take care of it for me."

I grimaced. "You willing to show me."

He glanced down at my one-inch heels.

"I've got hiking shoes in my trunk."

"Okay. Lemme report in. I'll be right back." He walked off toward the cruiser, while I retrieved my other shoes.

But Sheriff Sam and I did not find Marly.

One of the dogs did—the cadaver one—two hours later. As the sheriff had predicted, she was in a shallow grave at the edge of the swamp.

CHAPTER TWENTY-ONE

The Jacksonville ME crouched beside the body. It was face down, half covered with slime and mud.

I hovered nearby.

He glanced up, gave me an irritated look.

But I didn't move. I needed to see her face.

The ME was a dapper little man, with light gray hair and a dark gray suit that somehow stayed neatly pressed in the wilting heat.

Sheriff Sam stood a few feet away, his hat tilted back on his head.

To distract myself and rein in my impatience, I went back over the discussion I'd had with Sam a few minutes before the body was found. I'd pointed out that it wasn't safe for the trucker's wife and her son to stay out here in the middle of nowhere, especially with the man of the house on the road.

"Already thought of that. Joellen has a sister in town. I'll get her to pack some things and take her there."

I'd opened my mouth, but Sam held up a weathered hand.

"*And* I'll assign a deputy to watch the sister's place, and one for their house here."

The ME stood and brushed dirt off his gloved hands. "Marks on her neck suggests a garrote, but that may or may not be what killed her." He nodded to the Clover County deputy and one of my uniforms who were standing by.

They gingerly stepped down into the muck and carefully rolled her over.

The odds of asphyxiation by strangulation being the COD went down. She had a large red gash in the middle of her chest. The mud under her was a dark reddish brown.

The face was covered in mud, but the hair was right, dark and collar length, although hardly the carefully arranged bob that Marly usually wore.

"Any guess on the time of death?" I asked the ME.

He gave me a hard look. "Sometime in the last twenty-four hours."

"Can you narrow it down any?"

"Not until I get her on the table."

"How soon will that be?"

Another hard look.

I held his gaze. "People are dying, Doc."

"Tomorrow morning, eight a.m."

"I'll be there," I said.

"Mind if I come too?" Sheriff Sam said.

"Not at all, bring all your friends," the ME said, sarcasm dripping in his tone. He walked away.

I certainly didn't mind. Sam had as much right as I did. This kill was in his county. If only I could hand Marly's murder off to him, but I knew it had to be related to the others, in some way, shape, or form.

"I need to talk to the boy again," I said.

Sam used his hat to gesture for me to lead the way. Then he plopped it back on his head.

I looked up a couple of things on my phone as we hiked back across the field, almost landing my foot in a hole at one point.

Sam grabbed my elbow and kept me from a sprained ankle, or worse. His hand was warm on my arm.

We got to the road just as the mom and child were climbing into a Clover County cruiser. Sam called for them to wait.

We jogged to the car, and I crouched down at the back window.

Sam made a twirling motion with his finger, and the rotund deputy in the driver's seat lowered that window.

"Jamie, you said the moon was out, correct?" I asked. "Did you actually *see* the moon?"

"Um, I think so."

"Where was it in the sky? Can you show us?" I opened the door and he stepped out. His mother slid over on the seat, not willing to let her cub get too far away.

He looked all around the sky. "I don't remember," he said, with a tremor in his voice.

I stooped down. "It's okay, son. You're doing fine." I softened my tone. "So, you don't remember seeing the moon, but you thought it was out. How did the sky look?"

He chewed on his lower lip. "Well, it was dark, down here." He gestured toward the ground. "But the sky was kind of a lighter dark."

"Well, that don't make no sense," the deputy scoffed.

"Shut up, Pete," Sam said from behind me.

"Did you see any stars at all?" I asked the boy.

"There weren't many and the ones that was there was kinda faded."

"Was there any part of the sky that was lighter than the other parts?"

He pointed down the road, toward the eastern horizon. "Over there. I mean, it wasn't real light, but it was kinda light."

"Sunrise," his mother said under her breath.

I glanced up at her and nodded.

"Jamie, you have been a huge help. Don't forget to come visit us at the police station. I might even be able to find a hat that'll fit you."

His worried face abruptly brightened. "Really? That would be awesome."

"I'll get my assistant working on it."

Barnes stepped up, her hat in her hand. She plopped it on the boy's head. It covered his eyes.

We all laughed.

"Hmm, about two sizes smaller oughta do it," Barnes said.

Jamie's grin flashed under the brim of the hat.

Barnes plucked the hat from his head.

"Hey, how'd you get those shiners?" he asked.

"Jamie!" his mother exclaimed.

Barnes waved a hand in the air. "It's okay." She crouched down next to the boy. "Sometimes cops have to fight the bad guys, but I'm still here, so they didn't win."

Jamie whirled around to his mother, sitting in the cruiser. "Mom, I wanna be a cop when I grow up, so I can fight the bad guys."

The cops all laughed, but Mom didn't join us this time. She hooked a hand around the back of her son's neck and dragged him into the car.

As the cruiser headed off with Jamie and his mom, Sheriff Sam and I exchanged a look.

"Sunrise was seven-twelve this morning," I said.

He gave me a small smile. "That's what you were looking up on your phone, instead of looking where you were going."

"That, and the moon cycle we're in right now. We're only four days into a waxing moon. It wouldn't even be a quarter crescent yet."

"If the sky was just beginning to lighten," Sam said, "it would've been around six-fifteen."

I nodded. "Over two hours after we arrested the man we thought was our killer."

"You gonna cut Cleaver loose?" Barnes asked in a low voice. Cops and deputies were still milling around, knocking mud off their boots before climbing into cars.

"Not yet, but it's not looking good for us."

"Better for him, bad for us," Barnes said.

"Yeah. We can hold him on the drug possession charges though, which will keep him out of circulation, at least until he's arraigned tomorrow."

I cleared my throat. "I want to check out the other idea you had." Meaning her theory that Ronnie Malcolm and Cleaver might be in it together.

She looked confused for a second, then awareness dawned on her face.

"I've got another tidbit for you," Sam said. "There's a twenty-four-hour convenience store back down the road about a mile. I sent a deputy there to ask some questions. Seems there was a car pulled into their lot, off to the side, around five-thirty this morning. The clerk waited but no one came inside. So he went out front to have a smoke."

He pushed his hat back some on his head. "He saw a couple staggering down the road away from him, figured they'd realized they were too drunk to be driving. He got busy after that, people starting their commutes into Starling. Didn't give the car another thought."

"What'd the car look like?"

"A dark sedan was all he really noticed, maybe dark gray or blue. It was parked at the far end of their lot, away from the one outside light they have."

"Hmm, he didn't want his car to be seen anywhere near where he was taking her."

"That's what I was thinking," Sam said.

He pulled off his hat and waved down a county cruiser that was pulling out onto the road. "This is my ride. Keep me posted, Chief."

"I will. Thanks for your help."

Barnes and I headed for my car. I tossed her the keys. "You drive. I've got some calls to make."

First call was to Nate Jacobs. He'd been coordinating searchers when Sam and I had taken off toward the swamp. And that's the last I'd noticed him. When the search was done and our people were packing up and leaving, he was nowhere around.

My call went to voicemail after three rings. "In case you hadn't heard," my tone was a tad snippy, "we found Marly. Call me."

The Bluetooth speaker squealed a little as I disconnected, adding to my annoyance.

If Jacobs had gotten a call from dispatch, it would've been nice if he'd let me know. Another thought sent ice through my veins. I recalled my own speech the other night about this killer possibly taking out a cop.

I shook the thought off. Nate was a seasoned cop. He could take care of himself.

Then it dawned on me that he might have gone to do the death notification with the husband.

Sheez, what a roller coaster ride, from annoyed to worried to grateful. I was losing my grip. I really needed to go home and get some rest, now that Marly had been found.

A bit of guilt and sadness piled onto the emotional heap. Despite the odds against it, I had hoped we would find her alive.

Before making my other calls, I unsynced my phone from the Bluetooth.

I was scrolling through my contacts, when the phone rang in my hand. The main SPD number popped up on the screen. "Anderson."

"Sergeant Johnson, Chief. We got a call from a woman who was looking for Detective Bradley. She seemed kinda confused.

When I told her he wasn't in right now, she insisted on talking to the person in charge. Says she thought of something might be important, but she wouldn't tell me what it was. I told her you or the detective would get back to her."

"You tried Bradley?"

"Yeah. He's not answering."

Hmm, there was a lot of that going around, all of a sudden.

"Okay, what's her number?" I pulled out my pad.

"Agatha Price." He rattled off the number.

"Thanks." I disconnected, then punched the numbers into my cell.

"Hello?" An older woman, with a slight Florida accent.

"Ma'am, this is Chief of Police Anderson. How can I help you?"

"Um, one of your men called here earlier, askin' about my girl, and he said to call if I thought of anything else."

"Yes, ma'am."

Barnes glanced over from the driver's seat.

"I remembered that Cindy said she spoke to two police officers about the night that girl, Darla, died. One of the police told her not to tell anyone about their conversation."

I sat up straighter in the passenger seat. *Cindy?* Wasn't Stormy's real name Cynthia Price?

"So she didn't mention it to the other one," the woman was saying, "when she talked to him."

My heart rate jumped up several notches. "Did she say if the first one gave a reason for that request?"

"Yes, ma'am. He said he was from Internal Affairs and he was investigatin' the other detective."

My stomach clenched. "I see. Anything else?"

"No, that's all Cindy told me. Ya think I should be worryin' at this point. I still can't get her on her phone."

"I'm sure there's some logical explanation." No point in freaking the woman out quite yet. "Maybe she lost her phone. But we're already keeping an eye out for her, since we have a couple more questions about what she might have seen that night."

"Oh, good." The relief in her voice was palpable. "Tell her to call home the instant y'all find her, okay?"

"Absolutely, ma'am. Thank you for calling." I disconnected and sat for a moment, staring out the windshield. Jacobs had said that Bradley was duplicating his efforts. Had they both talked to Stormy, and one of them told her not to say anything about the conversation. Why would they do that?

And why would they say they were from IA? Our tiny department didn't even *have* an Internal Affairs division.

I suppressed a shudder. Was the killer pretending to be a cop—interviewing people to find out what they knew, and getting rid of the ones who might be able to lead us to him?

Barnes cleared her throat.

I looked her way. Her eyebrows were in the air, a nonverbal question mark.

Which I opted to ignore, for now. I needed to think through the ramifications of what I'd just learned before I shared it with anyone.

I'd been about to call her brother. I placed the call.

He answered on the second ring. "Hey, Chief, I got a uniform helping me canvas. No luck so far. And I got a call from Stormy's mother, but I was in the middle of talking to someone, a woman who was, amazingly, willing to cooperate. Not that she knew anything useful. Mrs. Price didn't leave a message, but I was about to call her back."

"That's okay. I already talked to her. She, uh, called the main number and the sarge handed her off to me." I was struggling to keep my voice casual.

"What'd she have to say?"

"She...got worried after you talked to her. I told her we were searching for Stormy and would have her call home when we found her. Look, leave the uniform there to keep canvassing. I want you to bring in Ronnie Malcolm."

A pause. "The kid at the convenience store?"

"Yes. Let's check out Barnes's theory–"

"More of a hypothesis," she mumbled under her breath from the driver's seat.

"Got it," Bradley said. "Anything else?"

"Yeah. Keep what you're doing on the down low for now."

Another beat of silence. "Sure. It is kind of a long shot."

That wasn't why I'd asked him to keep it to himself—I was back to trying to ferret out my leak—but I let him think that was the reason.

We disconnected.

"Uh, Chief," Barnes said. "*Down low* means something different in the gay community."

Heat crept up my neck. Thus the beat of silence.

I knew that, but it hadn't occurred to me that the term, which had made its way into the general vernacular, would be momentarily confusing to a gay man.

"You don't think of him as a gay man, do you?" Barnes said.

"I don't think of him as a man. He's one of my detectives."

One of my best ones, I'd thought. Now...I didn't know what to think.

I made my third call, to Kate Huntington. It went to voicemail.

"Hey Kate, Judith here. How likely is it that our perp has multiple personalities? Call me when you can."

A few seconds later my phone buzzed, indicating a text message.

It was from Kate. *Slim.*

Another buzz. *I'll call you later. In the middle of something.*

I nodded to myself and texted back. *Ok Thx*

Barnes pulled into the municipal parking lot.

I pointed to her car. "Time for both of us to go home."

She didn't argue.

But when I got home, I realized I might not have told Bradley about spotting Ronnie in the crowd at Cleaver's house. I texted him that information.

I got a return text. *Thanks. That gives me leverage. He's claiming he was home in bed all night.*

CHAPTER TWENTY-TWO

Despite the lack of clarity in the serial killer case and despite where I was headed now, I felt somehow lighter this morning.

Kate had called me shortly after seven last night. We'd talked for almost an hour, first about the case. She'd convinced me that people with Dissociative Identity Disorder—the official name for multiple personalities—are rarely dangerous to anyone but themselves. Then we'd chatted about mutual friends and acquaintances in Baltimore.

Dolph had been back visiting from Arizona a couple of days ago, she'd said.

My chest hurt a little at the thought that I'd missed him. Maybe I'd invite him and his wife to come to Florida. After all, it was one of the primary vacation destinations in the country. We could go to Jacksonville Beach or St. Augustine.

After Kate and I had signed off, I'd given up on getting all the mud off my hiking shoes, left them for another day. I'd gone to bed early and, for once, had slept well. No dreams.

Now I was headed for the morgue in Jacksonville to witness Marly Davis's autopsy. My second least favorite thing to do as a cop.

The building that housed the District Four Medical Examiner's Office was intimidating—a white cement facade with interior corridors of white cement block that continued the sterile motif. Inside the main autopsy room, I was greeted by the faint olfactory mix of disinfectants and death.

And it was really cold. I pulled my pantsuit jacket closed in the front and buttoned one button.

I was a few minutes early.

"I'm Judith Anderson, Starling's Chief of Police," I said to the morgue assistant. Did they call them *dieners* down here, as we did in Maryland?

No response, as he washed the body.

And you are?"

"Harold."

No indication if that was his first or last name.

"Pleased to meet you," I said, not really meaning it but trying to be polite. It was way too early in the morning for this.

"Likewise," he said, equally insincere.

"Do we have a solid ID?"

He nodded. "Your Detective Jacobs brought the husband in last night."

That reminded me that Jacobs had never called me back, but at least I knew he was alive and well and doing his job.

"And of course, her clothes and everything have gone to the lab?" I said.

He glanced my way. "Of course." The tone was neutral, the look irritated.

I opted to focus on the corpse, rather than continue awkward efforts at conversation. There were ligature marks on her wrists and ankles.

Marly had been bound at some point.

Like Darla.

Sheriff Sam showed up and flashed me a chipper grin.

I gave him a half smile back. *It's way too early for cheerful too*, I told myself. But I felt lighter still, with him standing nearby.

His face sobered. "You knew her?"

"In passing," I said.

He grimaced. "That tends to make it worse."

I wasn't sure if it would, in this case. I hadn't liked Marly Davis. But seeing her cold, naked body made me a little ashamed of that dislike.

The ME entered the room and, without preamble, informed us that there had been signs of recent sexual activity, either rough or non-consensual, he couldn't say which. No semen. Traces of lubricant from a condom. These things had apparently been discovered earlier, while gathering trace evidence from the body.

I thanked him for that information, surprised that the ME was doing the autopsy himself. Surely, he had several pathologists on staff.

"All my people are booked up for today," he answered the unasked question. "And I know you need to stop this guy."

"I really appreciate this," I said, now totally sincere.

He nodded brusquely, his expression grim, and turned on his recorder. "Deceased is a Caucasian female, fifty-three years of age..."

During the autopsy, I managed to keep my queasy stomach under control and not run screaming from the room. Both victories in my book. Although I'd long since become inured to dead bodies, watching them being cut open on a cold metal table was a whole other thing. After all these years, I still wasn't used to it.

And in the end, I didn't learn much, other than the fact that the perp had fed and watered his captive. She was not dehydrated and she'd had baked beans and Vienna sausages no more than two hours before her death. They were only partially digested in her stomach.

Yuck. Good thing I'd never been particularly fond of beans and Vienna sausage, because I was definitely off of them for the foreseeable future.

With a few nightmare-worthy images now imprinted in my brain, we exited the building. I welcomed the blanket of moist heat that enveloped my chilled body. After a deep breath of semi-fresh air—as close to fresh as city air ever is, I turned to the sheriff to say goodbye.

He surprised me by making an after-you gesture toward the parking lot, then falling into step beside me as I headed toward my car.

"Again," Sam said, "if there's anything I can do to help with the case, let me know."

"Can you send someone to talk to that convenience store clerk again? See if he remembers anything more about that car or the couple."

"Already done. I talked to him myself. His story meshed with what he'd told my deputy, and he had nothing new to add."

I sighed. "Thanks."

"Say, when all this is behind us and this guy is rotting in jail, can we grab a coffee some time?"

I gave him a sideways glance. "Sure. It would be good to coordinate some...uh, on things like when we can pursue a suspect across the county/city line, and such."

We stopped beside my car.

Sam touched the sleeve of my jacket. A small zing shot up my arm.

Static electricity?

I turned toward him.

He was smiling. "That wasn't exactly what I had in mind, but we can start there."

Confusion as my cheeks heated. He hadn't meant to zap me?

Wait, static electricity only happens in dry air, not in humid Florida.

Finally, his meaning sank in completely, and my neck and face grew even hotter. I quickly turned and opened my car door.

"Keep me posted." Sam tipped his hat.

"You do the same," I said, watching him out of the corner of my eye.

He was still smiling as he turned away.

Cocky bastard. But I found myself smiling as well, as I climbed into my car.

I was halfway to Starling when my cell vibrated in my pants pocket, reminding me that it had purred and vibrated twice during the autopsy, earning me dirty looks from the ME. He seemed to have excellent hearing for an old guy.

It was still disconnected from my Bluetooth so I pulled over onto the shoulder. Digging the phone out, I turned the ringer back on before answering. "Sorry, Bradley. I was in the morgue earlier."

"Anything interesting?"

"Not much. What's up on your end?"

"I got a search warrant for Ronnie Malcolm's apartment," he said.

"You did?" I said, surprise in my voice.

"Yeah, Jacobs isn't the only one with an in with a judge."

"What'd you use as probable cause?"

"The fact that he lied about several things. One, that he was home all night, when you saw him at the Cleavers' house. And two, he said he sometimes puts a note on the door of the store, saying 'be right back' so he can take a quick bathroom break, but it's never more than a few minutes–"

"Did anybody see you bring him in?" I interrupted.

"No, because he wouldn't come in. Insisted he had to stay and man the store. I questioned him there. Figured if I pressed the issue, he might lawyer up. But early this morning, I waited in the parking lot and stopped several of his customers. Three of them were regulars who said sometimes they knock and wait and knock some more and Ronnie never does come to let them in."

"So, more lies, and any alibis related to him being at work are worthless."

"Exactly. I'm headed to his place now to execute the warrant. Wanna come?"

"Text me the address and I'll meet you there."

I'd no sooner disconnected than my phone rang again. It was Barnes. "The Starke hospital called. Mr. Nelson is awake and coherent."

Hnmm, guess I won't be spending my morning digging through Ronnie's underwear drawer after all.

"Meet me out front," I told Barnes. "I'll be there in ten."

Benjamin Nelson looked a lot better than the last time we'd seen him, unconscious on a gurney with an intubation tube sticking out of his mouth. His broad face was ruddy now, rather than pasty white.

His blue eyes watched us with interest as we entered his room. "Good morning, ladies." His voice was rough, probably from that tube, but his tone was downright cheerful.

"Mr. Nelson, it's good to see you doing better." I introduced myself merely as Judith Anderson, flashing my badge at him quickly. I didn't want to get into why the police from another jurisdiction were interested in him and his communications, at least not until we'd gotten some answers from him. "And this is Officer Barnes."

She hung back, even though her face was looking better today. And she'd strategically applied makeup to cover the worst of the bruises.

"Are you feeling up to answering a few questions?" I asked Nelson.

"Sure."

"What do you remember about the day you had your heart attack?"

"I remember some guy bargin' into my house, sayin' he was a police detective, and the next thing I knew my heart was racin' a mile a minute and my chest hurt."

My own heart rate picked up. His heart attack happened *after* Bradley went into the house?

Nelson smiled. "And I vaguely remember you lovely ladies hoverin' over me. And then I woke up here. The docs say I had a real close call, and you two saved my life." His eyes were now shiny.

"Glad we were there," I quickly said, trying to cut the mushy stuff short. "We'd actually come to see you to ask about another matter. Did you know a young woman named Pearl Altman?"

"Why yes, she came to see me, oh, I guess about..." He scratched his head, making some of his graying dark hair stick up. "I'm not sure now. A couple of weeks ago? She said she thought she might be my cousin. She'd been doin' some of that genealogy research."

I leaned slightly forward. Barnes had her notepad out and was scribbling notes.

"What did Pearl say exactly?" I asked.

"Oh, I don't remember *exactly*. But she asked about other relatives in the area, past and present. I told her about my cousin Josh. His mother and mine were sisters and we were only a few months apart in age. We were inseparable, like brothers, until his family moved to Jacksonville. Then we didn't get together as often. Eventually we drifted apart, and he went off to college up north."

I was mentally doing the math. If Nelson was in his fifties and this cousin was the same age, they would not have been college age when Pearl was conceived. So why was this information a threat to anyone?

"Is there anything else you and Pearl talked about?"

"Oh, yeah," he said. "Josh's brother. He's seven years younger, one of them menopause babies. She asked if he had any children, and I said, yes, he has three, all teenagers now. But as we talked, I recalled that he got some girl pregnant when he was a junior in college. Apparently, she wasn't 'suitable.'" Nelson made air quotes.

My heart rate kicked up again.

"His mama paid that girl off and sent him to a different school for his senior year, somewhere in California, I believe. She was ambitious for her boys. Wanted them to go far, she always said. My mama was much more laid back about all that. She didn't get all that upset when I flunked outta college. Said that was fine, as long as I learned a trade."

He scratched his head again, dislodging more hair and setting off an avalanche of dandruff. "Course, Aunt Lucy, she might've been on the right track. Both her boys *have* gone far, and look at me—drinkin' too much, eatin' too much and havin' a heart attack at fifty-two. Josh is a surgeon up in Georgia, at some big hospital in Atlanta. And Mark, he's a lawyer and a politician, about to announce a run for state senate, last I heard."

My whole body tensed, my heart full out racing. "What's Mark's last name, Mr. Nelson?"

"Hayes." Nelson's chest puffed out with family pride. "Right now, he's the chair of the city council in that town just west of Jacksonville. The one that's named after some bird."

I glanced at Barnes.

Her eyes were bugging out of her face.

CHAPTER TWENTY-THREE

I worked hard to keep my expression neutral, despite my galloping heart. "Getting back to the day of your heart attack, can you describe the policeman who came into your house?"

Nelson shook his head slowly. "Not real well. I was kinda out of it. I'd been takin' a nap when some noise woke me up. Might've been him knockin' on my door. I sat up on the side of my bed, and the room was kinda spinning."

He waved a hand in the air. "I work night shift, sleep in the daytime. I'd had a few beers when I got home, to help me sleep. I guess I was still feelin' their effects some."

Some? He'd stunk of beer, but I didn't say anything.

"He comes bargin' into my bedroom, asks me if I'm alright. I think he said something about me not lookin' so good, and he put a hand on my shoulder. That's when my heart started racin'."

"Was he tall, short? Heavy, thin?"

"'Bout average, I guess. But I was lookin' up at him, ya know, from where I was on the bed...can't really say how tall he was."

And that was all we got out of him. He said he couldn't remember any more details. I honestly didn't trust the ones he'd already given us.

We would put together a photo lineup, including both Cleaver and Bradley. But even then I wasn't sure I'd trust him as a wit-ness.

"How did you know he was police?" Barnes said.

"I think he said he was." Nelson tried to snap thick fingers. "No, wait. He showed me his badge, one of them gold-colored ones that detectives carry. I seen that on TV."

I pulled out my badge and showed it to him again. "Like this?"

"Yeah, 'cept his didn't say Chief of Police." He leaned back a little, looked up at me, a surprised smile on his face. "You really a police chief? Skinny little thing like you?"

Not sure if the "skinny thing" was a compliment or an insult, I ignored it. "Yup, I'm Chief of Police in that city named for a bird—Starling."

"Ya don't say!"

I gave him my card and asked him to call me if he thought of anything else. "Is it okay if we ask your doctor some questions about your case?"

He nodded, rubbing his throat, which was probably feeling quite raw, with all the talking he'd been doing. "Doc already thought of that," his voice was raspy now. "He had me sign a waiver."

Outside his room, Barnes stopped me with a hand on my arm. Her face was pale. "It sounds like he's saying that he was conscious when Danny got to his bedroom. But that can't be right."

"He also said he remembered us, but I don't recall him opening his eyes the whole time we were giving him CPR. He's either making stuff up to make himself seem important, or his mind's producing memories to go with what the doctors told him. He was drunk when we got there, so even without the heart attack, he's not a reliable witness."

And I think I doth protest too much. That was an awfully specific memory, of the guy showing him his badge and putting a hand on his shoulder.

If Bradley had immediately run down that hallway, flashed his badge at Nelson, and injected him, then picked up the chair and broke the window himself...did he have enough time to do all that while we were clearing the front rooms?

A nurse paged Nelson's doctor for us.

He was a young Cuban-American—slight, with dark hair and light beige skin.

When I introduced us, he pumped our hands. "You're the officers who found Mr. Nelson. Damn good thing you started CPR right away, or he wouldn't have made it. He had enough epinephrine in him to give him two heart attacks. That combined with the alcohol..."

"How could he have gotten that much epinephrine in his system?" I asked. "Is he allergic to something? Did he use an epi-pen?"

The young doc shook his head. "It was a lot more than there is in an epi-pen, and way more than the body naturally produces."

"There's no pill that would produce that result?" Barnes asked.

"Nope, it has to be injected. And it dissipates pretty quickly in the body. As much as we detected, there had to have been even more to begin with. He's lucky there wasn't brain damage from it, 'cause it can restrict blood flow to the brain."

"Any sign of a puncture wound?" I asked. "Maybe on his arm or shoulder or upper back?"

"Not that I saw," the doc said. "But I can check again."

I thanked him, handing over another of my cards.

As I drove, Barnes fiddled with her phone in the passenger seat. "According to a couple of websites, epinephrine does have to be injected. Are you thinking the hand on the shoulder was disguising giving him a needle? He didn't complain of feeling anything sticking him."

"Maybe. If you know what you're doing, it doesn't necessarily have to hurt, especially if there's a fair amount of fat where you're giving the injection."

"*And* you distract the person by asking if they're okay. Not to mention he was full of pain-killing alcohol."

"Do we have a work history on Ronnie Malcolm?" I asked. "Does he have any medical training?"

"I'll text Dan...uh, Bradley."

"You know, it's okay for *you* to call him Dan."

She glanced my way, her cheeks pinking a little. Her phone pinged. "Yep, Ronnie trained as a paramedic for a while, but dropped out before finishing the program. Shortly after that, he started working for Tremont. Three years ago."

In my peripheral vision, I saw her chest rise as she took a deep breath. "Maybe he's confusing two memories. One of when the person who drugged him came in, and then maybe he was drifting in and out when Detective Bradley entered the room."

"I suspect that's what happened," I said, though I didn't feel nearly as sure of that as I sounded.

Granted, Nelson's picture should be next to the definition of *unreliable witness* in any detective's training manual.

Wait. Bradley had said he was convulsing when he got to the bedroom. "See if a large dose of epinephrine can cause convulsions."

I recalled my earlier speculation, that the perp might be posing as a cop to find out what people knew, and taking out the ones who knew too much.

After a moment, Barnes said, "It looks like high doses of epinephrine can cause seizures." She paused. "Are you thinking that Councilman Hayes is...*was* Pearl's father?"

Nice job of changing the focus, Barnes.

"The story sure fits together with what her grandmother told us."

"I wonder if he has any inkling that one of our victims was his daughter?"

"I plan to ask him that," I said. "And whether or not she contacted him."

"Okay, but why would our serial killer care whether or not we found out about all this? Why go after Nelson?"

Those were exactly the pieces of the puzzle that I was trying to rearrange in my brain. "If Pearl was killed to keep it quiet that Hayes had an illegitimate child in his youth, then it's likely that we have two killers." Which was what Kate had been saying all along, that Pearl's killer was a copycat.

I glanced over at Barnes.

Her eyes were wide. "Do you think Hayes is capable of murder?"

"Not really. I'd say that his wife was a stronger suspect. If she weren't dead too."

Barnes scrubbed a hand over her face, tucked a stray strand of dark hair behind her ear. "Okay, I see two possibilities. Either the same person who killed Pearl—to protect Hayes's reputation—also went after Nelson to keep him quiet. Or, the serial killer wants Pearl's murder to be lumped in with his kills. Not sure why, though."

"My psychological consultant thinks it's so we'll blame Pearl's killer for all the murders."

I paused. "And she thinks the original killer was done, after Darla got away that first time. He'd gotten his anger out of his system, and/or he had something good going on in his life that he didn't want to jeopardize. And then someone killed Pearl, imitating his MO."

"And that set him off again," Barnes said. "But what I don't get, why did Mrs. Hayes's murder have the same MO as Pearl's?"

"*That*," I said, "is a very good question."

I resynced my phone with the car's Bluetooth and instructed it to call the Bradford County detective in charge of Nelson's case.

I filled him in on our interview, finishing with, "It's looking more and more like our cases are related."

"Yeah," he said in a mournful voice. "Any idea who this mystery cop is?"

I told him my speculation that the serial killer might be posing as police, to find out what people knew, and killing them if there was any chance they might lead us to him.

"So he's mopping up," the detective said. "I'll go talk to Nelson later, see if his story changes."

I managed not to snort. No doubt it would change, but it would be interesting to see *how* it changed.

"No dark sedan registered to anyone at that trailer's address, by the way. Only a silver pickup."

"Somehow I'm not surprised," I said. "I'll keep you posted with any relevant developments on my end."

"Same here."

I called Foster and proposed the same theory to him.

"Quite possible," he said. "I'll tackle it from the angle of where he might get fake credentials, and check out any former JSO cops who left under a cloud."

"Thanks."

I was filling Barnes in on Marly's autopsy when we crossed the Starling city line.

Her stomach growled audibly, and I laughed. "If you can be hungry after what I just told you, then you definitely have the stomach for police work."

She grinned.

"Wanna stop for lunch?" I asked.

"Sure."

"Hmm, I'd love to talk to Ronnie again." I pointed my car toward Pronto's convenience store.

But Mrs. Tremont was behind the counter.

I nodded a greeting and headed for the glass doors where the prepackaged sandwiches were displayed. Picking out a ham and cheese with light tan bread that was probably supposed to be wheat, I grabbed a bag of chips and went to the counter.

"Where's Ronnie?" I asked in a casual tone.

"I insisted he take some time off." Mrs. Tremont's eyes were down as she rang up my food. Was she focused on what she was doing, or avoiding eye contact?

"Add a coffee to that, please."

"Ten-forty," she said.

"Chief?" Barnes called over.

I turned. She was holding up two individual-serving-sized cans—one of baked beans and one of Vienna sausages.

Oh, yeah! Circumstantial, but every little bit of evidence helps.

She brought the cans to the counter. "How handy. They're flip tabs so no can-opener needed." The corners of her mouth twitched. She was working hard to suppress a grin.

Mrs. Tremont rang her up. "You want a bag?"

"Please. Those are for my dinner. I'll take one of the hot dogs for lunch." She pointed toward the dogs rotating slowly in their cooker.

I poured my coffee while Barnes paid for her purchases and squirted some ketchup on her hot dog. We left the store.

She took a tentative bite of the dog, only wincing a little as she chewed, and followed me to my trunk. I opened the lid, blocking anyone's view from the store, and got out an evidence bag.

She lowered the cans, plastic bag and all, into it, then tried to hand me her pen.

I shook my head. "You spotted them. They're your evidence."

She juggled her hot dog into her left hand and filled in the information on the evidence bag.

I put the bag in my trunk and closed the lid.

Mrs. Tremont was staring at us through the store's plate-glass window.

Bradley waylaid us halfway across the bullpen. "You'll never guess what we found in Ronnie Boy's apartment."

I pointed to my office.

When the three of us were inside, with the door closed, I said, "What?"

"A four-inch hunting knife, with dried blood on it."

My heart galloped in my chest. For once, it was from excitement rather than fear or dread.

"I hightailed it to the FDLE lab," Bradley said, "and hung around while they did an initial analysis. Two different samples of blood, both human. One matches Marly Davis's blood type and the other matches Tremont's. Of course, we have to wait for DNA results to be sure, but..."

Nodding, I walked around my desk and sat in my chair. "Did you bring him in?"

"Yeah, I'm letting him stew for a while in the holding cell."

Barnes had settled into the new comfy visitor's chair—which had apparently been delivered while we were on our field trip to Starke. Her brother frowned at her and perched on the edge of one of the uncomfortable ones.

She gave him a smug smile, then said, "The knife ties Tremont more firmly to the serial killer, right? I mean, if his death was a robbery gone wrong or he was killed by Ronnie and/or his wife because they were having an affair, why would that knife also have Marly's blood on it?"

"Not necessarily," Bradley said. "Marly might have found out about their affair, or she asked the wrong question, and they thought she was on to them."

I shook my head. "Anybody else feel like we've got two jigsaw puzzles with all their pieces mixed together in the same box?"

"More like three puzzles," Bradley said. He held up an index finger. "Puzzle number one, we've got a serial rapist, slash, killer who started out in Jacksonville and moved to our fair city. Did he commit all of the murders? Or..." He raised a second finger. "Puzzle number two, Ronnie and Mrs. T took advantage of the opportunity to dispense with Tremont because they want to be together, and somehow Marly found out about it–"

"Wait." Barnes held up a hand. "Before you move on to puzzle three, we found out some things from Mr. Nelson, who is now awake and quite talkative." She filled her brother in on our meeting with Benjamin Nelson, notably leaving out the part about a police detective coming into his bedroom just before he had his heart attack.

"Well, that increases the chances," Bradley said, "that puzzle number three has a different killer murdering Pearl, and maybe Mrs. Hayes, and then going after Nelson."

"Or..." Barnes repeated Kate's speculation that the serial killer wanted all the murders attributed to his copycat, so he had gone after Nelson.

"But there were parts of the MO that were not released to the press," I said, playing devil's advocate. "Specifically, that the women were garroted, rather than strangled by hand. Pearl's killer had to have inside knowledge, or it was the same guy, who, for some reason, deviated from his MO in other ways."

"Or it was one hell of a coincidence," Bradley said.

"But let's look at the deaths since then." I ticked off fingers this time. "Darla, the one who got away and remembered about the stocking over his head, and maybe could have identified him." I touched another finger. "Tremont, who saw Darla talking to someone in a car the night she died."

Finger number three. "Karen Hayes, the MO matched Pearl's." I tapped my little finger. "Marly Davis, who had info she shouldn't have had, that maybe came from the killer."

My chest tightened. Four deaths on my watch. I rubbed a hand over my breast plate. "Three of those four kills were about cleaning up loose ends."

"Then there's Shelly Trent," Bradley said. "I seriously doubt she's still alive."

Barnes was shaking her head. "But neither Shelly or Darla could give much of a description."

"No, but if they saw him, they might recognize him," I said. "He wasn't willing to take that chance."

"And he's a serial killer," Bradley said. "He *enjoys* killing."

"And raping," Barnes said in a disgusted voice.

That reminded me. I held up a finger and picked up my phone to call Cruthers. I got voicemail and left a brief rundown of the autopsy, including the rough sex and/or SA and the traces of lubricant. "Ask Mr. Davis about birth control," I said. "Do they use condoms?"

I found it hard to believe that a middle-aged couple with grown kids would—most likely one or the other had tied something off to make more children an impossibility.

I disconnected and turned my attention back to the two people in my office. "*Why* were Pearl and Karen different? That's what I want to know."

Barnes and I were standing by the video screen outside the interview room, when it dawned on me that I'd never followed through on the janitor.

"Do you know how to do a background check?"

"Theoretically," Barnes said. "But I haven't done one yet."

"Do one on William Walker. He's the janitor for this floor. No rush. Whenever you get a chance."

Barnes gave me a questioning look but I didn't enlighten her.

Bradley entered the stark interview room with Ronnie Malcolm. He removed the young man's cuffs and told him to sit in the chair across the table from the video camera—so we all could see his face.

Bradley sat, his back to us. He held up the hand-cuffs. "Sorry about these. Departmental policy when we're moving people around." He pocketed them.

He was taking a bit of a chance, not cuffing Ronnie to the metal ring attached to the table. But I got it. He was being the good cop, building rapport. It was my preferred approach to interrogations as well.

Unless the perp was a total scumbag.

And Bradley wasn't taking much of a risk here. The kid was unarmed, the furniture in the room was bolted down, except for a rubber trash can in the corner. And two cops were watching.

I partially zoned out as Bradley identified himself and the detainee, ran through the Miranda again and asked if Ronnie understood his rights.

"Yes," the kid said.

Bradley paused, giving him a chance to lawyer up if he so chose. But he didn't ask him if he was willing to make a statement. Something we often asked before proceeding with an interrogation.

Good. I held my breath. We needed this guy to talk.

We needed to know if he was a viable suspect. If he lawyered up right away, we wouldn't know for sure that we had our man.

Wait! Why was I even thinking along those lines? We had the damn knife!

But something about this didn't sit right with me.

Bradley was starting off slow, gently confronting Ronnie with the information that customers said he sometimes closed the store for more than a few minutes.

He shrugged and his tanned cheeks took on a coppery hue. "I've fallen asleep in the back a few times. Working double shifts has been hard, since Mr. T died."

Bradley moved on. "One of our police personnel saw you in the crowd at Douglas Cleaver's house the other night, when you said you were home asleep."

"I...um, I heard the commotion and stepped outside for a few minutes to see what was going on. But then I went back to bed. Had to be at the store bright and early." He produced a sickly grimace that was probably meant to be a smile.

He was lying through his teeth. He hadn't yet arrived at the store the next morning, when Bradley went to talk to him. Only the part-time clerk was there. What time was that exactly? I couldn't recall, but Bradley would have it in his notes.

The detective pretended he'd bought the lie and moved on. "You said you don't know the reporter, Marlene Davis."

Ronnie relaxed slightly, as if he thought they were now on safer ground. "No. I mean, I know who she is. I've seen her on TV, but I never met her in person."

"So you didn't know she was killed yesterday?"

Ronnie's eyes went wide. He blinked twice. "No. I, um, didn't hear about that."

Bradley opened a folder on the table in front of him. He pulled out two photos and placed them in front of the kid.

"This is what Marly Davis looked like after her killer was done with her."

Ronnie quickly averted his eyes. "Shit, man. Why are you showing me that?"

"Because..." Bradley paused for dramatic effect, "we found this in your apartment." He laid another photo on the table, no doubt of the bloody knife.

Ronnie stared at it for a moment, the significance sinking in. His skin turned ashen under his surfer-boy tan. He slapped both hands over his mouth, and his body heaved.

Bradley pointed to the trash can in the corner. Indeed, that was why it was there.

Ronnie ran over and lost his lunch.

He'd angled himself to put his back to Bradley, perhaps to salvage some degree of manly dignity. But in so doing, he'd positioned himself sideways to the video camera.

I could see both his hands, clutching the sun-bleached tresses on either side of his head. No finger going down the throat. He wasn't faking tossing his cookies.

My own stomach lurched.

A psychopathic serial killer could fake a lot of emotions, but *vomiting*?

I was reading and signing off on reports when my desk phone rang. I grabbed the receiver before Barnes could answer, grateful for the interruption. "Anderson."

Damn. I forgot the Chief again. *Screw it!*

"Got two pieces of bad news, Chief," Bradley said. "My CI's still out cold and the doctors are not entirely optimistic that he'll ever wake up, and if and when he does, he might have brain damage due to blood loss."

"And?"

"Ronnie's got a lawyer now, and he's saying the kid has an alibi. He wants a meet, in fifteen minutes."

"Okay, in the larger conference room." Where the murder board wasn't. "I'll be there."

I'd barely hung up when my private line rang. Bracing myself for the possibility that it was the killer—even though we now had two suspects in custody—I picked up the receiver. "Chief Anderson."

"Chief, my admin said you wanted to speak with me." Councilman Hayes's voice.

I blew out air. "Yes. There've been some interesting developments. I'd like to meet in person, sir."

"I'm, uh, pretty booked for the next couple of hours. Can you come to the house at four-thirty? I've been trying to get home before my youngest boy gets off from school, since his mom..." He trailed off. "But he'll be up in his room doing his homework, by then."

"Sure, that works." I disconnected and gratefully signed off from my computer. The reports could wait.

I headed for the conference room.

Ronnie's alibi turned out to be Mrs. Tremont. Not a big surprise.

Bradley and I exchanged a look across the conference table.

"Ronnie couldn't have killed that woman," she said, before the lawyer could open his mouth. "He was with me...I mean..." She stammered to a halt, her face turning red.

"Mrs. T, don't–" Ronnie began.

The lawyer waved a hand in the air. "Y'all didn't do anythin' wrong," he said with a Georgian drawl. "There's nothin' to hide here."

"Uh...he wasn't *with* me," the woman continued. "We were talking. I called him and he came over. We were in the living room. Ronnie's been a good friend, these last few days, since my husband..." She trailed off, swallowed hard. "But that's all we are—*friends*. He came over about–"

"Wait." I held up a hand. To the lawyer, I said, "Have you told your client what Mrs. Tremont told you?"

He shook his head.

"Good. Mrs. Tremont, please come to my office and give me your statement." I ushered her out the door, then turned back.

"Mr. Malcolm, I suggest you tell Detective Bradley what really happened Saturday night."

Their stories jived. Mrs. Tremont had called Ronnie at four in the morning. "I knew I shouldn't do it, that I would be wakin' him up. And he had to be at the store later. But I couldn't sleep. I was just wanderin' around the house. Then somewhere around three-thirty, I started crying so hard, and I couldn't stop."

Tears had pooled in her eyes. She hadn't expected Ronnie to come to her house, only talk to her for a while on the phone. He'd insisted on coming over.

But she'd sworn "on everything I hold holy" that they had only talked. Ronnie had left at six to go home and grab a shower, before opening the store.

Ronnie had reported the same time frame to Bradley, and he'd continued to call his boss *Mrs. T.*

He was heading out to go to her house when he saw the police cars at the Cleavers' house and had walked over to investigate. That's when I'd seen him in the crowd.

Bradley had pressed him about his feelings for the woman, and he'd finally admitted to having a crush on her. But he likewise swore that they'd done nothing but talk.

I'd sent Mrs. Tremont on her way, and Bradley returned Ronnie to his cell.

In my office, Bradley got to the comfortable chair first. Barnes scowled at him and perched on the edge of one of the uncomfortable ones.

"What time were you at the store Sunday morning?" I asked Bradley.

"Seven-ten, right after it opened. The other clerk said Ronnie had called, told him he was running late but would be in by seven-thirty. I didn't want to wait. I was anxious to interrogate Cleaver."

He sighed. "I hate to have to admit this, but I don't think he's our perp. No way could he get to Clover County—even if he'd already had Marly Davis in his trunk the whole time—park his car down the road, and be seen by that little boy only fifteen minutes after leaving the Tremont house. By the way," he added, "I sent our CS team to check out Ronnie's car."

"He could have killed Tremont, though," Barnes said, "hoping that his murder would be pinned on the serial killer? He's got a strong motive there, and he could have easily lured his boss to the back of that bank. *Or...*" she dragged out the word. "Mrs. T did the luring and Ronnie did the killing."

"Maybe." Bradley scrubbed a hand over his face. "But then whoever killed Marly had to have gotten the knife from him, and put it back in his apartment afterwards."

"You gonna let him go?" Barnes asked me.

His lawyer had pushed for that, immediately after we'd taken the pair's statements, but I'd told him we'd get back to him.

I looked at my watch. "He's supposed to be arraigned in half an hour." And I was supposed to be at Hayes's house in an hour.

I was inclined to agree with Bradley, but the knife still gave me pause. And why had Ronnie lied initially about going to Mrs. Tremont's house? Unless their little get-together wasn't as innocent as they were making it out to be.

"Bradley, talk to the ASA. Ask that the prosecutor request own recognizance and a GPS monitor. Hopefully that will forestall the judge throwing the case out completely. And follow up with the other clerk to see when Ronnie really got to the store."

"What if he kills again?" Bradley said.

"We'll keep a close eye on him, but I doubt he will." If he'd killed at all, it was puzzle number two. He and "Mrs. T" had taken out her husband, hoping his death would be blamed on the serial killer. I was pretty sure that Ronnie was *not* said serial killer, however.

Bradley and Barnes trooped out, and I tried to focus on a few more reports, with limited results. I was relieved when it was time to leave for my meeting with Mark Hayes.

Gathering my briefcase and laptop, I took a step toward the office door. The phone rang.

My private line.

I swallowed hard and dumped my stuff back on the desk. Picking up the receiver, I barked, "Chief Anderson."

"Good afternoon, Chief," the mechanical voice said. "I see you've figured out that poor love-struck Ronnie isn't the killer."

CHAPTER TWENTY-FOUR

I'd sent Barnes home, figuring Mark Hayes would not want an audience when I told him what we'd found out about his family. I'd warned her to be careful, that the killer was probably still out there. But I hadn't told her about the phone call this time, loathe to admit that a serial killer was taunting me.

I had alerted Derek, the tech geek who was trying to track the number.

As I drove to the Hayes's home, a niggly feeling had my stomach uneasy. Was it about the phone call?

I gave up my attempts to lasso it and punched the button on my steering wheel to activate Bluetooth.

"Call Sheriff Sam," I instructed the female voice that asked how she could help me.

"Sheriff Pierson," he answered.

"Hi, Sam."

"Hey, Judith. How's it going?" He sounded genuinely pleased to hear from me. Might not be when he heard my news.

"Not great. It's looking like neither of the men we've arrested is our serial killer, or at least they didn't kill Marly Davis. They both have alibis for when young Jamie saw that man and Marly along the road."

"You've kicked them loose?"

"Not completely. We have drug charges against one of them, and one or both may be responsible for some of our other victims. I'm hoping the ADA will be able to get ROR and ankle bracelets, until we can gather more evidence."

"So our killer's still out there. I'll beef up protection for Jamie and his mom."

"Good idea. You sure you don't want this case."

"No thank you, ma'am," he said emphatically. "I always laugh when I see shows on TV where the cops fight over jurisdiction to *keep* a case."

I chuckled. The truth was we were usually more than happy to let some other agency have the headaches that came with a tough case.

"But let me know if we can help," Sam offered again.

"Thanks. I'll keep you posted."

We disconnected, as I pulled into the Hayes's driveway.

The niggly feeling was instantly back. I'd overlooked something, but I couldn't for the life of me figure out what.

Shaking my head, I stepped out of the car, checked my pistol in its holster at the small of my back and donned my black cotton jacket over it.

Mark Hayes ushered me into a spacious study. Its walls were paneled in a pale wood and accented with tasteful beach scenes. Other than an oak desk, the furniture was wicker, with thick, pinstriped cushions in pale green and tan. A potted plant, some tropical flora I didn't recognize, stood in one corner.

Definitely a man's room—but decorated by a woman. A woman intent on giving any visitors a good first impression. In other words, his wife.

"Nice," I said, making a show of looking around. There were diplomas on the wall above his desk, along with photos of him shaking hands with people who must be important. A well-worn black leatherette desk chair rested on a bamboo chair pad.

"My wife had a decorator do it, but she supervised, of course."

Of course.

I glanced again at the shabby desk chair. Karen Hayes had ambitions for her husband, but she'd also loved him, wanted him to be comfortable. My throat tightened.

"So, you have news?" Hayes asked.

"Not the news I'd like to be able to give you, but yes, some news. You have a cousin, Benjamin Nelson, who lives in Lawtey. Have you spoken to him recently?"

He shook his head.

"I take it you're not close."

He sighed. "We used to be, as kids. We were pretty much raised together. Our mothers were sisters."

"Is your mom..." I trailed off.

"No, she passed a couple of years ago. My aunt's gone too."

"Is your dad still with us?" I was hoping for some other relative, besides unreliable Nelson, to confirm the story.

He shook his head again, a slow, sad swing back and forth. "Technically yes, but he has Alzheimer's. We're losing him too, a little bit at a time."

"I'm sorry," I said, meaning it. This guy'd had more than his share of grief, and I was about to heap on more.

I leaned forward. "Councilman, your–"

"Mark, please."

"Mark, your cousin told us an interesting story. About a young woman you dated in college."

"Yes."

That's all he said, looking at me expectantly. His cheeks were slightly flushed, but no concern in his eyes.

"Mr. Nelson said your parents sent the girl away, paid her to give her baby up for adoption."

He sucked in air and heaved it out in a big sigh. "How we regret the mistakes of our youth. And it wasn't my parents, only my mom. But Dad didn't fight her all that hard." He turned his head, gazed sightlessly across the room, his inner eye focused on the past.

"Vivian was beautiful, inside and out. And so happy when she found out she was pregnant. We both were, once we got over the shock. We wanted to get married..." He trailed off, perhaps contemplating how different his life would've been, for better or worse.

"Any reason why she didn't get an abortion?" I asked as gently as possible. "It would have been less disruptive to her life."

"My mother forbade it. We're Catholic."

I maintained a neutral expression, but I really wanted to shake my head. The woman forbade an abortion but was more than happy to use her money to manipulate her son's and his girlfriend's lives.

"I wanted to get married anyway, but Vivian said no. Mother had convinced her that she would be ruining my life if she did–"

A soft knock on the door and it opened. A young man stuck his head in the room. "Dad, me and some friends are going out for pizza. Jayden's picking me up."

I was trying to place the face. Again, the sense that I'd seen him somewhere before.

Hayes gave him a fake smile. "Okay. Have fun."

The coin dropped in my brain. The telephone guys. He was the younger one who'd looked familiar at the time. He had the Jacobs features, like his mother and uncle.

Had the kid planted a bug in my phone? Why the hell would he?

"You were saying?" Hayes's voice pulled me back.

He'd actually been talking, but I didn't point that out. "I'm afraid my news is not good. The first victim here in Starling, Pearl Altman. We believe she was your biological daughter."

Hayes stared at me for a second, then his face slowly crumpled. He jumped up and paced across the room, away from me. Without turning around, he mumbled, "It can't be."

I ignored the denial. "Her death may or may not be related to the others. It's possible someone else killed her and made it look like the same MO as the serial killer's."

He didn't respond, only stood staring out a window at his backyard.

"Had you had any contact with Pearl or her mother over the years?" I asked.

He shook his head, again without saying anything. Finally, he turned, swiping at his eyes with the backs of his hands. "I'm sorry. I guess…" He trailed off and came back to sit on the loveseat across from me. "I guess I wasn't quite up for another blow just yet."

My chest ached. "Sorry to have to be the one delivering that blow."

He blew out air and sat back. "That must be the hardest part of your job."

"It is." I let the silence spin out.

His eyes suddenly went wide. "Do you think it could've been Vivian?"

"Pearl's mother?" My voice went up on an incredulous note. "Killed her own daughter?"

"No, killed my wife. Maybe she found out about Pearl dying and it stirred up old resentments."

I opened my mouth, but I couldn't bring myself to tell this man that his first love was also dead. "We can check into that," I said instead. "But there's a detail we didn't release to the press. Pearl and your wife were posed a certain way, and it was a variation from the serial killer's normal MO. Their hands were resting on their thighs." I demonstrated with my palms on my own legs. "Does that have any significance to you?"

His face paled. "My wife would do that, when I wouldn't go along with something she wanted me to do. She'd lay in bed on her back, with her hands on her thighs. I thought of it as her resigned look."

I felt my eyes go wide, but managed to stop my chin from dropping.

Hayes seemed oblivious to my surprised reaction. "Sometimes she'd do it while sitting watching TV in the evening, after we'd had an argument about something."

My heart racing, I asked, "Any argument?"

"No, only when I didn't want to do something she wanted me to do."

"Like run for state senate?"

He seemed to hesitate, then nodded.

So whoever killed his wife and Pearl was someone who knew Karen Hayes well enough to know her tells. More and more, it looked like those crimes weren't related to the serial killer.

"Pearl was searching for her biological parents, through one of those DNA sites. Are you sure she didn't contact you? Maybe some strange phone call that you thought was a prank at the time?"

He shook his head.

"And your cousin didn't contact you after he talked to her? That would've been around two weeks ago."

"I haven't heard from him in years, although I talk to his brother occasionally. He's closer to me in age. Um, Ben's kinda gone downhill."

You could say that. Out loud, I said, "I got the impression that he drinks too much, when he's not working."

"Working?" Hayes shook his head again. "He used to work for a sand and gravel company, but he lost that job over a decade ago. His mother owned the lot where his trailer is. I guess she left it to him in her will. I think his brother sends him money occasionally."

Hmm, yet another indication that Nelson was unreliable.

I stood up as I gave the usual "if you think of anything else" speech. Then I remembered the kid. "Does your son work for the phone company?"

As Hayes stood, his face showed the first sign of pleasure I'd seen. "Yes, part time. Brian's also a sophomore at UNF. And my daughter just started there this year."

I nodded, making a mental note to have Bradley check on that, to see if either Hayes child had ever crossed paths with Pearl at school.

Bradley! The niggling thought marched up and hit me with such force I took a small staggering step.

"You okay, Chief?" Hayes reached out, as if to catch me if I fainted.

I shook my head. "Yes, yes. I'm fine. I just remembered something I need to do."

I was really glad I'd sent Barnes home.

Her brother sat across my desk from me, scowling. "What are you saying, Chief?"

"I'm saying that we have a leak, and some of the stuff that's leaked, only the detectives would know."

I'd already asked who he'd told about Ronnie Malcolm being a person of interest. He'd denied telling anybody.

"So, as much as possible, I've been segregating information among you all. To see if our leaker would take a wrong step."

"Well, once we arrested Ronnie," Bradley said, trying and failing to sound nonchalant, "there were lots of people who knew he was in custody and why, or they could guess why."

"True, but the killer knew earlier than that. He knew to plant the knife in Ronnie's apartment, *before* you searched it and arrested him."

He had been lounging in the comfortable visitor's chair. Now he leaned forward. "Are you saying *I* told the killer?"

"I'm saying you told someone, and the info somehow got back to the killer. Maybe you were talking about it somewhere and someone could have been eavesdropping?"

I raised my eyebrows in a questioning look, hoping, *praying* he'd take the way out I was offering. I could chastise him for loose lips and we could move on.

He sat up straighter, his face red and taut. "I don't talk about active cases."

"Not even with your partner?"

He half stood. "Now you're accusing Brad of knowing a serial killer?"

I waved him back into his seat. "No, I'm just trying to figure out how the killer knew to plant the knife."

The bigger mystery was how he knew so quickly that we'd interviewed Mrs. Tremont and knew Ronnie had an alibi for Marly's murder. Other cops could've seen her come and go, but they wouldn't know that she'd alibied Ronnie. I had interviewed her in my office, with the door closed and shades drawn.

"I canvassed some of Ronnie's customers and his neighbors," he was saying. "Maybe one of them knows the killer and mentioned being questioned by the police. Or maybe one of them *is* the killer."

"Who helped you canvas?"

"The sarge assigned a uniform—Peters. But I didn't tell her what or who I was asking about. You'd said to keep that quiet. I was using her to speed things up with the neighbors. She went ahead of me, knocking on doors to see who was home."

My stomach queasy, I tried to decide what to do. I found it unlikely that one of the random customers or neighbors he'd interviewed happened to have an inside track with a serial killer. But it was a way that information could have somehow found its way to the killer.

Or the killer had planned to frame Ronnie for Tremont's and Marly's murders even before we were looking at the kid as a suspect? I shook my head slightly, my thoughts beginning to scramble.

It was getting late. "Time for both of us to go home," I said. "Maybe it will make more sense in the morning."

Bradley gave me a forced smile and dragged himself out of the chair.

After he left, I made sure all the blinds were closed and locked my door.

Then I tore my office apart, searching for a bug.

All I discovered was that Mr. Walker was very thorough when he cleaned my office. Even the mismatched blinds were spotless.

The cleaning service! I stood in the middle of my office and resisted the urge to smack myself in the forehead.

Janitors were among the invisible people who came and went with nobody paying them much mind. But they had a passkey to my office.

I'd never given it a thought since my desk was locked and my computer was password protected.

But had one of them planted a bug, and had now retrieved it?

I called Barnes.

"Chief?"

"Have you done that background check on William Walker yet?"

"No, sorry. I haven't had a chance to yet. I can come back in and do it now."

"No, that's okay. First thing in the morning will be fine."

I marched down the hallway toward the conference rooms, the large windows to my right offering up the remnants of the sunset. The lovely colors did nothing to lift my mood.

I examined every square inch of the conference rooms. I even stood on a chair and checked the tops of the doorjambs, as I had in my office.

No listening device.

CHAPTER TWENTY-FIVE

I did not sleep well.

There were the usual dreams—the woman lying on the floor, the officers coming to the door and asking for a dead woman. But woven between them were other dream fragments.

Bradley, a sickly grin on his face, holding a bloody knife.

Mark Hayes weeping and begging me to find Karen's and Pearl's killer, the mechanical voice from the phone laughing in the background.

Ronnie Malcolm blushing and telling me he had a crush on me. Then he morphed into my cousin Paulie, telling me he had a crush on me.

The janitor, Walker, smiling that pearly-white smile at me, telling me *he* loved me, as he pulled a woman's stocking from behind his back. And suddenly I was in a park, and Bradley and Walker were both chasing me across it in a spritzing rain.

I jerked upright in bed.

Giving up on sleep, I went into the bathroom and splashed cold water on my face to help me wake up.

Why is Bradley appearing as a villain in my dreams? He'd done a reasonably credible job of defending himself, had convincingly argued that he had not leaked about our interest in Ronnie.

I met my own gaze in the mirror, water dripping off my sharp features.

But nothing he'd said explained how the killer knew we were growing lukewarm about the kid, when only Barnes, Bradley and myself were privy to that conversation. Barnes was as tight-lipped as they come. And I sure as hell hadn't told anyone in the thirty minutes or so between that conversation and the killer's phone call.

I'd found no listening device in my office last night—and I'd even taken the phone apart. If there had been a bug in there during our conversation about Ronnie's alibi, someone somehow had to have gotten into my office while I was meeting with Mark Hayes and removed it.

When there were still detectives and staff in and out of the bullpen.

Probably not the cleaning people then. Someone would've questioned Walker letting himself into my office during the day.

I breathed out a sigh. I kinda liked Walker, didn't want to find out he was a mass murderer. Or even someone who took bribes to spy on me.

My stomach clenched. I'd liked Bradley too.

I dropped to the floor in my bedroom and did my sit-ups and push-ups, forcing the thoughts out of my head by focusing on my breathing.

As soon as I was on my feet again, the thoughts came back.

Not only was Bradley most likely the leaker, he'd leaked the info at warp speed.

I jumped in the shower and washed my hair, wishing I could wash away the doubts that had taken root in my mind and were growing like poison ivy.

I'd trusted Bradley, had even secretly wished that he was my second in command. Not that Nate Jacobs wasn't a competent detective, but he was a little too independent to be a good leader.

And he was an even worse follower. He'd yet to check in, since... I thought back, while rinsing my hair under the streaming water. Hell, I couldn't remember the last time I'd talked to him.

I rubbed conditioner into my hair, then rinsed it again and stepped out of the shower.

Great, I might have to discipline two of my detectives, right in the middle of a serial killer case.

Why the hell did I move down here?

I went through everything one more time while towel-drying my hair.

How did the killer find out so fast that we had all but given up on Ronnie as a suspect? There were really only three possibilities. The cleaning staff was a long shot.

It was more likely that either Barnes or Bradley was the leak and had called the killer, or someone who knew the killer, immediately after our meeting.

Did that mean one of them was an accomplice? Did they know the person they were feeding information to was the killer, or did they think he was a reporter?

Another thought made me freeze in the act of putting on my white shirt. There was a third possibility. What if one of them *was* the killer?

Okay, that's just plain paranoia.

I beat Barnes in by two minutes. She came into my office.

I stared at her face, into her eyes. The swelling had gone down, the bruises faded to a dull yellow-green.

No way is this earnest young woman a killer's accomplice.

"Chief?" she said, worry starting to cloud her eyes. "Are you okay?"

"I'm fine." I waved a hand in the air. "Find Bradley and tell him I need to see him as soon as possible."

My desk phone rang. She stopped in front of her desk and reached for the phone.

"It's okay. I've got it."

She nodded, glanced back over her shoulder, still looking worried.

I picked up the ringing phone. "Anderson," I barked, a bit more sharply than usual.

"Chief, I'm sorry I didn't check in yesterday." The voice sounded raw. It took me a second to recognize it as Nate Jacobs's.

"I was really dragging so I came home at lunchtime to grab some sleep, and I forgot to plug my phone in to charge. Its alarm didn't go off. I slept straight through 'til ten last night, and still felt tired when I woke up."

"You don't sound so good," I said. "Are you coming down with something?" He had been coughing lately, had said it was from allergies.

A slight pause. "Could be the flu, I guess. I feel achy."

Hopefully he hadn't already passed his germs on to others in the department. Just what we needed, a flu outbreak. Or worse. Ever since Covid, I got a little nervous when anyone got sick. At the peak of the pandemic, BCPD'd had a good chunk of its force down with it or in quarantine because they'd been exposed.

"Maybe you'd better stay home today," I said. "Where are we in the Davis investigation?"

"Cruthers asked for a couple hours off this morning," Jacobs croaked out, "so I was going to go talk to the husband again and–" He broke off, coughing.

"*I'll* go talk to Davis," I said. "You stay in bed and get better."

"Thanks, Chief. I'd argue that I'm okay, if I wasn't so damn sick."

I chuckled and we disconnected.

I heaved a relieved sigh. At least I didn't have to discipline *two* of my detectives today.

Barnes returned to my office. "Detective Bradley will be here shortly. I'm going to work on that background check now."

"Great. Thanks."

A few minutes later, her brother knocked on the frame of my open door. "You wanted to see me, Chief?"

I waved him in. "Close the door."

Before he could sit down, I said, "One more time, who did you tell about Malcolm being a person of interest?"

He rolled his eyes toward the ceiling. "No one."

The eye roll pissed me off, and helped me make the final decision between a warning or suspension.

Twenty seconds later, Bradley was slamming out the door, after tossing his badge and department-issue pistol onto my desk. Head down, he stormed across the bullpen toward the exit.

Barnes was in my doorway. "What's going on?" she asked, worry and confusion in her voice.

My stomach twisted, but I hid behind a neutral mask.

I gestured for her to come in. She stood in front of my desk, her body tense.

"After I answer that question, I will understand if you wish to be reassigned." I took a deep breath. "Detective Bradley is suspended, pending an investigation."

Her eyes went wide and her chin dropped. "An investigation into what?"

"I can't tell you that."

Silence stretched for several beats. "No, I don't want to be reassigned," she said in a tight voice. She walked out and sat at her desk, her back to me as she worked at her computer.

Now the question was *how* to conduct an investigation. We weren't big enough to have our own Internal Affairs people.

And I wasn't about to call up the former chief, despite his insincere offer that his help "was just a phone call away."

Normally, I would ask Bradley how such things worked. My throat tightened.

I swallowed hard, thought for a moment, and placed a call. It went to voicemail. "Nate, I hate to bother you when you're not feeling well, but I need some information regarding internal investigations. Give me a call back when you can."

Barnes emailed me, *background check* in the subject line.

I perused the information, trying to ignore the implications of her means of communication.

As I read, my stomach tightened.

I'd been right about the orthodontics. Walker had grown up in a ritzy section of Jacksonville. He'd received a bachelor's degree from a good college, gone on to graduate school.

But things went downhill from there. He'd been in jail three times, once for sixty days, then for ninety days, and then an eighteen-month stint at Raiford, the state prison. All for domestic violence charges, with three different women, the last one his wife of less than a year, who'd testified against him, claiming repeated abuse.

Kate's comment flashed into my mind. *Usually they're abusive with those families.*

My gaze landed on his release date. He'd been returned to society three years ago, five and a half months before the first sexual assault in Jacksonville.

How had we missed this guy?

The answer was found under current address. He lived in a cheap hotel on the other side of town, not in Starlingville. And he had no obvious connection to any of our victims here. But did he have any with the Jacksonville victims?

He had a master's degree in business. He was smart enough to pull off these crimes, to stay one step ahead of us, especially if he knew what was going on.

A well-heeled kid now reduced to cleaning offices for a meager living. Yeah, that would certainly piss him off, and obviously he already had anger issues if he beat up on the women he supposedly loved.

I called the watch commander—Sergeant Johnson was on duty—and ordered a BOLO put out on Walker. I wanted him brought in for questioning.

Donning my jacket, I walked out to Barnes's desk. When I told her I was going to interview Marly Davis's husband, she nodded but made no move to join me. I didn't press the issue.

"See if you can find out more about what Walker's been up to since his release from prison."

She nodded again.

In the car, I second-guessed myself all the way to the Davis's home.

Why hadn't I looked for our leak among the civilians who came in contact with the police department?

Because too much of the leaked stuff was info only the detectives knew.

But anyone could've planted a bug, in my office and/or in the smaller conference room where we'd discussed the case. Not just the cleaners but delivery people, the guy from the mail room who brought us our snail mail...

And it was quite a coincidence that the Hayes's oldest boy happened to be one of the installers from the phone company—and had access to my private line number.

I grimaced. The kid seemed pretty clean-cut.

But looks could be deceiving. The clean-cut exterior could be the calculated veneer of a psychopath.

I nudged my car through a group of paparazzi hovering in front of the Davis house and pulled into the driveway.

Okay, maybe *paparazzi* wasn't a fair term in this case. One of their own had been killed, and they wanted answers.

So did I.

Unfortunately, James Davis didn't have them. He was still pretty broken up, but reasonably coherent. And he couldn't imagine why anyone would hurt his wife.

Even though she's gone after multiple big names in town, when she had some dirt on them.

"Did she receive any threats here, letters or emails?" I asked.

He shook his head. "She never said that she did."

Because she hadn't wanted to upset him. It was obvious who the more fragile spouse was.

Cruthers had already taken her personal computer, with the husband's permission, and had turned it over to Derek.

I handed Mr. Davis my card. "Call me or Detective Cruthers if you think of anything else." I softened my voice. "Again, we're sorry for your loss."

I felt like a bit of a fraud, since I wasn't particularly sorry that Marly Davis was out of my hair.

My mind flashed to her body, lying in that muddy grave, and my insides tightened. Okay, I *was* sorry. Nobody deserved to leave the planet that way, not even annoying reporters.

Is James Davis truly a distraught and innocent spouse, or is he a good actor? On the drive back to 3MB, I contemplated that question.

Analyzing it intellectually, all signs pointed to the former—he was an innocent spouse. And the strongest indicator was the way she died.

A spouse who'd reached the end of his rope might kill her in a fit of rage, or maybe smother her in her sleep or arrange a fatal household accident.

If we'd found her buried in his backyard, then yeah, he'd be at the top of our suspect list. But hold her somewhere, report her missing, take her out to the boonies and walk her into a swamp, and *then* kill her? Very unlikely.

My gut was agreeing with my intellect, but still I felt uneasy. *Why?*

I let my mind drift, and after a minute or so, it came to me. If Marly *always* called when she was going to be later than she'd said, why had Davis waited until the next morning to report her missing?

I instructed my Bluetooth to call Cruthers.

"Hey, Chief. Just walking outta the doctor's office. What's up?"

"Are you okay?"

"Yeah. It was only a check-up. I'm fit as a fiddle, according to the doc."

"Good. I talked to Mr. Davis again. Nothing helpful there. Track down Marly's lawyer and see if you can find out what's in her will."

"You got it."

"And if they won't tell you details, ask for a yes/no answer to whether or not the husband benefits in any major way."

"Gotcha."

"Did you talk to Marly's boss about any threats she might have received at the office?"

"Not yet, couldn't reach him yesterday. It's on my to-do list for today."

"Good."

We disconnected, and I placed another call.

"Hey Judith, how ya doing?" Sheriff Sam's rich baritone was soothing.

"I've been better. I had to suspend someone."

"Oh, that's rough. Why?"

"Uh, I don't really want to get into that. But I was wondering how our smaller departments handle internal investigations around here? We don't have an IA division. Hell, we don't even have an IA *person*."

"Not a short disciplinary suspension then. You suspect the officer of something?"

"Yes." My throat closed anew at the thought of Bradley leaking information.

"Well, if you think it's serious enough, you can ask the state's Department of Justice to investigate. Otherwise, it's up to the sheriff or police chief to investigate."

"Damn."

"Yeah." He blew out a sigh. "There's a form you fill out to request an investigation from the DOJ."

"Okay. Thanks."

"No problem. Wish I could do more to help." Somehow, I knew he meant help with more than just the investigation.

"Actually..." Did I really want to say what I'd been about to say, that it was good to have a sounding board, a friendly ear? My trust level was a little on the low side right now. "Um, this helped a lot. Take care, Sam."

"You too, Judith." The warmth in his voice had me feeling slightly better as I disconnected.

Once in my office, I sank into the desk chair. *Should I have suspended Bradley so quickly?*

Maybe I could've kept a close eye on him instead. No, I couldn't risk him feeding any more info to the killer. My mind veered away from the paranoid thought that he could be the killer himself.

I shook my head. This wasn't like me, second-guessing myself. Feeling claustrophobic, I jumped up and opened the mismatched blinds.

I scanned the bullpen. Only one detective sat at a desk, Cruthers. He gave me a stony look, then turned away.

The word had apparently spread about Bradley's suspension.

Barnes again had her back to me at her desk.

My eyes stinging—I told myself it was from fatigue—I woke up my computer, intending to review reports.

A ping announced an incoming email. It was from Cruthers. Again, I tried to ignore the form of communication while reading its content. Mr. Davis had given their lawyer permission to tell us the gist of Marly's will. And the lawyer had immediately called back.

That was fast. Davis's quick cooperation was another indicator that he wasn't his wife's killer. But still we had to investigate all the angles.

Marly had left the thirty-thousand dollars she had in a retirement account to her son and daughter. James Davis got the house and the rest of their joint savings and investments.

Not enough coming to him—that he couldn't already access—to make murder worthwhile. But how much would he lose if they divorced?

I glanced over my shoulder. Cruthers was still at his desk. I hit reply and typed: *Make sure neither of them was having an affair. Talk to their coworkers, friends again.*

I heard him stirring, then he walked past my office, his suit coat slung over his shoulder. He never looked my way.

Hell, what have I done? The rapport I'd been building with my people, gone, *poof.*

Barnes was also away from her desk. I was alone, in my little fishbowl, amidst a sea of empty desks.

It wasn't that my people had to like me, but I needed their respect in order to do my job. And active dislike would make the work environment pretty damned uncomfortable.

My throat tightened. The pressure behind my eyes increased. Work was all I had.

Cut it out, Anderson. Pull up your big girl pants and get on with it.

I sat down at my desk and stared at my computer, which had been Chief Black's computer before me. Another aspect of getting to know my department that had been derailed by this serial killer—exploring the multitude of document files I'd inherited along with the computer.

Info about how internal investigations had been handled in the past might be in there somewhere. I grabbed my mouse and started searching.

I'd actually been a little surprised that Black hadn't wiped the hard drive before he retired, but I guess he figured that would be too blatant.

I wasn't surprised, however, to discover that the folder titled *Internal Investigations* was password protected. I figured out the password on the second try—*badcops.*

Sure enough, there was a document labeled *DOJ_investigation_request_form.*

What stopped me cold, though, was the file below that one. *Jacobs_investigation.*

CHAPTER TWENTY-SIX

The file was just the filled-in form requesting the investigation. The complainant was Captain Luis Martinez. The captain who had resigned two years ago.

The accusation was *receipt of bribes*. No indication of the outcome, but Jacobs couldn't have been found guilty or he wouldn't still have a job.

I didn't remember seeing anything in his personnel file about the charge or investigation. It would have made an impression. Indeed, if I remembered correctly two years ago was about when he was promoted to lieutenant.

Barnes returned from whatever errand she'd been on, interrupting my train of thought.

The phone rang and she answered it, still standing facing me. Her cheeks paled. "Hold on, please. She'll want to talk to you."

She put the call on hold and walked to my doorway. "It's the sh...sheriff of Bradford County," she stammered.

A lump of dread forming in my stomach, I picked up the line. "Chief Anderson."

"Hey, Chief." His Florida accent was thick. "I'm in Lawtey, and I'm afraid I got some bad news. Ben Nelson is dead."

"Heart attack?" I asked, watching Barnes, who was slumped in her desk chair.

"Can't tell for sure. They'd dried him out some while he was in the hospital. It looks like he came home and drank himself to death. The place reeks of beer and hard liquor. But we'll have to wait for the autopsy to know for sure."

"You might want to get some blood drawn right away. See if he's got high levels of epinephrine again. I don't know if it dissipates after death, but the doc at the hospital told me it only lasts a few hours, if you're alive."

"Good point. We got paramedics here, even though there wasn't anythin' they could do for him. I'll get them to draw blood and take it to be analyzed."

"Do you mind if we come out there and take a look at the scene?"

"Not at all," he said, "but bring a nose plug."

This time I didn't give Barnes the option of staying behind. "I'll need you to drive so I can check on some things."

After tossing the car keys to her, I climbed into the passenger seat of my own car and sighed. For the second time today, I asked myself if I'd made a mistake moving down here, taking this job.

I shook my head slightly, as Barnes pulled out of the municipal parking lot. "Do you know where Captain Martinez ended up after he resigned?" I asked her.

She glanced my way, then back at the road. "I'd heard he's with the Starke PD now." Her tone was neutral, too neutral.

I nodded. "Do you know anything about a bribery investigation a couple of years ago, involving one of our officers?" I didn't say which one.

"Before my time." She glanced my way again, her eyes hard. I could almost hear her thinking, *my brother would know*.

I disconnected my phone from my Bluetooth again, somewhat wary of having Barnes hear both ends of the conversation I was about to have. I placed the call.

"Hello?" Mark Hayes's voice was tentative, even though my name had to have come up on his caller ID.

"Chief Anderson, sir. Sorry to disturb you, but I have a question. Why did you all hire me? Why not promote from within?"

"Um, we didn't feel that anyone had quite enough experience to be chief."

"Uh huh, but why me?"

"You were the best qualified."

I didn't believe that for a New York minute. Certainly, others who had more administrative experience had applied. They'd done a nationwide search.

"Anything that made me uniquely qualified for the position?"

The sound of air being blown out. "All your references mentioned your integrity, in glowing terms."

"And you wanted someone like that because..." I trailed off, not really expecting a straight answer. But I would bet my last dollar that they'd suspected corruption in the department.

Woulda been nice knowing that up front.

My next thought was, *Did the old chief retire willingly or was he nudged out?* I didn't ask that one out loud.

Instead, I changed the subject. "I'm afraid I don't have much to report on the case. We thought we had our man, and he's still technically in custody, but I don't think he did it." I didn't mention that we'd thought we had our man *twice*, first Cleaver, then Ronnie Malcolm.

"I was afraid to ask," Hayes said.

Afraid?

"Why?" I blurted out.

Another sigh. "My family's beginning to get into a routine again. There's a huge hole in our household, but things are settling down. So I almost dread the upheaval that will come when you do have the killer under arrest. I mean it'll be a relief, but..." He trailed off.

That kind of made sense.

Damn, I should tell him about his cousin. Indeed, I should've led with that.

But I opted not to bring Nelson's death up now, especially over the phone and right after he'd said he was dreading more disruption.

We'd do an in-person notification after we'd seen the scene out in Lawtey.

"Thank you for your time, sir." We said our goodbyes and disconnected.

"Cruthers would know about that investigation," Barnes said, her voice more normal.

I gave her a small smile, acknowledging the peace offering. "Yes, he would. I'll ask him when we get back."

Near Lawtey, Barnes said, "What about Walker?"

"What about him?"

"Are you thinking he could be our killer? I saw he's employed by the cleaning service the city uses."

"I was checking him out for other reasons." Not a total lie, but still I felt my chest tighten. I hated lying to her when I demanded truth in the other direction.

The Bradford County sheriff hadn't exaggerated. As bad as Nelson's trailer had smelled before, it was now worse. Once past the putrid odors of the front rooms, our nostrils were assailed with the stench of beer and vomit, not a pleasant combination.

But not the scent of a decaying body—which had already been removed by the ME's people.

One of the Bradford County crime scene techs noticed me sniffing the air. "He hadn't been dead long, and the air conditioning delayed decomp."

I nodded. Barnes and I were standing off to the side of the room, near the doorway. I noted two pint-sized whiskey bottles, on the floor near the bed, along with quite a few beer cans.

The bottles were both open, with a little bit of amber liquid still in them.

A layer of dust covered most things in the room, except the cans and liquor bottles.

"I count ten cans," Barnes said. She was writing in her notepad.

I took a couple of careful steps over to the bed. The pillow was soaked. I leaned over slightly and sniffed. Mostly beer, not stale, with a hint of whiskey.

"Our killer isn't much of a drinker."

"Why do you say that?" Barnes asked.

"Because he overdid it. Downing *either* ten beers or one pint of whiskey, after a few days of sobriety, and Nelson probably would've passed out. You can't keep drinking when you're unconscious."

She stepped up beside me. "Why is the pillow wet?"

"I suspect the killer forced beer down his throat. Then he topped it off with the liquor, to make damn sure Nelson died." My voice caught on the last word.

My chest hurt. *Why didn't I get him protection?*

Because I'd assumed that once he'd told his story, he was no longer at risk. But the killer couldn't be sure that Nelson wasn't able to identify him, and this perp had shown us again and again that he didn't take chances with loose ends. I recalled Bradley's comment. *He enjoys killing.*

When I could trust my voice, I said to the techs, "Can I get a copy of your report?"

The one who'd spoken to me earlier nodded. I handed him my card.

Cruthers sat across from me at my desk. His bulky frame dwarfed the chrome and fake-leather visitor's chair. I'd offered him the new, comfortable one, but for some reason he'd chosen the familiar but uncomfortable alternative.

"Not much to report," he said, his tone and expression neutral. "Marly Davis's boss said there were some nasty emails, but they were all fairly vague, mostly along the lines of he should fire her, or she deserved to burn in hell. Nothing overtly threatening.

"No indicators, according to her coworkers, that Marly was having an affair. Main answer to the question, who would want to hurt her, was local bigwigs whom she'd relentlessly pursued for the sake of a story. Yourself included, Chief."

I nodded.

"The folks who worked for and with the husband all say he's a good guy, loved his wife, talked about her a lot. Best I could tell, they didn't have any true friends."

Considering Marly's personality, that did not surprise me.

Cruthers ran a hand through his shaggy hair. "Frankly, I don't think Davis has the balls to kill anyone."

"That's my take as well."

He leaned forward. "May I ask an impertinent question?"

I was mildly surprised by his word choice. *Impertinent* was not exactly cop-speak. "Ask away. I may not answer, however."

"Why'd you suspend Bradley?"

I took a deep breath, deciding how much to tell him. My gut said Cruthers was trustworthy, but my gut's track record hadn't been great lately.

"I've been trying to compartmentalize certain information."

"Because we've got a leak," Cruthers said. Statement of fact, not a question.

"A pretty serious one. We had another suspect in custody, besides Cleaver. Only Bradley, Barnes and I knew why he'd been brought in. Turns out he has an alibi."

I paused, sucked in air. "Within a half hour of a private discussion among the three of us about that alibi, I got a call." I pointed my chin toward my desk phone. "On my private line. From the killer, who knew what we had discussed."

Cruthers sat even farther forward, literally on the edge of his seat. "He called you *again*."

I nodded. "Neither call was long enough to track, and the voice was mechanically altered, so no helpful info there."

His eyes were wide. "You are one cool cucumber, Chief."

A quick debate. I could let Cruthers think I was emotionless, my usual *modus operandi*, or I could let on that I'm human. In the interest of rebuilding rapport, I opted for the less comfortable latter option.

"I wasn't all that calm, cool and collected at the time of the calls."

He nodded, his eyes sympathetic. "What's next?"

My stomach relaxed a little.

"Well, I think we can put Marly's husband at the bottom of our suspect list." I paused, thinking. There were so many balls to juggle in this investigation. Had we let any of them fall?

"Let's go take a look at the crime board," I said. "I'm feeling an itch for a marker and a whiteboard."

After a half hour in the smaller conference room, adding some notes to and then staring at the crime board, we'd identified a few loose ends worth tying up, but nothing that would really qualify as an active lead. One was Pearl Altman's tablet. We never had gotten a report on it from Derek, the tech geek.

But I wasn't really hoping for anything new there, unless she'd uncovered some other biological relative who didn't want to be found.

Cruthers started to push himself out of his chair, to go pursue the loose ends.

I held up a hand. "Were you aware of an investigation, a couple of years ago, into bribery charges against Nate Jacobs?"

Cruthers fell back into the chair. "Yes." His tone was wary.

"There's nothing in his file about it."

"The charges were dropped."

"He was exonerated?"

"Not exactly." He sighed. "Captain Martinez brought it to the chief's attention that he had a solid witness, who'd seen Neat take payoffs from drug dealers, twice."

"Neat?"

Cruthers smirked. "Neat Nate. My nickname for him, because he's always dressed so...neatly."

I suspected he'd been thinking of another word. *Prissy* maybe.

"How solid could a witness be who hung out around drug dealers?"

"Pretty solid," Cruthers said. "He was a priest. But he died in a hit-and-run pedestrian accident."

Holy crap, as Kate would say.

"Did they catch the driver?"

Cruthers shook his head.

I paused, debated, then asked the question anyway. "Did Martinez leave because of that investigation?"

Had Chief Black pressured him to resign? I didn't ask that one out loud.

Cruthers shrugged. "Don't know for sure, but the timing is suspicious."

I stopped in my tracks a few steps inside the bullpen. Bradley was standing next to his sister's desk, a good-sized, paper evidence bag in his hand.

I nodded acknowledgment as I passed him, not surprised that he followed me into my office.

He closed the door behind him. "Can I close the blinds?" he asked.

I nodded again and sat behind my desk.

Once the blinds were all closed, except for the inevitable gaps, Bradley placed the evidence bag on my desk. "I found this in the trunk of my car, under the mat, when I was looking for some tools."

He paused, took a deep breath. "It's a zippered navy-blue canvas bag—the kind banks used for deposits. The zipper clicks into a lock on one end. Not that it did much good. This bag has a large slit in one side. There's dried blood on it, Tremont's most likely. It's empty."

I wrote the date, time and my signature on the evidence bag, as its recipient in the chain of custody.

"You should've left it in place, called for one of us to come get it," I said, keeping my voice neutral.

"I'd already picked it up before I realized what it was." His voice was stiff. "I did take pictures, after the fact. And I'm happy to let the crime scene boys look for trace evidence."

"I'll arrange it. Thank you." My tone was as formal as his.

"My CI died. Never regained consciousness."

"I'm sorry."

He nodded, stone-faced. "I'd like permission to look into it, unofficially. He was an addict, but not an intrinsically bad kid. He didn't deserve to be gunned down like that." He paused. "I know you must be stretched thin." His voice sounded almost normal. "I can take this off your plate."

He was a suspended officer. I should give him some song and dance that sounded like I was saying no when I was really saying yes, but I wasn't up for the game. "Sure," I said. "Go for it."

"Thanks." He turned and left, closing the door behind him.

I called the city's personnel office. Something I should have done days ago, although then I only had one position to fill. Now I might have two.

I requested an internal posting for a detective position, and that they advertise externally nationwide as well.

"We have to advertise internally for ten days," I was informed, "and you have to interview any internal candidates that meet the qualifications, before we can advertise externally."

I blew out air. Of course, there would be bureaucratic hurdles to jump. But I wasn't ready to tell anyone I might have more openings to fill. That would set the rumor mill a twitter for sure. And there was a chance that Bradley was innocent of wrongdoing.

"Okay," I said. "But be prepared to advertise externally as well."

I called Foster in Jacksonville, planning to plant a certain seed.

But before I could do so, he said, "I talked to Shelly Trent's aunt again. The night her husband died, she'd gone to bed early with a migraine. She thought she heard voices downstairs but they weren't raised, just normal conversational volume. She decided it must be the TV. The next morning, she found him dead in his recliner."

"Was the TV on?"

"Nope."

We were both silent for a beat. Then I said, "Not conclusive."

"No, but it's got my Spidey senses tingling."

"Mine, too. But why would this perp go after the uncle?"

"The uncle was there, at the time," Foster said. "He'd just gotten home from work when Shelly literally ran into his arms. He sent her inside and took off for the alley, but he didn't find anyone there."

I didn't remember seeing that in the case file. "Maybe the rapist was hiding in the alley, saw the uncle, and wasn't sure whether or not Trent had seen him."

"Maybe," Foster said. "We may never know for sure, with Trent gone."

Which of course, was the killer's intention.

"Hey, I've got an opening for a detective over here. I don't suppose I could tempt you to jump ship?"

He chuckled. "Not likely. I'm too close to retirement."

I hadn't expected an affirmative answer, but the seed was now planted in the JSO. Maybe someone over there would rather compete in a smaller pond.

We disconnected and I called up Shelly Trent's case file on my computer. Several pages back, I found the interview with the uncle. It hadn't registered the first time I'd skimmed the file, since the uncle hadn't seen anything helpful. And I hadn't known then that he'd died shortly thereafter.

I shivered, as another realization hit me. If Mr. Trent was killed by our perp, he had most likely let the killer into the house willingly. His wife hadn't heard any arguing or sounds of a struggle.

It was someone he trusted. *Like a cop.*

My stomach grumbled, reminding me that I'd never had lunch. Actually, I couldn't remember eating breakfast either. I checked the time. Four-twenty.

Jacobs hadn't called me back. I called again and got voicemail. "Never mind. I found the info I needed. But call my cell and let me know how you're doing."

Worry niggled. From harsh experience, I knew the downside of living alone—no one there to call for help if you were seriously ill. I'd almost died of meningitis in my thirties. I'd had a headache at bedtime, then woke up a few hours later with cramps, chills and every joint in my body aching so bad I could barely move. If my phone hadn't been right there on my nightstand, I don't know what would've happened.

I'd take myself out for a late lunch, and if Jacobs hadn't called back by the time I'd finished eating, I'd go to his house to check on him.

Barnes came into my office with a phone message, from the gun shop. The background check had been completed and I could pick up my Glock.

Excellent. I added that errand to the agenda, and told Barnes my plans.

Pointing toward the tiny bathroom, I said, "See if you can get maintenance up here to oil the squeaky hinge on that door. It's starting to drive me crazy."

She nodded. "What happened to the buddy system?"

Good question. It had gone by the wayside when we thought we had our killer in custody. But I really wasn't up for Barnes's presence as I ate. Things were better between us, but there was still some tension.

"It's broad daylight. I'll stay alert. And I'll probably go home after I check on the lieutenant." I gave her a stern look. "But you get a uniform to walk you to your car when you leave. That's an order."

I figured she was much more at risk than I was, since the killer had already gone after her once, and he didn't like loose ends.

Before leaving the building, I took the bank bag to our tiny crime lab to have the blood analyzed.

What was Bradley's motivation for bringing it in?

The implication was that someone had planted it in his car. And him being a good cop, he'd turned it in, even though it could incriminate him.

But could it be an elaborate ruse to throw suspicion off himself?

Barnes was still staying with him. His idea, she'd said. The argument that going home would put their parents at risk had convinced her.

And that was the strongest evidence against Bradley being the killer's willing accomplice. No way would he tolerate his sister being attacked.

Unless that botched attack was another elaborate ruse. If he was a psychopathic killer, some or all of his affection for his sister could be faked.

I shook my head and tried to push the whole mess aside while I took a much needed meal break.

After picking up my new-to-me gun, I found a little Italian place near the gun shop. I ordered a full meal, combining lunch and dinner so I wouldn't have to cook later. But I ended up asking the waiter to box most of it up.

Paranoia and depression are powerful appetite suppressants.

I called Nate again from my car. Three rings and it went to voicemail.

Okay, either he was *really* sick, in which case it was good that I was going over to check on him. Or... I suspected he sometimes ignored my calls.

Maybe it was time to confront him with that suspicion.

And, depending on how he was feeling, I might ask him about the bribery investigation. It would be interesting to see his reaction.

Nate's home was much larger than I'd expected, a red brick mini-mansion with a white-pillared verandah, in an upscale neighborhood.

I double-checked the address. Yes, this was it. And a white SUV was in the driveway.

The property was at least a half acre, but a bit overgrown, the grass high. The workload of a police lieutenant didn't allow a lot of time for yard work. A good argument for condos, in my mind.

Some palmetto bushes encroached onto the sidewalk, and a nearby pine tree needed a good pruning. Several branches hung low over the walk.

Ironically, baskets of bright red flowers, suspended from the porch ceiling between the pillars, were thriving. I chuckled softly. I never would've pegged Jacobs as the hanging-geranium type.

I was gingerly stepping along the cement walk, when the back of my neck tingled with that creepy feeling of being watched. I stopped and did a slow 360, scanning the neighborhood.

The only people on the street were an older couple walking a small dog, farther down the block.

I shrugged, turned back toward the house. I skirted around one of the palmetto bushes and ducked under the drooping pine bough.

Pain shot through my scalp. *Damn*, I'd snagged my hair on the branch.

I reached up to untangle myself, and encountered leather. A gloved hand clamped over my mouth.

CHAPTER TWENTY-SEVEN

Adrenaline shot through me as I was slammed on my back, behind the palmettos.

A man with a distorted face landed on my chest, his knees pinning my shoulders. One gloved hand shoved painfully against my mouth.

In the other, he held a large, open pen knife.

Self-defense training kicked in. I flung my legs up to hook them over his hoodie-clad shoulders, with the intention of flipping him off of me.

He poked the knife against my neck. I froze.

"Move again and I'll slit your throat," he growled.

I let my legs drop back to the ground and lay still, my heart and mind racing. I willed myself to stay calm. I'd been trained for such scenarios. I'd find my opening.

"I'm going to remove my hand from your mouth," again a low growl, unnatural. Not his real voice. "But you're not going to make a sound, because you don't want to involve civilians, now do you?"

I squinted, trying to make out his features despite the distortions caused by the stocking. But the shadow under his hood was too deep.

"Blink twice if you understand."

I blinked twice.

He removed the hand from my mouth but not the knife from my throat. His free hand went behind him.

"See, you have some things in common with Marly." A twisted smile creased his distorted face. "You've got good sense, and you don't want others to get hurt."

Cold metal against my right wrist and the snick of handcuffs closing. Then he was flipping me over so fast I didn't have time to react. My other wrist was captured in the cuffs.

A sinking feeling inside. My mouth went dry. My options had just narrowed considerably.

He sat on my butt and laughed, the cadence the same as the mechanical laugh of those phone calls.

To calm myself, I took inventory of what I knew. I was pretty sure he was white. And I'd had the impression of bulk earlier, but maybe that was due to the loose hoodie. He didn't weigh as much as I'd expected. A thin guy.

Walker? No, this guy moved like a cop.

Bradley?

My chest ached. I had hoped...

A subtle prick on my upper arm. *Shit, is he drugging me?*

I squirmed. He laughed again. He might not be as heavy as I'd assumed, but he was still heavy enough to keep me pinned to the ground.

Stinging scalp as he grabbed my hair. Hot breath against my neck and ear. "I took Marly in her own driveway," he whispered. "Pointed out that I'd had hours of hand-to-hand combat training, unlike that wimp of a husband of hers. She never made a peep."

That made me want to scream my head off, just to defy him. But damn him, he was right. I couldn't risk civilians getting hurt trying to rescue me.

I was a cop. Protect and serve.

Pressure at the small of my back. He held up my Glock. "Sweet piece. I'll add it to my collection."

A twinge of grief over my short-lived ownership of the *sweet piece*.

"Your backup gun, on the other hand... I'll be sure to plant that on whatever schmuck I decide to frame for your murder."

My heart sank. I'd been hoping I could get to the little pistol somehow.

Definitely Bradley. Only he and Nate knew about my revolver.

I tried to focus on the Glock. It was fuzzy.

And my brain was foggy. What the hell had he drugged me with, that it was already taking effect?

"Roofies," he whispered in my ear. "Ground up and dissolved in a little water. Injected. Takes effect even faster than a tampered drink."

How the hell did he know what I was thinking? It had to be Bradley. *He* knew me that well.

Because he was *so* easy to be with, easy to talk to. *Shit!*

Flashes of greenery as he dragged me, crouched low behind the bushes himself, toward the back of the house.

Was he trying to frame Nate?

Screw it! I sent signals to my mouth to open and scream.

Nothing happened.

Grey mist. Everywhere I looked...grey mist.

A moaning sound. I realized it was coming from me.

Someone was running hands over me. "Chief, Chief, wake up." An urgent whisper.

I managed to open one eye. A foggy image of Bradley's face.

Memory flooded back. Pain shooting across my scalp, thinking my hair had snagged on the tree, his threat to hurt civilians...

The bastard!

I struggled, trying to fight him, but my hands were bound behind my back.

"Chief," he whispered.

Nate Jacobs's face appeared over his shoulder.

Relief washed through me.

Bradley leaned closer. "It's–" His eyes went wide. He disappeared from my view.

Weird sounds. Slowly my mind translated them as a scuffle. Then the sound of something being dragged.

I vaguely registered a prick on my arm.

I drifted for a while, no longer afraid. Then I fell asleep.

The body in the kitchen, I couldn't get away from it. I was clawing at the kitchen door, but I couldn't get it to open.

I looked over my shoulder. The body seemed bigger, darker.

Desperation surged through me. I had to get away.

Then it was on me, enveloping me, whispering in my ear in a deep, growling voice, "You're doomed. You couldn't save me. You can't save yourself."

I tried to shake myself awake.

It didn't work.

I was stuck in the dream, which I now knew was a dream. But that made it only slightly less terrifying.

The body was back on the floor. It rose slowly and turned to face me.

A horrifying, decayed skeleton stared at me, from the outline of my mother's body, my mother's face.

"Time to let it go, sweetheart."

My heart pounded. My eyelids flickered open.

Dark shadows.

I blinked, trying to focus my eyes.

Where the hell am I?

Slowly the answer seeped in. I was in a basement.

Shrouded shapes in the semi-darkness. Some ambient light filtered from small windows high above my head.

"'Bout time you woke up," a voice out of the darkness.

I squinted but couldn't make out any form that resembled a person.

A few feet away were dusty boxes, and beyond them, what had once been a white chest freezer, now speckled with rust.

I spotted feet, and my breath caught. They were bound at the ankles, sticking out from behind the freezer.

Black, bulky oxfords, with velcro straps.

My stomach clenched at the sight of those shoes, although I couldn't figure out why. The acidic taste of tomato sauce rose in the back of my throat. I swallowed hard.

I was sitting against a cement-block wall. My brain sent a signal to my hands to push myself to a stand. Nothing happened.

I realized I couldn't feel my hands. It was cool down here, clammy with humidity, but not cold enough to make my hands go numb.

What had I been drugged with? Could it have affected my circulation?

A flash of memory, a voice growling, "Roofies."

My legs stretched out in front of me, my black slacks intact. My shoes were gone, as was my ankle holster. My bare feet were blocks of ice.

I told my knees to bend, to bring my feet up underneath me, not at all sure those feet could hold me if I did manage to stand.

My knees obeyed. I blew out a sigh of relief.

They rose until they were almost touching my chest. I glanced down the front of me, to make sure my numb feet were where they needed to be in order to stand.

Dried blood on my shirt startled me. Then I remembered the knife pricking my throat. On cue, the cuts on my neck throbbed.

Carefully, I leaned my head forward to look down at my feet. A thin cloth, crisscrossed between my ankles, flesh colored.

Not sure what it was, I ignored it and wiggled my shoulders to ease my back up the wall.

"You might as well stop trying." A figure stepped out of the darkness, its face distorted, my Glock in its hand.

Confused, I shook my head. *Am I still dreaming?*

Moving my head was a big mistake. The room swam. My stomach roiled.

Swallowing tomato-flavored bile, I tried to sort out reality. Nate had *saved* me from the killer—Bradley. Who was now tied up behind the freezer?

I looked past the figure's legs. Yes, those were Bradley's shoes, on their sides, trussed together against the far wall.

Then who the hell was this guy? My focus returned to the distorted face. I took in the white tee shirt over dark dress pants. He was too short to be Bradley.

Did he have an accomplice? Had the accomplice turned on him for some reason?

Where was Nate?

My gaze moved to the shoes of the person in front of me.

Expensive black leather wingtips.

That answered both my questions. Nate Jacobs was standing in front of me, and no, he wasn't Bradley's accomplice.

He was the Midnight Killer.

CHAPTER TWENTY-EIGHT

Jacobs pulled off the stocking that distorted his features. "Don't bother with trying to scream. Hear that music?"

Rock music vibrated faintly from above us. I hadn't noticed it before.

"I play it occasionally, so the neighbors are used to hearing it. It disguises any sounds my guests might make that manage to get past these thick cement walls."

Guests?

Darla! She'd been tied up. He'd held her for a few hours, before killing her. And Marly... A shudder ran through me.

"Even the windows are thick," he pointed out conversationally. "They're those old-fashioned glass blocks folks used in basements decades ago. Let light in but nobody can *see* in."

"I take it you didn't have the flu," I said, figuring that keeping him talking was preferable to whatever alternative he had in mind.

He snorted. "Hell no. I was just taking some time off, so I could plan my next move. And then that phone message asking about that damned bribery investigation."

I almost blurted out *what phone message*, then realized he'd misinterpreted my request for information about how to conduct an internal investigation.

"I knew I had to make a move sooner instead of later. Get rid of you before you figured too much out. And *then*," he grinned, "you announced loud and clear that you were coming to visit poor little ole me."

He *had* bugged my office, and the bug was still there. Where the hell was it?

Jacobs held his arms out wide. "Step into my parlor, said the spider to the fly." He let out a noise, a cross between a snort and a chuckle.

Pacing around the cluttered space, he began regaling me with his exploits, bragging about the crimes he'd committed right under the JSO's noses.

Rubbing it in that he'd committed even more, right under *my* nose.

I wanted to remember every detail, so I could nail his ass once I found a way out of here, but the residual Rohypnol in my system was making me drowsy. I kept drifting off.

"It's easy to get a woman to trust you when you flash a badge," he droned on. "I should've tried that approach much earlier, but I was always worried about being identified if they happened to get away. So I was using the blitz attack from behind. And a couple of them did get away. But I've fixed that now..."

My chin drooped toward my chest.

"Hey," he yelled, "Am I boring you? Because I can always liven things up." He walked over and grabbed a knife up off the freezer lid.

My heart stuttered. It looked suspiciously like the one that should be in the evidence room—the one Bradley had found in Ronnie Malcolm's apartment.

A slight movement caught my eye. Bradley's shoe had moved. Was that a soft moan?

Jacobs hadn't seemed to notice. "I'll keep you awake!" He started toward me, brandishing the knife.

"It's the drug," I quickly said. "I'm actually quite fascinated."

He narrowed his eyes at me. "I'm actually quite fascinated," he mimicked in a falsetto.

He snapped his fingers. "I know what will keep you awake. Let's play a game." He tossed the knife back onto the freezer. It slid across the dingy white top and fell behind it.

I held my breath, hoping it didn't land point down, praying Bradley would be able to get his hands on it.

Jacobs didn't notice the knife's disappearing act. He seemed downright manic.

I wondered if he was literally high, on drugs.

Psychopaths get off on power. Kate's words in my head. More likely, then, that he was riding a natural high because he'd captured the big prize—me.

He paced to the freezer, turned, pointed a finger at me. "You," he boomed in a game-show-host voice, "are contestant number one."

Looking down, he kicked Bradley's foot. "Maybe I'll let your boy toy be contestant number two, if he ever wakes up."

He whirled back toward me. "Your question, *Chief* Anderson," he sneered the title, "is which victim was *not* my kill?"

I pretended to think about it. "Tremont."

"Bwaah." He made an obnoxious buzzer sound. "The badge worked really well on him, too. No problem luring him into the back parking lot. I told him I had some more questions, but we could sit in the air conditioning in my car, where I had my recorder. He followed me around back and started to climb into my passenger seat. I garroted him and dragged him behind the dumpster. Then..." He mimicked a stabbing motion.

Jacobs pretended to swoon. "It was almost as good a feeling as the women, overpowering a man like that."

I shuddered.

He grinned.

I needed to work harder at hiding my reactions. Not easy when you're trussed up, half frozen, and dopey from residual Rohypnol.

"Guess again," he said.

"Karen."

"Bwaaah. That bitch! She's had it coming for years. Those damned geraniums, for one thing. She came by and watered them every week, even though I told her not to. She even sent her brat Brian over to mow the lawn. Said it was a disgrace.

"But this time she went too far. First, she shits in my nest. Then she comes waltzing in here, acting like she still has a half interest in the place, yammering about how she needs to use *our* parents' freezer for a bunch of burgers and spareribs. Well, *I* needed to *shut her up*."

My brain had snagged on his sister's earlier sin. "Shitting in your nest?"

"Yeah. Even dumb animals know not to shit where they sleep, but she has to make a kill in *my* part of town, and set it up so it looks like *I* did it."

"She *knew* you were a serial killer?"

"Of course not. But I'd told her about 'these cases I'd heard about in Jacksonville,'" he made air quotes. "It was fun watching her freak out at the thought of being raped and killed."

"You told her your MO, including the stocking used to strangle the women?"

"Yeah, but she mucked it up, posing the girl like that, instead of leaving her sprawled out for all the world to see her." He grinned again. It was not a pretty sight.

"And of course, she couldn't rape her. Not the right equipment." He put a hand on his crotch and hefted his junk through the pants.

I managed not to wince or throw up.

"So Pearl was the one who wasn't your kill."

"Yes, but you don't get the prize, 'cause I told you."

"Karen killed her because Pearl had tracked down her biological father, your brother-in-law."

Bradley's feet twitched.

"I suspect Pearl called their house," Jacobs said, "and Karen answered. She probably set up a meet. Amazing that she had it in her to kill somebody." His tone was downright proud. "But she couldn't have some stupid girl messing up her boy's chances of getting elected. And she wouldn't have let him stop with the state senate. She wanted the schmuck to be President someday. As if he has the balls to run this country."

I was tempted to steer the conversation toward politics. Anything to keep him talking, until...

Until what? Realistically, I wasn't going to get my numb hands loose from the handcuffs behind my back. But maybe Bradley had the knife and was cutting himself free.

"Why did you pose Karen like Pearl?"

"It seemed fitting. And I was thinking that if you did catch on that those two kills weren't connected to the others, maybe you'd blame Mark."

He shook his head. "When we found Pearl, I figured I'd catch the guy who did her and then all the killings, hers and the ones in Jacksonville, would be blamed on him. So I posed Darla like Pearl. I'd been keeping my eye on the little junkie, trying to decide if it was worth the risk to take her out. When she started remembering more details..." He trailed off, shook his head again in mock regret.

"But after I talked to old man Nelson, I knew my stupid sister had killed Pearl. That changed everything. I couldn't take the risk that she'd be caught and blab about me telling her the MO."

"That's why you tried to kill Nelson, so we wouldn't make the same connection."

"Exactly. If only y'all had taken a little bit longer to get there," Jacobs drawled.

"Why," I asked, "did you even tell me about Nelson, if you didn't want us to talk to him?"

"I figured I'd better mention him, in case you or Bradley or someone looked at Pearl's phone records and saw the calls to him in Lawtey. But I thought you'd be satisfied when I said he was a dead end. But no..." Jacobs rolled his eyes. "You had to go out there and follow up yourself. *You* signed his death warrant."

Guilt squeezed my heart. I shoved the feeling aside, focused on this bastard's words.

"I was almost to Starling on 301, had to turn around and hustle back to his place to beat you there."

He began pacing again, muttering now, as if he were talking more to himself than me. "That dunderhead, Doug Cleaver. I should've figured in the he's-too-dumb-to-have-planned-all-that factor. Shit, he's too dumb to live. Planting those trophies, trying to frame him, that was my one mistake."

In retrospect, I could think of several mistakes he'd made, but we hadn't caught on to them—yet. My insides felt like lead. How had we...how had *I* missed the clues?

But I hadn't completely. I'd just suspected the wrong cop. My chest tightened. I shoved the guilt aside again. It wasn't helpful.

"His buddy Ronnie made a much better patsy," Jacobs was saying. Then he babbled on about the things he'd done to Marly Davis.

I really wanted to tune him out, but I needed to mentally record every gory detail.

Because I *was* going to get out of this mess. And I *was* going to arrest this bastard.

I'd never been a believer in the death penalty. I knew it wasn't a deterrent, and cops and prosecutors weren't infallible. You couldn't take back dead if it turned out an innocent person had been convicted.

But right now, I was glad I'd moved to a state that still had the death penalty, and used it. I was going to watch this man fry.

Excellent! I was getting pissed. Good old energizing, fear-cancelling anger.

But despite the anger and my efforts to concentrate on Jacobs's words, I started to drift again. Between the remnants of the drug and exhaustion… It must be the middle of the night by now. I shook my head slightly, blinked my eyes.

"What, you're getting sleepy on me again?" A big grin split his face. "I know what will wake you up. Let's stick your head in the freezer. You'll love the view. My sister certainly did." He cackled as he strode across the floor, grabbed my arm, and hefted me to my feet.

He half dragged, half carried me to the freezer.

My mind scrambled for a way to use this to my advantage. My hands and feet might be out of commission, but I could elbow him in the gut, slam him against the wall… Then what?

We'd reached the freezer. He threw the lid open, grabbed the back of my hair and painfully yanked my head forward.

Inside the freezer, the frozen face of Shelly Trent stared back at me.

I screamed and reared back, went over backwards. My butt and then my head slammed against the concrete floor.

Pain exploded.

The room dimmed. I fought to stay conscious.

The darkness won.

CHAPTER TWENTY-NINE

Brain fuzzy, I stared up at floor joists. I was now lying on my back. Some kind of white panels were between the joists, where the underside of floorboards should be. *Styrofoam?*

Soundproofing. The rock music thumped from a distance.

My hands were now tied to something above my head. But the bonds felt soft. Not the handcuffs he'd tightened way too tight before. My hands were tingling, waking up.

I looked down the length of my body, trying not to move. I didn't know where Jacobs was, and I didn't want him to realize yet that I was awake.

I was on a metal cot, my feet tied to it. The flesh-toned cloth, that I now realized were women's nylons, looped around each ankle and then under each lower leg of the cot.

I was still clothed—a relief, but also confusing. Why hadn't he tried to rape me yet?

Not that I was in a hurry.

My feet were ice cold. The pins and needles in my hands were becoming excruciating.

My insides felt heavy. As if I were already dead. My chest ached and my throat hurt. I admitted to myself that I might not get out of this alive.

A shoe scraped on concrete.

I turned my head toward the sound. Pain shot through my skull and down my spine, making me gasp.

When the room stopped spinning, I registered sunlight streaming weakly through the thick windows high on the walls. It was daytime. Jacobs had turned off the glaring overhead light. The corners and edges of the room were full of shadows.

I was a little surprised that Neat Nate didn't keep his lair cleaner. It was quite dusty down here.

Another scraping sound. I blinked, forced my eyes to focus. A dark form was leaning against the wall, where I'd been sitting before.

Bradley, and he was awake, watching me. He gave a small nod.

And for some crazy reason, I felt hopeful. Even though he was trussed up just as I had been.

Footsteps on wood, high on my left.

I slowly turned my head, keeping the pain bearable.

Jacobs was descending the stairs. The white tee shirt remained, but it now topped a pair of loose cotton pants, covered with tiny Jacksonville Jaguars' logos. Pajamas?

My brain wasn't working right, focusing on stupid things.

No wonder. I had to be concussed.

He stepped into the space between Bradley and me, held his hands out in an expansive gesture. "Look who's joined the party. Pretty Boy Bradley finally woke up."

He glanced down at himself. "Oh, sorry for the casual attire. I had to fend off a well-meaning Barnes, making a wellness check."

Bradley's face blanched.

"I assured her it was only the flu, and I should be able to return to duty by tomorrow." He turned toward me slightly. "I considered inviting her to join our little get-together. But she really is a good choice as an assistant. Very diligent and eager to please, like a loyal puppy. I'm thinking I'll keep the little bitch on, once I'm chief."

His eyes sparkled with amusement. He was intentionally looking away from Bradley while he baited him.

I glanced over. Bradley's cheeks were now red, but there was something odd about how he was sitting. He'd twisted around some and was leaning a bit to the side.

I caught a glimpse of metal and he waggled his fingers at me.

My eyes went wide before I could catch myself. *Damn!*

Jacobs whirled around.

But Bradley'd already straightened, his back against the wall. "You bastard," he spat out, giving Jacobs the reaction he wanted.

"Yes, I am, actually," Jacobs said, in an amused voice. "My mother was pregnant with me when she married old man Jacobs. They were already engaged, when she was raped. Being good Catholics, abortion was out of the question. They moved the wedding up, and he reassured her that he would raise the child as his own."

Hallelujah, my hands had passed the pins-and-needles phase. I could wiggle my fingers, and more importantly, I could feel them wiggling.

"And Lord knows, he tried to 'beat some sense into me.'" Jacobs made air quotes, then his face darkened. "The night before I left for college, he told me the truth. Said my real father had been identified recently, thanks to DNA. And he'd been diagnosed with antisocial personality disorder. He was a psychopath."

My feet were still frozen lumps. I sent signals for them to move around in tiny circles.

They obeyed—as much as the nylon bonds would allow—and began to tingle as circulation returned.

"I was pretty upset at the time," Jacobs was saying, "but I also remember thinking, 'Well, that explains a lot.' The old man said he'd still pay all my college expenses, on one condition." His voice edged toward bitter. "That I never came home again."

Then he chuckled. "I think my stash of dead cats and mice in the bottom of the freezer might have been the tipping point for him."

He raised his hands again in the expansive gesture. "I had the last laugh, though. Mom wouldn't let him cut me out of their will. So I ended up owning the old homestead, after I used some of the other assets to buy Karen out."

He brushed his hands together. "But enough of all that. It's time to get this party going." He leaned over me. "I've been waiting for you to wake up. It's no fun raping a comatose woman."

My stomach heaved.

"What are you planning to do with us?" Bradley quickly demanded. I suspected he was trying to turn Jacobs's attention away from me.

It worked. Looking at Bradley, he said, "I thought I just told you." He made an obscene gesture, thumb and index finger making a circle, the other index finger going in and out.

My stomach heaved again. I willed myself not to vomit.

"Oh, you mean *eventually*." Jacobs grinned at Bradley. "Well, I plan to keep you alive for a while. I discovered with Marly that a drawn-out relationship can be *so* much more satisfying than a quick rape and kill. What is it the profilers call it? Ah, yes, the killer's MO is *evolving*."

I forcefully steered my thoughts away from imagined scenes of Marly's last hours. I needed to focus.

Jacobs gave Bradley an appraising look. "I might even do you," he repeated the obscene gesture, "just to see what it feels like."

Bradley blanched again.

"But to get back to your original question. Eventually, I'm going to take you two out to the boonies and set it up so that you, Pretty Boy, will look like the killer. And I the hero, who came swooping in to rescue the chief here. Only I was too late. Alas, she was already dead."

He swung his head back and forth slowly, an expression of truly mournful regret on his face.

Kate was right. The smart ones really can imitate normal emotions.

"You see, y'all thought I was setting up poor Ronnie, but after Dougie let me down as a patsy, I decided to go for the big fish. I was setting *you* up," he pointed at Bradley, "by making it look like you were setting Ronnie up."

Jacobs laughed, then turned his attention back to me.

Bradley had distracted him long enough for me to get myself under control. And for my mind to clear some. I had the beginnings of a plan, if only Jacobs would cooperate.

I stared at Bradley, willing him to read my mind. *Wait.*

He gave a slight nod.

Meanwhile, Jacobs was busy cutting the nylon bonds around my feet with the pen knife he'd pulled from his pajama pocket. "Don't know what I did with my hunting knife last night." He grinned at me. "I was a little excited about my big haul—you!" He grabbed my pants legs' cuffs. "No matter. It'll turn up."

With a flourish, he yanked my pants off.

I'd known it was coming, but still my neck and cheeks heated, even as cool air raised goose bumps on my thighs.

Anger surged. I was not going to let this bastard see me squirm.

His gaze was on my face.

Then again... I turned my head slightly to the side, faked a whimper. Watched him out of the corner of my eye.

His chest was puffed out, his face grinning. He stepped back from the cot and hooked his thumbs in the waistband of his PJs.

I had been slowly lowering my now-loose feet to the cement floor, on either side of the cot.

Trying to ignore that the only thing between me and this monster was a thin pair of panties, I shook my head back and forth, gritting my teeth against the pain ping-ponging inside my skull. I hoped I looked like a terrified woman, trying to deny the reality of what was happening.

I *was* a terrified woman, but I wasn't in denial.

His gaze was intent on my face, the grin wider.

Good!

He shoved down his pants and bent at the waist to lower himself on top of me.

Praying this worked, I contracted my stomach muscles, as if doing a sit-up, and bucked upward, bringing the cot with me. My head butted his with an audible smack.

Searing pain brought me to the edge of passing out.

He staggered back, tripping over the pants pooled at his feet.

Bradley sliced through the bonds on his ankles with a quick stroke of the hunting knife.

Jacobs went down. Bradley launched himself on top of him. Thundering feet, coming down the stairs.

All that happened in the second or two before the cot, still attached to my hands, pulled me over backwards.

The ringing of metal cot legs hitting the floor, jolting my body.

Pain exploded, consuming me.

CHAPTER THIRTY

My head was full of cotton candy. Had I passed out?

Cops swarmed around me. *Where the hell am I?*

Bradley climbed to his feet, hauling Jacobs up with him.

Memory flooded back—the basement, the attempted rape...

Bradley yanked one of Jacobs's arms high behind his back. The pervert yelped. His nose was bleeding.

Despite the throbbing in my head, I grinned.

Cruthers scanned the room, his pistol out in front of him. "Anybody else here?" Several uniforms had spread out, weapons drawn.

"Nope, just us." Bradley slammed Jacobs against the basement wall.

Barnes rushed over to me and plucked at the knots at my wrists.

"Good to see ya, man," Bradley said over his shoulder to Cruthers. "Can I borrow your cuffs?"

His conversational tone struck me as funny. Hysterical laughter bubbled in my throat. I clamped my lips tight to keep it from escaping.

"Gloria," Bradley said in the same casual voice, "you wanna get the chief's pants for her, please?"

The laughter escaped through my nose, in the form of a snort.

The hospital room was quiet, for a change.

Barnes sprawled on a chair next to my bed, snoring, a magazine abandoned on her lap.

I was regretting letting the paramedic talk me into coming here, but not being able to stand up without the world spinning had made his arguments hard to resist.

The ER doc had been equally persuasive about admitting me. "How many times did you lose consciousness?"

"From the drug or the conks on the head?"

He'd given me an exasperated look. "My point exactly. You're severely concussed and moderately dehydrated. Do you want to end up with brain damage?"

So now I was trying to get some rest. In a hospital. Good luck with that.

Every half hour or so, someone came in and poked and prodded, took my vitals, held up fingers and asked me how many, and/or tried to give me more pills.

And each time they exited the room, they left the door to the noisy hallway open.

Barnes would get up and close it again, and we'd have another twenty to thirty minutes of peace.

After her brother had reassured her he was okay, she'd insisted on riding with me in the ambulance. And I'd insisted that she take my statement, while my recall of what Jacobs had said was still fresh. Fortunately, the conks on the head hadn't messed with my memory.

I gave up on sleep and hit the button to raise the head of my bed, wincing some. When I was semi-upright, I eased against the pillows and the pain subsided.

A light rap on the door.

Barnes jolted in her chair, the magazine sliding to the floor.

"Come," I called out, bracing for more poking and prodding.

But Detective Cruthers and Sergeant Collins entered the room, looking everywhere but at my face, their cheeks ruddy.

"What is this, Humiliate the Chief Day?" I quipped. "First you see me without my pants, now you get to see me in one of these." I plucked at the front of my too-big hospital gown.

They laughed and the tension eased. Barnes grinned at me.

"How ya doin', Chief?" Cruthers asked.

"I'm alive, for which I am quite grateful. What's happening?"

"The CS team is still at the scene," Cruthers said. "Johnson's supervising. The ME's got Shelly Trent. He'll do the autopsy as soon as she's thawed out."

The image of that shocked frozen face... A shiver ran through me, which I tried to hide.

"And Jacobs?"

"He hasn't asked for a lawyer, but he's not talking."

"How did you all know to call in the cavalry?" I asked.

"Barnes called me." Cruthers nodded toward her. "I thought she was joking, at first."

I turned my head gingerly toward my assistant. "How'd you figure out what was going on?"

"When you didn't come in this morning, I called your phone, and immediately got voicemail, *twice*. You'd said you were going to check on Jacobs before going home last night, so I–"

A light rap on the open door. A doctor, tall and dark-haired in blue scrubs, stood behind Cruthers and Collins.

"Come in," I called out, even though I was anxious to hear the rest of Barnes's story.

Cruthers and Collins drew apart to let him pass.

Only it wasn't a doctor. It was Bradley. He stepped into the room, dragging a portable IV stand.

I fought the urge to jump out of bed and give him a huge hug, reminding myself that wasn't part of my management style. Not to mention, I wasn't sure my legs would even hold me up at this point.

His sister had no such restrictions. She bolted out of her chair, raced over, and threw her arms around him. "You sure you're okay?"

Laughing, he gave her a one-armed hug, his other hand steadying the IV stand. "I'm fine. Just a little dehydrated."

"Did they admit you?" I asked.

"I wouldn't let them. My doc said that was okay as long as I stayed around long enough to get rehydrated." He jiggled the IV stand. "I escaped from the ER when he wasn't looking."

"But you took a blow to the head too," I said.

He chuckled. "Guess my head's harder than yours."

"Not surprising," his sister teased.

"Okay, start at the beginning," I said. "How did you come to be in Jacobs's basement?"

"I was checking out the other victim in the drive-by," Bradley said. "Reggie Diaz. And I saw the indicators that he might be somebody's CI. I asked Officer Barnes to check. She said he belonged to Jacobs."

As my assistant, she had access to the confidential informants list. But she shouldn't have given out that information without my permission.

Anderson, get a grip. Under the circumstances, I was damn glad she did. But still, we would have a little talk, at another time.

"My gut was starting to scream," Bradley was saying. "This Diaz gives my CI the info about the trophy box in Cleaver's room. And then he asks for a meet, supposedly with more info, and they're both gunned down? Way too many coincidences."

Bradley smiled. "Like you, Chief, I'm allergic to them. I called Jacobs. No answer, straight to voicemail. So I decided to drop in on him. No answer when I rang the bell or knocked, which seemed strange since he was supposed to be home sick. I thought maybe he was sitting out back. I went around, and lo and behold, the back door is unlocked. Seemed careless of a police officer. I opened the door, calling out my name and that I was entering the house. No response." He stopped, took a deep breath.

"Well, that was because he was setting me up. The door to the basement stairs was slightly ajar, so of course I checked it out, found you down there and was checking you for injuries when you came to. I saw your face shift, Chief, but I wasn't fast enough to stop him from grabbing me from behind. We struggled for a few seconds and then he hit me on the head with something."

My chest tightened. At that point, I'd had no idea I was in Jacobs's basement, and I thought Bradley was the enemy and Jacobs was rescuing me. My stomach hollowed out. *How'd I miss the signs?*

But I hadn't completely. I'd figured out a cop was the leak, maybe even the murderer. I'd just suspected the wrong cop. Which was Jacobs's intention.

"Next thing I knew," Bradley continued, "I'm lying behind a noisy appliance, and a knife drops from heaven." He grinned. "I thought maybe I heard angels singing."

I gave him a small smile. "I was praying that Jacobs wouldn't notice the knife had slid off the freezer. But he was high on the fact that he'd kidnapped me."

"Yeah," Cruthers said, "that would've fed right into the bastard's narcissistic ego."

He paused. "Boy, it feels good to say it out loud. I *never* liked the creep."

I should have tried to suppress my grin, but I didn't.

"He was jabbering away," Bradley said, "and I was half out of it. He didn't completely make sense. All I knew was I was tied up and I now had a knife. But the space between the wall and the freezer, it didn't allow for much squirming around. The best I could manage was to slide the knife up inside my jacket sleeve, figuring eventually he'd haul me out of there."

He looked at me, his face suddenly more serious. "But when he did, the first thing I saw was you, Chief, out cold on that cot."

He sucked in air. "I figured I needed to bide my time. I pretended to be groggier than I was. As soon as he had me sitting there by the wall, I sliced the sleeve of my jacket to get the knife loose and then worked on the bonds on my wrists."

Bradley frowned. "That was my favorite suit." He swayed a little on his feet.

Barnes led him to her chair.

I gingerly shifted my head to look at him. "Why didn't you call for backup?"

"Because I wasn't thinking Jacobs was the killer. I wanted to talk to him, see if he might know why Diaz would set Cleaver and my CI up like that." He scrubbed a hand over his face. "When I realized the back door was unlocked, I was actually afraid someone had broken into his house and *he* was in danger. But I didn't want to sound a false alarm."

Especially since you were suspended, I thought. Guilt that I'd doubted him made my insides queasy. I owed the man an apology, but not in front of a crowd.

I turned to Barnes, standing next to the chair. "You were saying, before half the department descended on us?"

"When your phone went to voicemail," she said, "that had me worried. You never turn your phone off. So I called Dan...Detective..."

I swallowed a chuckle, not wanting to interrupt her.

"...Bradley to see if he knew where you were, but his phone went straight to voicemail too. That really gave me the heebie-jeebies, that I couldn't reach either one of you. I went to your apartment, rang the bell several times, no response, and I'm remembering how you said you were going to see Jacobs last night.

"So I went to his house. He took a long time coming to the door, even though his car was in the driveway. But finally he did, wearing pajamas. I didn't want to admit that I'd lost track of you. I pretended I was checking on him, to make sure he was okay.

Oh, and by the way, did the chief stop by last night? He said you had but didn't come in, 'cause he might be contagious."

Bradley and I exchanged a grim look. An icy shiver ran down my spine. She had come so close to becoming another victim.

"I was walking away," Barnes said, "when I spotted something under a bush. I crouched down, pretended I was tying my shoe. It was a black low-heeled pump, like you usually wear. And suddenly all the pieces came together. I picked the shoe up with my pen, held it in front of me as I walked away, so he couldn't see it from the house. When I got to my car, I called Detective Cruthers."

I turned to Cruthers, my eyebrows raised. "That was enough to get a no-knock warrant?"

"That, and Foster called early this morning. Said he'd tried to call you first. He'd found another case he thought might be related. An attempted SA, same MO. The gal didn't see his face, but she got a real good look at the knife he was wielding. Sounded like the hunting knife we had in custody. I went to the evidence room, to send Foster more detailed photos of it, and Phil, the officer on duty, couldn't find it."

Cruthers paused for breath, glanced around the room. "Then I caught up with Derek, but before I could ask about Pearl Altman's tablet, he asked *me* if we'd ever figured out why or how it had been wiped clean. He'd reported that to Jacobs, who'd told him not to bother writing it up, that he would include it in his own report."

I shook my head, then wished I hadn't when a throbbing pain started up again. "He supervised the crime scene techs in her dorm room. He must've taken the tablet when they weren't looking—who knows what he found on it—then wiped the hard drive before he took it to Derek. He couldn't just dispose of it, because I'd already seen it."

"Oh, another thing," Barnes said. "I found something in your office this morning." She made a small circle with her thumb and index finger, the size of a dime. "About this big."

"The listening device! Where the hell was it?"

"On top of the lower hinge on the bathroom door, painted to match the hinge. Maintenance said they couldn't get to the squeaky door until Friday. So I brought some oil from home. When I looked more closely at the hinge, it didn't look quite right."

"Jacobs let on that he still had a bug in my office," I said. "That's how he knew to get all dressed up in his rapist costume and lay in wait for me."

Bradley frowned. "I caught a glimpse of a suit, just before he clobbered me."

I nodded carefully, not wanting to set off the pain again. "He was either on his way out to get the knife from the evidence room or had recently come back. He was wearing dress slacks and shoes, when I came to the second time. But why was he obsessed with that knife?"

"He probably wanted it to plant on me," Bradley said, "so all the crimes would be tied together and blamed on me."

"Hey," I said to him, "didn't you see my car? It was parked at the curb in front of his house."

"It wasn't when I got there."

"We found a big garage on the back of his property," Sergeant Collins spoke for the first time since entering the room. "Four cars in it. Yours, Chief. His sister's, Bradley's and–"

I held up a hand. "Lemme guess, the mysterious dark sedan."

"Yup," Collins confirmed. "Older model, dark gray, stolen, fake tags."

"Anything on Marly's car?"

"Sheriff Pierson found it," Cruthers said. "Three-quarters under water in another swamp. Wiped clean."

My chest warmed at the mention of Sheriff Sam.

"I think I've got the timeline now," Cruthers was saying. "I'm gonna go confront Jacobs with it, see if I can get him to slip up."

I held up my hand again. "Before you do, I want to say something."

They all looked at me.

I had to swallow the lump in my throat before I could speak. "You are one hell of a team, and I'm proud to work with you."

At my invitation, Bradley met me for breakfast at a local diner, the morning of my first day back to work.

I'd been out two days. One in the hospital and one at home. The doctor had wanted me to stay home through the weekend, but by Thursday midday, I'd been downright stir-crazy.

I owed Barnes an apology. I was no better at being a good patient than she was.

Thursday afternoon, I'd worked from home, doing the paperwork for commendations for both Cruthers and Barnes. Then I'd called Sergeant Collins and suggested he apply for the detective position that had been posted. I also planned to encourage Armstrong to take the sergeant's exam, to replace Collins.

Once settled in our booth, I ordered eggs and bacon, extra crispy. Bradley went with his usual pancakes and wimpy turkey sausage.

"I hear you've been giving out commendations right and left," he commented, after the waitress poured coffee and bustled off.

I swallowed a grin. "Yes, I figured our rescuers deserved recognition."

His expression said, loud and clear, *What about me? I'm the one who took a rap on the head for you.*

Just to be ornery, I dragged out the suspense. "So what happened to that gal, Stormy—Cynthia Price—from the NA meeting?"

Bradley was in the process of taking a sip of coffee. He smiled as he lowered his cup. "She called me yesterday, after she heard we'd caught the Midnight Killer."

His face sobered. "Jacobs had talked to her first. She'd gotten a bit of a look at the driver of that car, the guy talking to Darla Monkton–"

"Whom we now know was Jacobs."

"But all she'd seen was his forehead and some of his hair, in the light from a street lamp. She said Jacobs kept asking her questions, mostly about the hair—what shade of brown was it, and how long."

"Damn. He was leading the witness, trying to steer her away from short and blond and toward implicating you."

Bradley nodded. "Then he told her to keep their conversation to herself, that he was IA, investigating the Starling PD detectives working the case."

"He probably let her live so he could use her as a witness against you later."

Bradley nodded again. "When she heard that Tremont had been killed, she figured whatever dirty cop Jacobs was investigating would be coming after her next. She took off, went up to North Carolina and stayed with a cousin."

Our food arrived and we dug in.

"I wonder what set him off?" Bradley said, after a couple of bites. "And why did he begin so late? I thought serial rapists, slash, killers started such activities in their teens or twenties, not their early forties."

I had asked Kate those questions when she'd called to make sure I was okay. Belatedly, I'd realized *I* should have called her—because of course a serial killer kidnapping a female police chief, who subsequently helped overpower him, had made the national news.

I was such a rookie in the friendship department.

I did catch Dolph, and my cousin Paulie, before they'd heard it on the news.

And Sheriff Sam, who had heard already from Cruthers, so he knew I hadn't been seriously injured. He said he was extremely grateful for that, since I owed him a cup of coffee. We'd bantered back and forth about who owed who, since he'd originally issued the invitation.

My chest warmed at the thought of that conversation.

I cleared my throat. "My psychologist...friend in Maryland said it was likely a combination of things, beginning with his wife's suicide."

Cruthers had found several domestic violence complaints from his neighbors, the first year after his parents died and he and his wife moved into their house. But the wife always denied there was anything wrong. Then the DV calls stopped, but one neighbor called repeatedly, complaining about noisy music.

Three months later, the neighbor had died of a heart attack. According to the report, Jacobs had found her in her backyard.

"Guess there's no point in exhuming his neighbor's body," Bradley said.

It was eerie how he could read my mind. Or maybe we just thought along the same lines.

I paused, half a strip of bacon almost to my mouth. "I called her daughter. The woman lingered for a day and a half after the heart attack. If he used epinephrine, like he did with Nelson, it would've dissipated long before she went into the ground."

I popped the bacon in and crunched. Nice and crispy.

Bradley nodded. "Wanna bet he soundproofed that basement about the time the DV calls stopped? I'd also bet our CS guys are gonna find the wife's blood down there, along with Darla's and Marly's."

I'd been in the process of picking up more bacon, but suddenly it wasn't quite so appetizing. Cops have iron stomachs, but in this case, I'd come too close to having my own blood splattered around that basement.

"Not taking either of those bets." I picked up my fork and worked on my eggs instead. "I thought the wife was a suicide." I hadn't looked up the records on her, hadn't really wanted to know the details, considering...

"She was. Hung herself."

I winced.

"I'll bet, though, that he dragged her down there many a time before he beat her, so the neighbors wouldn't hear."

I stared at my plate for a second, swallowed hard.

"What else did your psychologist friend say might have contributed?" Bradley asked.

I took a deep breath. "That he'd probably dealt with his anger and need to dominate women by abusing his wife. But then the wife kills herself. According to Kate, that would've made him furious. How dare she deprive him of his power over her. And shortly after that, Martinez accused him of taking bribes."

"Yeah, the timing fits. The first two SAs were not long after his wife died." Bradley forked a chunk of turkey sausage into his mouth.

I nodded. "And his first attempt at murder, with Shelly Trent, was shortly after Martinez filed his complaint." I ate some more eggs, which helped ground me.

"I wonder," Bradley said, "how he managed to control his anger during his dormant periods."

"Kate thinks he reverted back to raping but not killing his victims. She suggested checking neighboring states for *any* unsolved SA cases. And I've got Derek checking his GPS history and credit card records for long road trips on his days off. We'll see if there's any overlap."

Bradley shook his head slowly. "I suspect Chief Black was covering for him regarding the domestic violence. They were real buddy-buddy."

I nodded again. "There was no mention of the DV calls in his personnel file. In most departments, there would be a note, even if no charges were filed. Especially if there were multiple calls."

"Black tended to downplay DV cases anyway. He was old school—what happens between a man and his wife is their business, yada, yada."

My turn to shake my head. "How'd he last as long as he did?"

Bradley snorted. "Connections. He was the former mayor's brother-in-law. When the new mayor was elected, Black immediately started talking about retiring."

No doubt in my mind now—the new mayor and/or the city council had given him an ultimatum, retire or be fired.

Bradley waved a syrupy fork in the air. "I suspect Black only filed the investigation paperwork against Jacobs because Martinez made such a stink."

We ate in silence for a couple of minutes.

"Chief, don't answer this if you don't want to." Bradley was looking down at his substantially diminished pancake stack. "I mean...I may be totally out of line here," he glanced up, "but why do you stiffen or wince at mentions of DV or women being strangled or hung?"

I stared at him, my mouth falling open. The memories swirled.

I took a deep breath, pressed my palms against the tabletop. "My father was abusive," I said in a clipped tone. "But my mother put up with it, and then he left her for another woman. This case stirred up some of those memories."

I didn't tell him the rest. That my mother, who should've left the bastard years before, fell apart after he left her. That she drank and popped pills, and tried to kill herself several times, once by hanging. I had found her, saved her, each time. Until the day I was too late.

Bradley was now staring at me, then he dropped his gaze. "I'm sorry. I shouldn't have asked."

"No." I stopped, took another deep breath, felt strangely lighter. "It's okay."

He raised his eyes, met mine. "We all have baggage."

I heaved a sigh. "I guess that's true."

To change the subject, I said, "Speaking of DV cases, who interviewed William Walker?"

"I did. He seemed genuinely surprised about the listening device. And chagrined that he'd never noticed it when he cleaned your office. I don't think he planted it."

"No, most likely Jacobs did himself. There were several times my office was unlocked when I wasn't there. Barnes was usually there, but she wouldn't have thought anything of him going in to leave me a note or whatever." I shoved away my not-quite-empty plate. "Back to Walker, I'd been thinking about hiring him to clean just our floor, as an SPD employee, but–"

"He might very well be interested," Bradley said.

"You think I should hire him? Despite the DV history."

"Yes, I do. He said he's had a ton of therapy, most of it court-ordered, but nonetheless it helped him sort out a lot of stuff. His dad beat him and his mother when he was a kid. Now, he's going to school during the day, to become a couples' mediator, specializing in DV cases."

"Wow. Occasionally a DV case can have a happy ending."

Bradley smiled and polished off his pancakes.

I stood, dropped bills on the table. "We should get going."

He followed me out of the restaurant. On the sidewalk out front, I stopped suddenly.

"Oh, by the way, *Sarge*, I need you to take the lieutenant's exam, as soon as you're eligible."

He stared at me, eyes wide.

"My second in command should really be at least a lieutenant."

Sergeant Bradley and I walked into the bullpen, and suddenly everyone was on their feet, clapping. Not just the detectives—most of the uniforms were there too.

Word's spread already about Bradley's promotion?

That made no sense. I hadn't told a soul about my intentions to promote him.

Jan, the head dispatcher, was there as well. And the CS team and Derek, the tech geek. Sergeants Johnson and Collins, and Phyl Gladstone.

And they were all looking at me.

I managed to maintain a calm exterior, but something had turned all warm and gooey inside my chest. I wasn't sure what to do with that.

A plastic banner, reading *Welcome Back*, stretched across the top of my office wall. A large vase of gaudy flowers sat on Barnes's desk.

Standing beside her chair, she pointed her chin toward them. "They're from Councilman Hayes."

Through the door to the office, I glimpsed copper-colored custom blinds. No gaps. *Alright!*

And a bouquet of red roses on my desk. I suspected they were from Sam. More warm, gooey feelings.

I mock glared at Barnes, waving a hand at the banner, then around the crowded room. "Was this your doing?"

"Nope." She grinned. "I don't recall who suggested it, but everybody was on board."

I knew damned well who had suggested it.

But I let her get away with the lie, this time.

AUTHOR'S NOTES

If you enjoyed this book, please take a moment to leave a short review on the book retailer of your choice. Reviews help with sales and sales keep the stories coming. You can readily find the links to these retailers at the *misterio press* bookstore (https://misteriopress.com/bookstore/). The next book in the series is *Fatal Escape*, set a month after the end of this story.

This book was proofread by multiple sets of eyes, but proofreaders are human. If you noticed any errors, please email me at kass@kassandralamb.com so I can have them corrected.

Heck, email me anyway. I love hearing from readers!

And you may want to sign up for my newsletter at https://kassandralamb.com to get a heads up about new releases, plus special offers and bonuses for subscribers. You will also receive a free novelette, *The Tell-Tale Bark*, the prequel to the Marcia Banks and Buddy Mysteries, AND a free novella, *Sweet Sanctuary*, the prequel to my traditional mystery series, the Kate Huntington Mysteries.

Also, *misterio press* has a readers' group on Facebook (https://www.facebook.com/groups/misteriopressmysteries/) where we chat with readers and also offer giveaways, contests and other goodies. Please stop by and check it out!

I had so much fun writing this spin-off from my Kate Huntington mysteries. I loved the new challenge of writing a police procedural, and it was a great opportunity to peek in on Kate and see how she and the gang are doing. (All my books are listed at the end of these Author's Notes.)

One of the positives of writing police procedurals—there's no need to justify how often your protagonist stumbles over dead bodies. I have at least four books planned so far for this series, and I'm sure more ideas will come to me.

The downside of writing police procedurals, if you are not a law enforcement officer, is struggling to get it right! Much gratitude to the Cops and Writers group on Facebook and its fearless leader, Patrick O'Donnell, for their assistance with all things LEO related. And extra gratitude to Patrick for beta reading this story and pointing out all the things I got wrong about the police. Lessons well-learned for the rest of the series.

Any mistakes that remain are mine, or they are things that I fudge a little to make the story work. For example, pulling a rookie in to be a police chief's assistant and taking her along to crime scenes and briefings would be quite unorthodox indeed.

Also, big thank-yous to my sister authors at *misterio press*, Shannon Esposito, Vinnie Hansen and Candace Carter, who all helped to shape this story and make it better.

And my eternal gratitude to my wonderful editor, Marcy Kennedy. I was very relieved when she told me that Judith had a distinct "voice" from Kate and my other main character, Marcia Banks.

Once again, Melinda VanLone came through with a great cover, capturing my vision for the series. Thank you, Melinda!

And last but not least, love and gratitude to my husband, my final proofreader. Any errors you might have noticed are not his fault; I tend to tweak things right up to the final publication deadline, and I sometimes introduce new boo-boos.

A quick note about Covid. When I started this book, I set it in the fall of 2021, assuming Covid would be behind us by then. It wasn't. But after writing a book for a different series, set in the spring of 2021, I just wasn't up for more taking masks on or off and people asking each other about vaccination status. Therefore, I went with my original plan and wrote this story as if Covid was mostly in the past. After all, it is fiction!

Starling is a made-up city, based loosely on the real city of Starke, Florida. Bradford County and the town of Lawtey are also real places. I like to use real settings whenever possible. It's fun for locals to be able to say, "Hey, I know that place."

The St. Johns River is real, but the tributary that runs through Starling, the Sofki River, is fictitious. The word *sofki* comes from the Creek language. It was a staple of the Seminole people's diet, a type of porridge or soup made from corn and vegetables, and sometimes fruit or meat. It was left simmering on the fire throughout the day, so folks could have some whenever they were hungry. I figured that was an appropriate name for a fictitious tributary of the St. John's River, which provides daily sustenance to a huge array of wildlife in eastern Florida.

If you're wondering about Judith's cousin, Paulie, he will be making an appearance in a later book. There are some other mentions in this book that I left hanging as well. They'll be brought to fruition later.

In the meantime, if you haven't already read the Kate Huntington mysteries, I now have that series bundled into four collections that will save you several dollars on the individual book prices. Check those collections out on my website (https://kassandralamb.com/books/)

ABOUT THE AUTHOR

Kassandra Lamb has never been able to decide which she loves more, psychology or writing. In college, she realized that writers need a day job in order to eat, so she studied psychology. After a career as a psychotherapist and college professor, she is now retired and can pursue her passion for writing.

She spends most of her time in an alternate universe with her characters. The portal to that universe, aka her computer, is located in Florida, where her husband and dog catch occasional glimpses of her.

In addition to this new police procedural, Kass has completed the ten-book, traditional mystery series, The Kate Huntington Mysteries (set in her native Maryland, about a psychotherapist/amateur sleuth), plus four Kate on Vacation novellas (with the same characters). She is also the author of the Marcia Banks and Buddy cozy mystery series, about a service dog trainer and her sidekick and mentor dog, Buddy. There are eleven stories out in that series, which is set in north central Florida. Book twelve is planned for early 2022.

Kass's e-mail is kass@kassandralamb.com and she loves hearing from readers! Her website is https://kassandralamb.com, and she's also on Facebook, Goodreads, Instagram, and Bookbub. And she blogs about psychological topics and other random things at https://misteriopress.com.

She also writes romantic suspense under the pen name of Jessica Dale (https://darkardor publications.com/jessicas-books/).

~~

Please check out these other great *misterio press* series:

Karma's A Bitch: Pet Psychic Mysteries
by Shannon Esposito
Multiple Motives: Kate Huntington Mysteries
by Kassandra Lamb
The Metaphysical Detective: Riga Hayworth Paranormal Mysteries
by Kirsten Weiss
Dangerous and Unseemly: Concordia Wells Historical Mysteries
by K.B. Owen
Murder, Honey: Carol Sabala Mysteries
by Vinnie Hansen
Blogging is Murder: Digital Detective Cozy Mysteries
by Gilian Baker
Full Mortality: Nikki Latrelle Mysteries
by Sasscer Hill
ChainLinked: Moccasin Cove Mysteries
by Liz Boeger
To Kill A Labrador: Marcia Banks and Buddy Cozy Mysteries
by Kassandra Lamb
Steam and Sensibility: Sensibility Grey Steampunk Mysteries
by Kirsten Weiss
Never Sleep: Chronicles of a Lady Detective Historical Mysteries
by K.B. Owen
Bound: Witches of Doyle Cozy Mysteries
by Kirsten Weiss

At Wits' End Cozy Mysteries
by Kirsten Weiss
Payback: Unintended Consequences Romantic Suspense
by Jessica Dale
Steeped In Murder: Tea and Tarot Mysteries
by Kirsten Weiss
Travels of Quinn
by Sasscer Hill
Maui Widow Waltz: Islands of Aloha Mysteries
by JoAnn Bassett

Plus even more great mysteries/thrillers in the misterio press bookstore.

www.ingramcontent.com/pod-product-compliance
Lightning Source LLC
LaVergne TN
LVHW091020080826
845145LV00002B/308

9781947287303